Marriage by Arrangement

Anne Greene

Marriage by Arrangement

Contact Information: titleadmin@pelicanbookgroup.com

Scripture quotations, unless otherwise indicated are taken from the King James translation, public domain.

Cover Art by Nicola Martinez

White Rose Publishing, a division of Pelican Ventures, LLC
www.pelicanbookgroup.com PO Box 1738 *Aztec, NM * 87410

Publishing History
First White Rose Edition, 2013
Paperback Edition ISBN 978-1-61116-290-5
Electronic Edition ISBN 978-1-61116-289-9
Published in the United States of America

Dedication

I dedicate *Marriage by Arrangement* to my precious Savior, Jesus Christ, and to my loving family.

Praise

Masquerade Marriage

Filled with rich Scottish language and descriptive passages, this book literally tosses you back in time to a land where men fought to be free from the tyranny of the English…I literally sat and read all day, pausing only to feed the kids, so compelling is the story. I laughed and even cried. The emotions run deep as Megan and Brody slowly see past the pretense of their marriage and fall for each other, only for fate to step in.

Definitely one to read, this will have you riveted to your comp/e-reader/book and one you'll want to read again. ~ Clare, Happily Ever After Reviews

English Peerage

DUKE. After the royal family, the duke ranks highest. The duke is always addressed as *Your Grace,* though familiars may address him as Duke. He will never be addressed by his family name.

MARQUESS. Next in rank is the marquess. He is also addressed by his *title* rather than his family name. If he is the Marquess of Queensbury, he is called Lord Queensbury, rather than Lord Churchill or whatever his family name. His wife is the marchioness. May be called Lady Queensbury.

EARL. Below the marquess is the earl. His wife is the countess. Addressed by his title, not his family name. Addressed as Earl of Spencer or Lord Spencer. Wife addressed as Countess of Spencer or Lady Spencer.

VISCOUNT. Below earl is the viscount. His wife is the viscountess. Never addressed as Viscount of Bradford. Addressed as Lord Bradford or Bradford.

BARON. The lowest inherited titled rank is baron. His wife is a baroness. Simply addressed as Lord and Lady.

SIR. Lower ranks simply addressed as Sir. As in Sir Richard Burton. Knights addressed as Sir, but the title is not inheritable.

DOWAGER. When a titled lady is widowed she becomes a dowager.

1

Castle Drummond, home of Lord and Lady MacMurry, near the Village of Kirkmichael in Lowland Scotland—April 19, 1746.

"I won't run." A shudder skipped down Lady Cailin MacMurry's spine, and she stared at her younger sister. "I'm committed."

"No, it's not too late for you to flee. You must, because I heard another scandalous rumor about Duke Avondale." Lady Megan MacMurry grasped Cailin's arm.

"I won't listen to gossip." Cailin pulled away from her sister and lifted her wedding bouquet to inhale the white rose fragrance. If only the sweet scent could overcome Megan's words, and her own misgivings. Though many arranged marriages turned out badly, surely God would give her a loving one. After all, since her earliest years, she'd prayed for a happily-ever-after love.

"Ask yourself why such a grand noble would stoop to marry a Scottish lass whose Papa is but a Baron? Why did he not choose the daughter of an English duke or a marquess or even an earl and receive ever so much more dowry and prestige?" Megan tilted her head and lifted elegant brows.

Why indeed? Cailin clutched her enormous diamond engagement necklace. The thing felt heavy with responsibility.

"The man's an English duke. He owns palaces all over England." Megan planted her hands on her slender, mossy-green silk covered hips. "Every noble lass in the land should be offering to give her right arm to be in your shoes. And yet they are not."

New knots formed in the nape of Cailin's neck. She held her finger to her lips. "Too late to turn back now. The wedding chorus has begun." She forced her feet to take the first step, and then began the slow glide from the stone castle's rear archway through the garden towards the rose arbor.

With a jerk, Megan lifted and straightened Cailin's cumbersome satin train. "In truth, beyond his wealth and titles, our family knows little about the English duke." She gathered up her own long skirts, and ran ahead to lead Cailin down the flower-strewn path.

Seven bridesmaids stopped giggling and chatting and moved to their places in front of Megan to head the procession.

Beneath her veil, Cailin smoothed her frown.

Papa had chosen to take this path in light of the violent upheaval following England's latest battle with the Highlanders.

Her marriage to the duke would shelter her family with his great cloak of protection. Neither the English nor the Scots would dare invade a castle guarded by the powerful duke's coat of arms.

More goose bumps shivered down her spine. Surely, jealousy fueled the flagrant tittle-tattle. She pulled in a deep breath, straightened her shoulders, and took measured steps in time to the music towards the loch gleaming in the late afternoon sunlight. She would not let whispers spoil her wedding. She laid her hand lightly on her father's offered arm.

Their procession passed the scores of guests assembled on both sides of the flowered path. Ahead, her groom stood beneath the rose bower, sunlight from the loch gleaming on him, the pastor, and his groomsman.

Her heart fluttered.

The duke looked the perfect picture of manhood. He towered above his shorter groomsman and the pastor. Sun glinting off his iceberg blue satin coat, heavily laced with gold, almost blinded her. His chocolate eyes gazed past the dazzling crowd of guests and focused on her. Beneath those beckoning eyes, the straight bridge of his nose above softly smiling lips formed the most handsome face she'd ever seen.

Her pulse quickened. Butterflies flitted from her stomach to her heart and back. As she reached her groom and the chamber music died, her high-heeled slippers sank into the grassy moor, but her foreboding dissolved like fog before the sunshine.

The rose bower in the garden where she and the duke stood together and promised their fidelity was pure romance with its lush greenery, heavy scent of roses, and panorama of softly rolling, newly green glen. Though she didn't know the man she wed, she repeated with all her heart to love, honor, and obey him as long as she should live.

Marrying a man one had barely met happened more often than not to daughters of lords. So why were her knees shaking? Her attractive groom, with his mahogany hair, wide shoulders, and square jaw, held her hand gently in his warm, strong grasp. Rumors were just rumors, and, truth be told, if he was not perfect, neither was she.

A breeze loosened strands of brown hair from the gold band that tied the thick mass behind his muscular neck to dance around his face.

She was glad he had not powdered his hair. Her throat tightened. Loving him would be easy.

Oh God, please let him love me.

She would love him so greatly, with everything inside her heart. Surely, he would love her in return. She would work hard to make certain her marriage turned out differently from her mother's. There would be no coldness, nor violent arguments between her and her grand duke. No sleeping in separate parts of the castle. No making their daughters' lives miserable with the dislike they bore one another.

As the magnificent sunset painted him gold, the duke's chestnut eyes stared into hers with promise, his inviting lips tipped upwards at the corners, and his demeanor was affectionate and approving.

Joy burst through her chest, and she gave him a brilliant smile. Yes, her marriage would be happy. A storybook marriage, like Cinderella's.

The English parson the duke had brought with him raised a hand in blessing. "I now pronounce you man and wife. You may kiss the bride."

She handed her heavy bouquet of roses and lilies to Megan and tipped her chin up.

The tall, lithe, young duke stepped forward and lifted her expensive Brussels veil. She was so very fortunate he was not old.

She closed her eyes.

He touched his lips to hers.

Oh! Her eyes flew open. The bridal kiss had been so short…and disappointing. The pledge in his gaze had led her to expect so much more. She frowned.

Their first kiss was like melding lips with someone on stage, acting a part.

He dropped his arms and moved back.

Megan handed her the wedding bouquet.

Guests surged forward, surrounded them, and poured out congratulations.

She swallowed. So, in obedience to Papa, she had made vows to a complete stranger…vows that could not be broken.

Though the cold kiss dropped a mantle of heaviness over her heart, she shook off the shroud, smiled, and lifted her chin. She'd done her duty. Now the family was safe.

She had her whole life to discover what manner of man she'd wed, and her whole life to make him happy. She firmed her wobbly smile. And come sickness or death, she *would* make him happy.

Nearby musicians, seated next to the newly constructed dance floor, struck up the music for the traditional four-reel.

The duke took her hand, his groomsman took Megan's, and the four of them stepped onto the dance platform.

She draped her silky train over one arm and lifted her heavy skirts. As her new husband led her through the lively dance, his hand felt strong holding hers, and firm and sheltering on the small of her back. She smiled into his dusky eyes.

He smelled of manhood, expensive scent, and new clothes.

Her heart flip-flopped. Perhaps he'd been nervous and the impersonal kiss had no meaning. Heat warmed her cheeks. Tonight he would kiss her in a quite different manner.

Too soon, the dance ended.

Other guests stepped onto the wooden platform. The musicians slowed the tempo and glided into a Mozart minuet. The wooden floor filled, vibrating under the thud of many feet, and couples overflowed to the grassy glen.

Her husband bowed and left to claim Mums for the Parents' Dance.

Carried along by well-wishers, she lifted her skirts and stepped down onto the grass.

Megan slipped to her side. "Now, while all the guests are busy, I won't be missed. I must make my bid for freedom and escape." Her sister's whisper tickled Cailin's ear.

"I have a few minutes while no one is expecting anything of me." Cailin edged away from the swirling dancers. "The guests will think I left to attend to my personal matters. I'll see you off." She lifted her skirts and glided through the garden after her sister. They hastened around the garden maze, through the purpling heather thinly spread over the spongy peat moss, past the herb garden, and sprinted straight for the carriage house.

Four horses harnessed to Papa's carriage pawed the gravel path.

Her hand on the carriage door, Molly, Megan's maid, stopped frowning. Her booted foot quit tapping. A grin brightened her homely face. She handed Megan a white, folded gown, gathered high her ankle-length woolen skirts, hopped up into the carriage, and took up the multiple reins.

Cailin pulled Megan into a hug. "Do be careful."

Megan nodded. Green eyes sparkling, her wedding gown draped in her arms, she climbed the step, and settled inside the open carriage.

Molly gave a chirrup and slapped the reins, and the vehicle lunged forward spewing gravel and dust.

Cailin watched, hugging her arms, pebbles pricking the soles of her thin slippers, until Papa's carriage clattered down the drive, and turned into the road leading to Inverness.

Oh, God, I pray Megan's doing the right thing.

She pressed her lips together. Despite her own wedding excitement, she must keep her sister's secret, or Papa would send an army of servants galloping after Megan and stop her.

Cailin turned and hurried back, her high-heeled slippers sometimes sinking into the grass. She held her veil in place, draped her cumbersome train over one arm, and rushed through the violet shades of descending dusk on a line to the candle-bright castle. She drew a deep breath as a stiffening breeze blew in scents of moor and wood.

People would gather soon inside the ballroom and expect to see her.

She panted so, she could scarce hear the crickets chirping as she rushed over the rough ground and onto the stone walkway leading to the front door and the entrance hall.

She hadn't soiled her wedding dress, but she brushed a clinging straw from her skirt and straightened her satin-clad shoulders.

Already she missed Megan. All her life she'd counted upon her sister to hold her hand before she entered her bridal chamber. She'd expected her sister to help shoo away the butterflies that swooped through her stomach no matter how often she tried to talk them away. She had scarcely been around men, and the duke was a stranger. She frowned. And his kiss had held so little promise.

Another terrifying thought swirled through her brain like a ghost. Since Papa had betrothed Megan to a cruel man, what type of man had he selected for her? Were safety and titles and lands more important to Papa than both his daughters' happiness?

She shivered.

Gasping for breath, she nodded to the full-liveried doorman who opened the door for her and entered the stone castle, glad to be inside, away from the promise of rain. The servant knew better than to gossip about where she might have been.

Her quick footsteps clacked against the polished granite of the long entrance hall. She had stayed too long with Megan.

Already the guests assembled in the ballroom.

She glanced at the vaulted ceiling where daylight was fast fading through the thick-paned windows.

Oh God, please take away my fear.

"Cailin, come in. Everybody's waiting." Several of her bridesmaids stood at the open double doors to the ballroom, eyes dancing, faces flushed, and beckoned.

Clutching her bouquet, she choked down the lump in her throat, lifted her white skirts, and entered the ballroom. Just inside the doorway, she stopped and caught her breath.

Flowers lined every nook and cranny. The sweet scent of English roses almost made her dizzy. She blinked. The ballroom was a fairyland, with tall candles, white bows with flowing ribbon tails, and flower garlands tucked into every possible space. The floor-to-ceiling mirrors that lined all four walls reflected candlelight, guests, and gaiety.

Papa had gone to great expense on the decor.

Joy bubbled over her anxiety like fresh water cascading down a dangerous cliff. Surely if Papa had done all this for her, he had secured a worthy man as her groom. She glanced into one of the mirrors to adjust her veil, and then faced the festive scene.

Tall beeswax candles cast a warm glow throughout the guest-clogged chamber perfectly reflecting the rosy luminance growing inside her heart. How could she be so happy one moment and so uncertain the next?

The lilt of music from the string quartet surrounded her. She and her bridesmaids swept past three white-draped tables laden with elegant food and five more overflowing with beautifully wrapped gifts.

As formally attired men and beautifully gowned women gathered around her, she smiled in response to their congratulations.

Mums rushed to her side and spoke in a low voice with her sweet Lowland burr so different from Cailin's own boarding-school English accent. "My dear, though we had but a few days to prepare, your wedding couldn't be more exquisite."

She kissed her mother's smooth cheek. "Thank you for a truly wonderful day. Yours was the tasteful hand guiding Papa's iron gauntlet."

Knowing Papa, Mums had no voice in Papa's choice of a husband for her, but Mums planned the wedding and reception.

Mums beamed.

"And Mums, you look splendid. That lavender silk is absolutely perfect."

Above her mother's low-cut bodice, a heavy diamond necklace twinkled against her ivory skin.

Diamonds sparkled in her ears and in her shimmering blonde hair that barely showed strands of gray.

"Thank you, dearest." Mums's soft, gloved hand felt warm under Cailin's chin. "You positively glow. His Grace cannot help but be pleased."

Warmth banished some of the butterflies flitting inside her stomach. "Oh, Mums!" She slid her arm around mother's narrow waist. "Thank you."

The clatter of feet on the polished parquet floor shifted her attention to the athletic, debonair man approaching like a royal ship with all flags flying.

Insignificant, less colorful vessels followed the duke's wake.

Was His Grace always surrounded by so many attendants?

A splash of contentment washed over her. How lovely to be an important part of her new husband's dazzling entourage.

"Your Grace." A shy flutter ran through her heart. She dropped a curtsy to the duke.

Beside her Lady MacMurry dipped even lower.

"Oh, the both of you, do address me as Avondale." Her new husband awarded her a stiff smile. "After all, we no longer need stand on formality."

Perhaps he was nervous.

"Thank you, Avondale." She leaned closer to the elegant duke and gazed into his eyes, but found his attention focused on the stringed quartet. Moths swooped into her stomach.

Was the flesh and blood man she had pledged herself to somewhere inside this handsome façade? Or was this stranger playing the role of the real man? Who was this person to whom she was bound for life?

"I say, Cailin. These Scottish tunes please me not. Don't your musicians know any good English melodies?"

"Why, yes…Avondale. Mums, would you see to it?"

Of course, her groom must think of his English guests before he could concentrate on his bride. The thought returned the smile to her heart, but didn't banish all the alarm peeking around the edges.

With the Highlanders defeated just two days past at Culloden, even Lowland Scottish tunes seemed no longer in vogue, though their Lowlanders, unlike the Highlanders, remained ever faithful to England and King George. Thank God, they'd taken no part in The Rising.

Mums nodded. "Certainly, dear. I'll make my way over to the musicians presently." She strolled off in a swirl of lavender silk, leaving her flowery scent behind.

Cailin slipped her arm through her husband's and couldn't keep her gaze off the muscular sword-wielder wrist that emerged from the lace edging his jacket sleeve.

Today she would not let thoughts of wounded and dead Highlanders intrude on her happiness. She would celebrate her Wedding Week in the best English tradition. With God's help, she would see this arranged marriage overturn the norm. No matter what she had to do, she would make Avondale happy and pray God he would return the blessing.

As they continued their circuit of the room, her new husband pulled away. So she stepped closer and rested her hand lightly on Avondale's arm. He bowed and spoke pleasant words to each person he encountered.

Apprehension curled like wisps of fog through her heart. Avondale's manner towards her seemed so very…remote. As if she were only another member of the fawning company surrounding him. Barely noticing her, he seemed intent on making each person he met adore him. Where had the affirmation gone that she'd seen in his eyes as they pledged themselves to each other?

To gain his attention, she squeezed his satin-encased arm. A trill rippled up her spine. Avondale's bicep felt tight with muscle. What other surprises had he in store for her?

Rather than turning his attention to her, he sniffed with apparent dissatisfaction the new smoke, called a cigar, which he'd plucked from his gold satin vest and rolled beneath his patrician nose. He slid the offending brown oblong into the breast pocket of the portly groomsman who hovered over him. "Get rid of this."

"Avondale," a high-pitched voice called from the entry.

Her husband instantly pivoted to face the front-hall, bronze eyes twinkling above a wide smile. "Ah, finally appears my royal mother." He raised his cultured voice. "Over here."

A hush settled over the room, leaving the music sounding loud.

Tightness gripped her throat, but she would not pant for breath.

Last evening when the duchess arrived, Cailin had a momentary meeting with the intimidating woman. The encounter had not gone well. The woman had barely acknowledged her.

Cailin blinked rapidly and raised her chin. With

time, she would surely grow to love Avondale's mother. How could she not when the lady looked a petite, though much older image of her aristocratic son?

"My mother's pleasure is of utmost importance." Avondale's gaze was flinty and compelling. "You must make her happiness a priority."

Her heart twisted. "Yes, of course," she murmured.

But not because the duchess's good graces had been ordered, but because her own duty as a wife included bringing harmony to the House of Avondale. She gave the approaching duchess her most heart-felt smile.

The dowager stopped a few feet away and gazed at her with lifted brows and narrowed eyes. The tiny woman's cool expression made Cailin feel as if she was interviewing for a position as lady-in-waiting rather than being welcomed as a daughter-in-law.

Unable to keep her smile from wavering, she bit her lip. Would the dowager accept her love? She tightened her hand around Avondale's bicep. Regardless, she would strive to be an obedient, dutiful daughter-in-law.

The duchess thumped a ribbon-decorated rosewood cane on the floor. The hard tap of her folded fan stung Cailin's arm. "I'm sure you'll be a great asset to my son." The plump, long-widowed dowager's low-cut gown of black silk with silver stripes accented her fair skin and elaborately coiffed white hair. She held herself stiffly straight and made flabby arms and a ponderous bosom appear high-fashion.

Duchess Avondale's retinue of dandified aides and sparkling ladies crowded around the short woman like soldiers around their commander. All eyes dissected Cailin.

Her cheeks grew hot. Heat spread from her face through her body. Perspiration made her bouquet almost slip from her hand. She dropped her gaze from the aloof hazel eyes to the woman's neck, and then clamped her lips to keep her mouth from falling open.

A necklace of large matched pearls hung around the wrinkled neck. The perfectly round, luminous pearls were so exquisite they had to be the famed Heritage Jewels given to the First Duchess of Avondale by Queen Mary in 1699.

Shaking off her awe, Cailin stepped forward and embraced Her Grace, the Dowager Fourth Duchess of Avondale. "I'm so pleased to become your daughter."

The woman smiled distantly, her expression cool as the snow atop Ben Nevis, and backed from Cailin's embrace without returning the hug. She slipped her hand through Avondale's offered arm.

Cailin pressed her hand over the smarting ache in her chest.

"That Scottish music is quite too awful." Duchess Avondale's shrill voice echoed through the crowded room. She thrust her gold filigreed fan over her jeweled ear as if the Lowland Scottish air, causing many a foot to tap, gave her an earache.

Every nearby Lowland face registered consternation. Behind their pearl-handled fans, the Scottish women whispered. Fashionably dressed men shifted their feet and ducked their heads.

But the English, dotted among the crowd, nodded, and their condescending expressions echoed the dowager duchess's sentiments.

Cailin glanced across the room and caught Mums

finally speaking to the musicians. The music squeaked to a halt.

"Oh dear, the duchess doesn't know the difference between Lowland and Highland tunes." The sudden silence caught the sotto-voiced whisper.

From long experience, Cailin knew that in seconds each Lowland Scot would cover his discomfort with whatever tactic he normally used to cope with English arrogance.

As the notes of an English minuet tinkled to a weak start, each returned to the festivities, pretending the English duchess had not insulted their music.

She peeked at Avondale, expecting him to explain the dowager's rude snobbishness.

Instead, his breath warm against her cheek, he murmured in her ear, "I say, where does your father hide his good cigars?"

Concealing her hurt at his callousness behind her fan, she smiled. "Why, in his study."

He raised a dark brow, but tucked her hand inside his unoccupied arm. "I see."

With the dowager clinging like a rudder to Avondale's right arm, she lightly held his left, smiled, made small talk, and accepted toasts and applause. Soon her good sense overcame her hurt.

The duchess had probably not heard her speak of her happiness in joining the family. Surely, her new mother-in-law had not meant to snub. And, of course, Avondale would not scold his mother. A man must honor his parent.

Despite the dowager's haughty attitude, every invited guest pressed forward, seeming eager to meet a bona fide duke and duchess and say something witty so the two would remember them.

Other than Avondale's unexpectedly distant behavior, Cailin discovered her first taste of being titular-almost-royalty exhilarating. After all, she was Avondale's wife, and, as such, she would be the person closest to him in all the world. His mother and aides would soon return to court, and she would have her husband to herself.

She smiled brilliantly, but her wedding bouquet trembled in her cold hand. Unaccustomed to English court life, the crowd's adulation began to unnerve her. The three of them plowing through the massed guests grew unwieldy.

Somehow, as Avondale, his royal mother, and she circulated through the ballroom, the swirl of people bestowing good wishes separated her from the charismatic man she'd married. She found herself deserted, a small island in the sea of celebrating people.

Standing on tiptoes and gazing over the heads of her guests, she watched Avondale, with the dowager duchess clinging to his arm, stalk to the center of the ballroom.

Obsequious English earls and marquises, followed by Lowland Scottish lords, trailed her husband and mother-in-law as if tied to the polished couple by invisible strings.

A sick feeling invaded her stomach, and she silently chided herself for not staying with Avondale.

Then Papa slogged through the crowd to her side. "Congratulations, my dear." He gathered her into a dress-wrinkling hug.

She buried her face into his chunky neck. Smelling his tweedy everything-is-all-right-in-my-world scent soothed her stomach.

Though he dropped his arms, she clung to Papa's hug. Somehow, at all costs, she would do her duty to the daunting, aloof dowager. With God's help, she'd close the distance between the English duchess and herself.

Hiding the sick feeling churning her stomach, she tugged Papa along as she embraced friends, kissed babies, laughed at precocious children, sampled goodies offered by loving hands, and performed all of the niceties expected of her. After all, she was the obedient daughter, so God would surely bless this marriage. He rewarded those who obeyed Him.

Occasionally she glimpsed Avondale inside his circle, his mother still clamped to his arm. A dagger of discontent snagged the common sense she worked so hard to hang onto. Her smile slipped.

Avondale really might pay a bit more attention to her. She fisted her hands. Should she make a scene and insist? No, she must trust God that her husband's negligence would change. Given time, she would love him into change.

When her husband arrived in their chamber to claim her, even her new mother-in-law could not invade her bridal bed. And she would be alone with her husband. Like a kitten snuggling into a cozy chair, happiness slowly settled into her heart.

But Megan's last words as she leaned out the carriage window to wave good-bye nagged her thoughts. *Cailin, you are too trusting. Where there are rumors, there must be a basis. I'm not sure Papa has your best interests in mind wedding you to the duke, but he certainly has his own.*

Cailin rubbed gentle circles on her throbbing temples. If only Megan had said nothing.

Feet, aching inside her satin slippers, and candles, three-quarters burnt in the hanging candelabra, proclaimed the evening celebration would soon end.

Presently she'd have Avondale to herself. Beneath the expensive handmade lace, her neck and chest heated, yet her hands remained icy.

No matter how diligently she tried to cheer herself, she'd never felt so alone.

2

A trumpet signaled.

Cailin glided to the center of the rose-scented ballroom. Her seven bridesmaids fluttered from various parts of the crowd to surround her. The beauty of their pastel gowns in the different hues of the rainbow, reflected in the full-length mirrors that paneled all sides of the ballroom.

She glimpsed herself as the white-satin center of the pastel maypole of laughing ladies. Each carried red, yellow and pink English roses. Her group of bridesmaids presented an enchanting picture.

She smiled. Of course her loving God would not allow her to wed an unworthy man. How could she have thought differently?

She shook her head. Her fears were just that. Unfounded misgivings based upon rumors. How could this wedding not be happily-ever-after? She pulled in a deep, calming breath.

"Your Papa's given you the biggest prize of all." Lady Lorna Stewart's voice held more than a trace of envy. "Your groom is the best match any titled lady could make. You are so fortunate, Cailin. How did your Papa pull it off?"

"Yes, Avondale's unbelievable isn't he?" Cailin tucked an errant golden curl behind her veil. "Papa's always been an astute businessman."

"He's outdone himself this time."

"And yet, do you not think Avondale seems a bit distant?"

"Heavens no! Everyone loves him." Lorna winked.

Cailin smiled. "I think he seems a bit stiff. He no doubt has wedding nerves." She squeezed Lorna's hand. "I know I do." She glanced over her attendants' heads at Mums, who nodded. "Now it's time for my final wedding ritual."

"Good." Lorna's almond eyes lit her elfish face, and her lavender gown flounced as she did a pirouette and turned her face to the double doors. "This is the part I've been waiting for."

Gently shoved by her chattering bridesmaids, Cailin wended her way to the doors and the stairway beyond. Most guests paused from their festivities and turned to watch. She strolled through the open hand-carved mahogany double doors and glanced over her lace-covered shoulder at the smiling faces of friends and relatives and the more austere faces of the English gentry.

As the music from the ballroom died, her bridesmaids clapped gloved hands, creating a muffled crescendo and raising the scent of lavender and rose water. The flowers wreathing their long curls trembled, raising another flowery scent.

Every sense heightened, she climbed to the landing at the curve of the staircase and rested her hand on the smooth satin entwined around the banister. Drawing in a deep breath, she prayed in her heart as she spoke. "It's been an almost perfect day. I've had a perfect wedding. And I'm wife to an ideal man." She suppressed a sigh. If only her words could vanquish her contrary ups and downs of happiness and anxiety. She was too level-headed to believe that wishing Avondale to be a good husband would make him so. A favorite verse slipped into her mind.

And the LORD, He doth go before thee; He will be with thee, He will not fail thee, neither forsake thee: fear not, neither be dismayed.

She gripped the banister. She would believe this verse.

Aunty Moira, her navy satin contrasting with the gay colors of the other guests, pressed through the chattering crowd of ladies and joined the younger single lasses gathered at the bottom of the stairs.

Cailin motioned to her favorite aunty and her best friend, Lorna, to join her on the second landing, and then whispered, "What do you think of Avondale?"

A frown skimmed across Aunty Moira's face. "He's a tall, handsome, personable man." She shook her head so her abundant chestnut curls danced. "We'll trust in God, that he's a good one." She tugged Cailin's slightly tangled train, and the brilliant satin fell gracefully into place so that it eddied to the bottom of the wide marble steps. "You knew that once your papa made up his mind, there was no changing him." Aunty Moira's feather-soft kiss tickled Cailin's cheek. "God will honor your decision to obey your parents."

Cailin bit her lip. Even Aunty Moira's words didn't keep her from walking a scary, though exciting path.

Lorna grabbed her hand. "I just now heard a story of Avondale's strange—"

"Shush!" Aunty Moira pressed a finger against Lorna's lips. "Never mind that prattle. God's in control, Cailin." Her favorite Aunty turned and scampered down the stairs like a lass.

The love Aunty left behind slipped genuine cheer

into Cailin's tight chest. She smiled at the sparkling crowd of ladies massed below her, each face gazing up with expectant eyes and laughing lips. Her friends. How dear they all were.

But where was Avondale? Surely he wouldn't miss this final ritual.

She leaned over the banister, searched the crowded entry hall, and glimpsed her new husband's mahogany hair, his blue satin jacket clinging to his muscular back as he retreated into the study with Papa and a few other men.

A sliver pierced her heart. Her hand flew to her mouth. "Avondale didn't stay to watch." She fought an elusive sense of things between Avondale and herself not being…quite right.

"Nobody's perfect." Lorna fluttered her lashes. "But believe me, he's still the grand prize. I've never seen a groom look so royal. You're so fortunate, Cailin. Count your blessings."

Beneath her billowing lavender gown, Lorna tapped her foot creating an inviting sound. "I can't wait to dance the night away." She winked. "But tonight you'll be spending the evening alone with Avondale."

Cailin's pulse fluttered faster than the allegro tempo of the music. She backed against the railing to steady her shaking knees. She and Avondale…alone for the first time. She hid her hot face inside her fragrant flowers.

"Please toss your bouquet to me," Lorna whispered. "I so long to meet a handsome duke like yours." Her effervescent friend flitted down the edge of the stairs, missed Cailin's train by centimeters, and positioned herself in front of the chatting, laughing, pushing ladies. She raised her arms, hands outstretched.

Cailin's bridesmaids, cousins, and friends stopped chatting and jostled for position. Other single ladies, including Aunty Moira and Aunt Aley, and several single lady friends of Avondale's, joined the excited women.

With the satin toe of her shoe, a favorite older pair as tradition dictated, she pushed back her yards and yards of satin gown, shifted her bouquet, and let the flowers tumble over her other arm. She hated to part with them. Like saying goodbye to her innocence. Nevertheless, she turned to face the bright tapestry hanging on the stair wall, gazed at her favorite embroidered hunting horse jumping a hurdle, and tossed her bouquet over her shoulder.

A scream from below announced her spinster Aunty Moira caught the bouquet. A tittering laugh rose around the trim figure in navy. Aunty Moira merely smiled a secret smile.

Cailin turned, gazed down at the cluster of women and winked at the happy spinster. Although intelligent, still fresh-faced and pretty, the thirty-year-old had little chance to make good the bridal bouquet's promise. The lively lady had no prospects and no dowry.

Out of the kindness of his heart, Papa had taken Mums's baby sister to live in the castle. And when Aunt Aley's husband died before she could bear a son, Mums's newly penniless older sister moved into the castle as well.

But thinking of her aunts couldn't distract her today. Her thoughts flew like homing pigeons back to what would happen tonight after the sun set.

Lorna scampered to her side and slid an arm beneath her veil and around her waist. "You're blushing. I know what you're thinking."

Together they climbed the remaining stairs.

Lorna leaned close and whispered, "Tonight what we've been giggling over, and secretly dreading since we started wearing long skirts, will no longer remain a mystery." Her mischievous face held a wide grin. "At breakfast tomorrow, you truly must tell me all about your wedding night." Lorna squeezed her waist. "If you don't find happiness in His Grace's arms, there is no happiness to be had." Lorna's lips cooled a spot on Cailin's hot cheek. "You will share all, won't you? Promise."

Alarm bubbled up and left a strange taste in her mouth. "I shall be too embarrassed." Her smile quivered until her chin trembled. She gripped the stair railing and gave Lorna an uncertain smile.

Wispy hat lopsided, her eyes wide, her hands fluttering, Mums climbed the steps to join them at the second floor banister. "Dearest, let's spend a few minutes in your room before I return to our guests."

"As you like." Cailin nodded.

Lorna led the way to the passageway that turned at a right angle away from the corridor leading to the family's rooms. "It's so exciting that your Papa gave you this entire corridor of rooms in honor of His Grace."

Mums nodded, her hand reaching for Cailin's. "You are beginning a new chapter in your life." A tear sparkled on Mums's cheek. "You are leaving childhood behind, and I could not be more proud of you, Cailin Mountebank, Fifth Duchess of Avondale."

Cailin swallowed a lump that tried to clog her

throat. She'd never before seen tears shimmering in Mums eyes. She squeezed her mother's gloved hand. There'd always been some indefinable degree of reserve between the two of them…as if Mums knew secrets she wouldn't share. Perhaps being wed would draw them closer.

Hand in hand, they entered the elegant suite of rooms furnished with velvet, linen, and silk, and hung with bright tapestries.

Mums carefully unpinned and lifted off Cailin's veil, then draped the voluminous lace over the window seat. "Come, dearest, sit on the bed while I remove your slippers and hose." She patted the kingly bed.

Cailin climbed the three steps to the massive bed, struggled with her train, and then smoothed her dress behind her before she perched beside her mother on the lush velvet spread.

Lorna scampered up and collapsed on her other side.

Cailin's heart fluttered. She was sitting on Avondale's bed. Goose bumps danced across her arms. She tried not to think of her groom. Impossible. Every item in the room spoke of him in one intimate way or another. The huge bed and hand-carved wardrobe filled with his undergarments made her stomach flutter and her cheeks burn. She would soon discover what Avondale was like beneath his breeches. She shivered.

The room smelled of some indefinable male scent. Strange and mysterious, but incredibly enticing. She dropped her gaze to her hands, unwilling to let Mums see where her thoughts skimmed.

Sinking back into the soft mattress, she could

scarce catch her breath enough to focus on why Mums was here.

At full dark, Avondale would arrive.

Cailin glanced out the window at the setting sun. Despite the tiered candles lighting his bedchamber, shadows already clung to the room corners.

She wriggled her bare toes and peeked at her flowing gauze bed gown lying ready across the red velvet settee.

"Here, dear, Lorna and I will unbutton your wedding gown and help you out of your stays."

She slid from the bed and turned her back. Both women began unhooking the tiny buttons that ran down her back between her shoulder blades. Fingering the lace of her bed gown brought more heat to her neck. The lace ended just where the roundness of her breasts began. She fanned her face. She'd never worn such a revealing garment. Perhaps she could lie in bed with the coverlet pulled to her neck when Avondale arrived. Or perhaps she could blow out—

"Wasn't Megan a beautiful maid of honor?"

Cailin jerked. She could have slapped Lorna.

But Lorna babbled on, oblivious to the warning look she threw over her shoulder at her friend. "Megan's green silk brought out the alabaster in her complexion and set her hair on fire. I couldn't gain any of the gentlemen's attention until she disappeared." Lorna unhooked the last tiny round button, and the wedding gown slipped down from Cailin's shoulders.

Mums lurched to face Lorna. "What?"

"Did I say something wrong?" Lorna's gray-green eyes widened, and then she shrugged and straightened the circlet of fresh flowers that had tipped askew on her forehead. "No woman this side of Perth has a chance at snagging a fine lord for a husband until Megan announces her betrothal." She grinned at Cailin. "At least now, one of you two sisters is wed and out of the running."

"Where is she?" Mums yanked the gown so hard the train slithered across the wooden floor like a writhing snake.

Cailin stepped out of the dress, reached behind Lorna, and selected a bottle of scent from the night stand. She smoothed some of the cool liquid onto her neck and shoulders.

Her mother's puckered brow revealed her age like no amount of smiling ever could. "Leave it to Megan. She's up to something." Mums cocked her head. "Hmm, I don't believe I've seen her since the wedding dinner." She pursed her lips.

Cailin frowned at Lorna.

Mums certainly wouldn't have missed Megan until tomorrow had bubble-headed Lorna not mentioned her.

"Don't fret, Lady MacMurry. No doubt Megan's snared the Earl of Mabry's attention, and the two of them tripped off into the garden to get a breath of air." Lorna's eyes twinkled. "With Cailin married, Megan reels in the other rich catch. But then, that's what your husband arranged, isn't it, Lady MacMurry?"

Mums ignored Lorna's saucy question.

"I'm most certain Megan would gladly hand Lord Mabry over to you on a silver platter if given the opportunity." With Mums attention on hanging the wedding gown in the wardrobe, Cailin frowned at Lorna and put a finger to her lips. "She detests the man."

Lorna's brows rose, and she slapped a small hand

over her mouth.

"That's beside the point, Lorna. I am sure Megan, like Cailin, will fulfill her duty to our family." Mums lifted the sleep gown over Cailin's head and pulled the fine, thin gauze down over her hips. Under cover of the nearly transparent garment, she unlaced Cailin's new stays and slipped the undergarment off. "I don't recall seeing Megan after we retired from the reception line." Mums eyes narrowed as if trying to recall. "Oh yes, she danced the four-reel with that peacock, Reginald, Earl of Sutcliffe. But after that—"

"You wanted to talk with me while I change?" Cailin knew she must steer Mums to a safer topic. With the revealing bed gown clinging to her skin, she felt naked and grasped one of the huge fluffy bed pillows from the group on the bed. She held the round softness tight against her breast. The room seemed to chill, and the rose scent she had smoothed on suddenly sickened her.

"Oh, yes." Mums glanced at Lorna. "Would you mind giving my daughter and me some time alone together?"

Lorna giggled. "I shall see you in the morning, Duchess."

When the door closed after Lorna's rustling gown, Mums leaned close. "Don't be frightened tonight, darling. I'm sure His Grace will be a gentleman."

Something in her mother's voice transformed the delicate shivers running down Cailin's spine into pricks of ice. She shivered and climbed into bed. "Are some grooms not gentlemen?"

Mums smiled an enigmatic smile.

Doubts and conflicting thoughts tumbled through Cailin's mind until she felt lightheaded. A new thought fought to the surface of her jumbled feelings. She fingered the soft gauze of her bed gown. "Did Papa make you happy on your wedding night?"

Mums twisted a corner of the coverlet in her hand. "Happiness has nothing to do with marriage. You will fulfill your duty to our family." She cleared her throat. "The secret is to relax, dearest." She turned to a tray sitting on the nightstand. "Perhaps this one night you should take a glass of port." Mums's warm hand cupped hers around a stemmed glass of sparkling wine, and then she lowered her eyes. "Whatever Lord Avondale wants...just do it."

"What might he want?" She took a sip and returned the glass to the nightstand.

Her mother squeezed her hand, kissed her cheek and slipped off the bed. She stood with hands on her hips, regal as a queen. "I'm so proud of you."

Before Cailin could respond, Mums rushed out the door, leaving lavender scent twining through the room.

Beneath the silken sheets, Cailin pulled her knees to her chest, her heart drumming so hard her head spun. What was this mysterious thing called marriage? What might Avondale want? Mums seemed so somber. Cailin pulled the satin coverlet to her chin and waited.

What if the whispers about Avondale were true? After they pledged their vows, why had he grown so cold?

Darkness gathered inside the chamber.

3

Avondale drew in a deep breath, let the smooth tobacco flavor fill his chest, blew out a perfect circle of smoke, and snuffed his cigar in the cut crystal saucer. He lowered his boots from his new father-in-law's huge, hand-carved walnut desk and slowly rose. "I'll take my leave now, gentlemen."

The room full of men stumbled to their feet and bowed. Elbowing and subtly pushing one another for position, each tried to shake his hand. The sound of deep voices rose to a crescendo.

Drat, he hated all this attention. Hated all the bowing and scraping. Hated always being surrounded by nobles and gents pretending to be his friends, when each really wanted to pluck him like a chicken to be roasted. If they didn't want money or favors, they wanted whatever his power could give them.

"No. No. Please don't bother to accompany me. I'll deem it a favor if you forestall any idea of coming along. Leave me to my own devices." He turned on his heel, strode from the den, and shut the door firmly against the commotion inside.

Hand still on the doorknob, lively music besieged his ears. Was peace to be found nowhere?

His valet appeared.

"No, Hennings, I have no need tonight for your services. You may go on to the servants' quarters. Perhaps they have a dance going on there as well." He forced a smile through stiff lips. "Goodnight."

"Very good, sir." Hennings stood as if rooted to the spot like the solid oak tree of a man that he was.

Avondale grunted. It was no secret to him why his royal mother insisted on such a brute of a man to take care of his toilette. Well, tonight the man would leave his sight, or he'd have Hennings's blood.

He grasped the hilt of his ornamental sword, glared the warning, pivoted and stalked in the direction of one of the doors he knew led to a garden. No footsteps followed.

With the first burst of cool air on his face, some of his tension eased. He unfisted his hands. If it wasn't for his ducal responsibilities, he'd give his entire fortune to be alone. Though only night sounds surrounded him, the music and noise banged and churned inside his brain like a commoner's shivaree.

Several couples, dotted here and there among the stone benches set among the trees, looked up from their apparent trysts and gazed at him.

He ducked inside the maze hedge. Here shadows were darker, and light from the torches burning outside the castle didn't penetrate. He stopped and listened. No footsteps from Hennings that he could discern. He leaned against the prickly branches and gazed up at the night sky. The wind had blown away the rain, but black clouds obscured the moon. A fit night for his wedding.

Was his bride waiting?

Some of the muscles in his chest loosened, but the nape of his neck remained as rigid as if he wore an iron neck shackle. And so he did. Chained by duty, and now by vows.

Mind boggling, what a title could buy. For once

the accident of his noble birth benefited him. His bride's ethereal beauty had stolen his breath. Under her veil, golden curls cascaded to her slender waist.

He grunted. He needed a son. Would her delicate body bear such a burden?

If the girl were as intelligent as she looked, his royal mother had pulled off a wonderment. Mother had said the locals named her the Golden Goddess of Castle Drummond.

He rubbed the back of his neck. He needed more than unbelievable beauty. He needed more than a goddess. He needed a miracle.

He'd give her everything he could, but she had a right to so much more.

How long before the trust faded from her great sky-blue eyes?

4

Cailin woke slowly. Smiling, she reached across the huge bed to touch the warm silk of her new husband's nightshirt. Her hand felt only the cool satin hollow of his empty pillow.

She stiffened. A feeling of loss crept over her as if Christmas had passed, and she missed the celebration.

Wide awake, she arched her back and stretched her legs. Perhaps she overslept. Except the sun slanting yellow rays through the long bank of deeply-recessed windows told her that wasn't so. Still, wherever Avondale was, she'd see him again soon.

She rolled over and kissed the empty hollow of his pillow.

So, this was what being a wife meant. Savoring a remnant of the relaxed nest of joy she'd fallen asleep with, his arms around her, her head snuggled against his muscular chest, she pushed upright against her double stack of satin pillows. She slipped out from between the rumpled satin sheets, slid down from the bed, and pirouetted around the room.

Catching a glimpse of herself in the cheval mirror each time she passed, her eyes sparkling, her cheeks rosy, she was totally unembarrassed with the extremely low-cut transparency of her bed gown.

He'd said she was beautiful.

Already she loved this massive room with the different shades of cream and white pouncing on the splashes of brilliant red. Avondale's bedchamber. And hers.

She ran her hands beneath the long, full sleeves of her gown and stroked her arms. Today, she would have preferred breakfast in bed, shared with Avondale. But wedding guests awaited her appearance.

That must be it! Avondale had gone downstairs to extend hospitality to their guests.

Conflicting emotions of joy and loss ran through her. After their closeness last night, she felt as abandoned as a stray kitten.

His absence this morning marred last night's glorious sense of the two of them being one.

She so desired to see Avondale's dear features in daylight. Had she pleased him even a fraction as much as he pleased her? Though he was gone, he'd left his warmth and masculine love bursting inside her heart.

Marriage was so different from what she'd expected. She was a woman now, complete and loved. There had been nothing to fear. The duty to be performed had turned out to be a delight.

She burned to talk with Megan. To be wed on the same day had really been a touch from God. She couldn't wait to compare experiences. She could never share what happened last night with Lorna. Nor with Mums. Only with Megan.

She frowned. Raised in a house full of women, she and Megan had known so very little about men. How had Megan fared last night? Had she been as surprised? And had her Highlander made her as unexpectedly happy? Had he left her glowing all over?

Oh, I hope so! Who knew duty could be so pleasurable?

Hoof beats thundered from the stable and grew

fainter as they crossed the moor. The distant blast of a hunter's horn sounded. So that's where her new husband, and probably most of the wedding guests, had gone.

Because she'd slept so soundly, Avondale had thoughtfully not awakened her.

Very well. She could eat breakfast in peace. She scooted across the room, digging her bare toes into the thick carpet, and pulled the bell cord.

In a much shorter time than usual, Jenny, her plain Irish features bright with questions, flounced in to help her dress. The nosy lass must have been waiting just outside the door.

Cailin couldn't keep the triumphant smile off her face as she wiggled her bare toes in the silky softness of the red Oriental rug.

Jenny winked slyly, raised her rust-colored brows, and lifted both her hands in question.

Cailin let her obvious contentment answer.

In the years Jenny had served her, the maid proved far too free with her tongue. But what harm could knowing she was a happy wife be?

And the moment she glimpsed Avondale's face, she would find the answer to her own question clearly written there. Pray God she would read the answer she sought.

She threw up her arms in sheer joy and twirled around the room. Surely she'd pleased him. How could she not have?

****

Driving rain had blotted out the sunlight. While the dreary afternoon wore on, Cailin tried hard to hide her irritation from the few ladies in the drawing room as she ran her fingers lightly over the harp strings.

Early on, the promise of a sunny day evaporated into storm clouds. Although rain slanted smartly against the thick window panes, Avondale had not yet returned from the wedding hunt.

"I suppose Megan is still out following the hounds." Aunty Aley gave a petulant sniff. "And in this weather. Such a handful, that child." If it was possible, she held her plump figure even stiffer than its usual rigidity an inch from the back of the damask sofa.

Her widowed aunt relished stirring up gossip. Rather than answering, Cailin plucked the notes of a tune Aunt Aley particularly favored.

"His Grace is a sportsman?" Lorna doodled at her drawing board.

"Yes. I understand he's quite dedicated."

Cailin strummed harder, but paid scant attention to the melody she played. Thoughts pounded her mind much like the drumming rain slammed the window.

Where was Avondale?

All the other guests returned before the deluge started, and his absence had grown embarrassing. As guests trudged in, tired and muddy, each asked about him, gave her a deeply questioning gaze, and then retired to bathe and change for dinner.

Lorna slashed her quill viciously against her parchment. "During his wedding week? I think Avondale neglects his bride."

Cailin winced and played a sour note.

"La, la, ladies. Men enjoy doing the unexpected." Aunty Moira wet green floss between her rosy lips and re-threaded her needle. "I'm sure the rain delayed His

Grace. More than likely he took shelter someplace and will return directly when the downpour ceases."

"It looks as if the rain will never stop." Cailin rested her cheek against the smooth curve in the rosewood harp and tried not to frown.

Had Avondale been hurt? Or lost somewhere on their vast estate? Why did he not return?

"His Grace seemed so attentive to you when he said his vows." Lorna's big gray-green eyes looked dreamy as she stared out the window at the blowing rain. "Perhaps he's not—"

"And he shall soon be at your side again. Do not fret, lamb. Men will behave like men. Would we wish them different?" Aunty Moira plied her needle through her tapestry panel and looked as content as a kitten curled inside a willow basket, her dainty slippered feet, peeking beneath dark blue satin flounces, tucked close to the fire crackling in the wide fireplace.

Cailin plucked another false chord and dropped her hands to her lap. She scooted her chair back from the harp and rose to pace the shadowed room.

Why had her new husband disappeared so quickly this morning? She puckered her forehead. What could lure him away from her arms? Was this his way of telling her she'd not pleased him? Now he was conspicuously absent. Guests were whispering.

"His Grace is accustomed to so much more society than our country castle affords. London has sparkling soirées." Aunt Aley waved her hand dramatically. "As well as the theatre and smart entertainment." Her round cheeks waggled with an aggravating air of knowing things the rest of them could only imagine. "We country folk must seem quite boring."

To what else was Avondale accustomed? Cailin gripped her arms under the folds of her loose silken sleeves and continued pacing. Perhaps he kept a secret lady friend whose company he sought. She let her hands droop motionless on the arched neck of the harp. She'd heard titled Englishmen, more often than not, kept mistresses.

"Yes. Oft times His Grace attends court." Aunt Aley stabbed her needle threaded with black floss into her section of the tapestry panel. "I understand all manner of unspeakable acts occur with the German majesties. And the English at court are little better."

The heels of Cailin's hands jerked against the heavy harp, knocking it off balance. She grabbed the wood and fumbled the instrument upright before it fell to the polished granite. She lowered her chin and hid her horrified expression behind her veil of golden hair. Despite courtly customs, she would not share her husband.

"Thank God for your beauty, lamb." Dear Aunt Moira's hazel eyes silently expressed sympathy. "Although you have not yet been to court, when you do you will be prized by the nobles there."

Aunty Moira's words didn't ease the anxiety curdling her stomach. She yearned to be prized by only one noble. She could still feel the magic of his hands on her skin.

"Do you have a headache, Cailin?" Aunt Aley's yellow teeth gleamed across the gloomy room. "You look positively ill. Last night must have been quite trying." She thinned her lips. "We do understand. Except Moira, of course." She glanced around the drawing room. "And Lorna."

Cailin's stomach clenched.

Obviously, Aley hadn't enjoyed her husband.

"On the contrary." She rose, wandered to the window and gazed out onto the dark, rain-drenched moor. "Last night was perfect."

Today was the problem. Why was Avondale doing this to her? Was English society so different that a man wasn't considered scandalous if he ignored his wife the day after they wed? She clenched her hands behind her back and stared out the tear-stained window.

"Oh, do stop drooping about like a love-sick turtledove and play for us." Aunt Aley stamped her foot. "Now, lass."

She refused to let Aley taunt her into a spat. Gliding back to the harp, Cailin slid into the chair, and plunked a few random strings. She would let neither Aley, nor Avondale upset her. Her frown softened and her fingers moved into "Beautiful Savior" of their own accord.

Father, only You could arrange such a fine marriage for me in such a breathtakingly short time. You promised, Your plans for me are plans for good and not for evil. I rest in Your goodness.

And she did rest—as best she could. After all, God was sovereign. He remained in control. Nothing could happen to her outside His will. But the tension remained in her neck, and each passing moment stiffened the muscles in her shoulders until her head began to ache.

As if they had a mind of their own, her fingers plucked a new song. After only a few seconds, she realized she played a love ballad. She smiled, and the sweetness inside her chest almost relaxed her stiff muscles.

Certainly Avondale pleased her last night. And he

would surely return by dark. Would their second night together be as delightful as their first?

The mother-of-pearl inlaid, double drawing room doors opened.

Jenny pushed the tea cart into the room and paused.

"Over here." With a ring-laden hand, Aunt Aley patted the brocade cushions of the sofa. "Come, sit next to me, Cailin. As long as His Grace is not here, I'll do the honors."

"Yes, Aunty." Cailin rose from the needlepoint chair behind the harp, skirted around the rosewood instrument, and settled beside her aunt.

Aunt Aley was in one of her moods. She would have stood up to her overbearing aunt, but she didn't give a fig who presided at tea.

But she did so want her husband. Sitting here, beside her where he belonged. With her, every day during her wedding week. How could he snub her so?

With a clink of tongs on the good porcelain, Aunt Aley dropped two morsels of sugar into a cup of tea and passed it to her. "Don't be such a dreamer." Her voice sounded sharp above the homey crackling of the fire. "Weddings aren't made in heaven. His Grace would not have married you at all had he not wasted his inheritance on self-indulgence."

She winced. Tea spilled into her saucer and burned her thumb.

"Aley, everyone knows the truth of what you say, but no one need repeat it." Aunty Moira clucked her tongue. "True, His Grace's income disappeared. But who is to say his wealth went for decadence? Let's just praise God that the duke's presence protects us from the English, and for whatever reason, Cailin makes a charming duchess. His Grace is fortunate indeed."

She shuddered. Papa didn't believe Avondale's money was gone.

"Decadence in the worst form. So say all the reports I've heard from England."

"Gossip you mean. Fie, Aley, hold your tongue." Moira shook a finger at her older sister.

"But we know little of the man except he has an unparalleled pedigree, five titles, and extensive lands near Stirling, as well as throughout England." Aunt Aley passed a particularly inviting plate of flaky scones. "His Grace shows excellent manners, makes a fine appearance, and has lived his entire life in the lap of luxury." She slapped the tongs onto the inlaid table and smiled, showing just how much she enjoyed gossip, hang whomever it hurt. "You know there are a great many stories of irresponsibility." She leaned forward and lowered her voice. "And shadowy deeds. And he does spend a good deal of time at court. I have heard worse—"

"Rumors." Aunty Moira bit delicately into a scone doused in clotted cream.

Cailin pinched her lips.

"Where there's smoke, there's fire." Aunt Aley smacked a scone into her mouth and licked her lips. "I've heard—"

"The duke rides horses well, and he flirts only the least little bit," Lorna interrupted, helping herself to a teaspoonful of clotted cream. "Just enough to give the impression he's a rogue. That's so romantic."

Cailin stirred her tea, glad her friend had chosen not to ride on the hunt with the rest of the wedding guests. She needed all the bolstering she could get. Hearing that Avondale didn't flirt raised her spirits.

Perhaps there was no mistress. Or perhaps he had no need to flirt because he had a mistress who—

No, no, no. She would not think along those lines.

Still—she stirred her tea so fast the best part of it slurped into her saucer. Why had she slept so late as to miss riding on the hunt with him and the wedding guests? And why hadn't Avondale awakened her? Now that dark had fully come, why was he staying away?

"Does he attend church?" Aunty Moira passed the scones without taking one.

"I understand his attendance is sporadic." Cheeks full of scone, Aunt Aley pinched her mouth together, making her double chin more prominent, and helped herself to the largest pastry left on the tea platter.

"If anyone has her ear to the keyhole, it's you, dear sister." Aunty Moira huffed and reached for the jelly platter. "Lorna, I would think one dollop of raspberry jam is adequate over your clotted cream. You shall spoil your girlish figure."

Cailin could have kissed her aunty for changing the subject.

Aunt Aley would pounce on this new topic like a hawk on a mouse.

"Moira, you may as well eat. Retaining your slim figure won't provide you any more opportunities to marry. What silliness for you to catch that bridal bouquet. Depriving yourself is a useless discipline." Aunt Aley's steely eyes sparkled. "You may as well eat your fill."

Aunty Moira winked at Cailin.

Cailin found it hard to believe the plump, disagreeable Aley was Mums's middle sister.

"Nothing done to God's glory is useless." Aunty

Moira sipped her sugarless tea, her gray eyes twinkling.

"You have always been such a dreamy dolt. Retaining a girlish figure isn't..."

Cailin let their chatter fade until it became little louder inside her mind than the driving rain on the slate windowsill. She refused to believe the whispered stories about Avondale. Yet, there had to be a grain of truth in the rumors, else they would not have traveled all the way from London to their country place in the borderlands.

Her hand trembled as she sipped the spicy tea. Where was he? She had run eagerly to the long window in Avondale's bedchamber and stared out for hours after the downpour started. Finally, she came downstairs to the drawing room and waited as all the other guests streamed in.

Still, Avondale had failed to return. Cailin fiddled with the teacup handle. One would expect a new husband to be impatient to rejoin his bride. She kept her gaze fixed on the delicate, blue flowers painted on her teacup.

At least Aunt Moira and Lorna took up for Avondale.

Mums had retired to her room with a reproachful look and an ice cap on her head.

She, too, should have begged off with a headache, but she had expected Avondale any minute. And she preferred company rather than face her husband's empty bedchamber. Perhaps she should have chosen the lonely room. Aley's gossip set her imagination on things far better left alone.

Surely he would return tonight for dinner. He must realize his absence made tongues wag, even if he cared not a sniffle about her feelings. Every guest here recognized his insult.

She slapped the dainty hand-painted cup against the cart's gold-gilded railing, spilling most of the remaining tea into her saucer. She didn't care. What motive could Avondale have for insulting her?

Aunty Aley glared. "Cailin, whatever are you doing?"

Her feeling of loss, regardless of how cheerfully she fought it, grew until her pasted-on smile felt as heavy as the muddy boots the guests had left in the entry. True, she hailed from the country, but she'd never heard of another groom ignoring his bride quite so blatantly.

"Perhaps the king summoned His Grace." Aunty Aley smirked. "I've heard they visit brothels together."

Cailin stood and stalked from the drawing room.

Avondale had some answering to do.

****

Thankful he'd not left his favorite black stallion in England, Avondale jumped into the saddle and took command of the prancing animal. He never used the decorative spurs attached to his knee-high boots. Instead he leaned forward in the small saddle. "Go boy, go."

The beautiful animal surged forward. Just as dawn broke, Avondale headed him on a direct line to the rugged loneliness of the Highlands. His thoughts clattered inside his head louder than the horse's thundering hooves against the rocky soil.

Cailin was so sweet. So beautiful. So loving. But she'd wanted answers.

Beneath his scarlet riding jacket, rivulets of sweat formed between his shoulder blades.

He couldn't give her answers. Not now. Maybe never.

When he'd refused, she'd asked if they could read that old black book together. He swiped an arm across his forehead. He could give her that much.

5

Cailin tossed restlessly in the luxurious bed. Avondale had still not returned from wherever he had gone. Her head pounded. She gritted her teeth and knotted her fists against the anger swirling in her veins.

Finally, she rose and padded barefoot to the wash bowl in the dressing room and brushed her teeth again. She returned to the dark, cavernous bedchamber and threw open a window.

Moonlight had faded into deep shadows when dark clouds rolled in. She thrust her head out the window and let the wind caress her waist-length hair, but the coolness couldn't blow away her frown. The wind was no substitute for the caresses she yearned for. Nor did her anger fade.

Avondale had come to bed so late last night. And tonight, he was even later.

She rubbed a hand across her eyes. Even had she been sleepy, she would have stayed awake. Tonight she would ask him again. Insist he answer.

She left the window open, hurried across the cold granite, and crawled back into the warm bed to snuggle beneath the sheets. The big clock in the corner ticked second by second, still he did not come. She would creep downstairs and peek into Papa's study. She slung her legs over the side of the bed.

The door swung open.

Avondale tiptoed into the room, moved silently across the rug into the dressing room, and closed the door behind him. His clothes rustled as he undressed.

She sprang up and her fingers trembled as she lit a candle. She opened the door.

He spun to her, eyes wide, mouth open, his face a mask of startled guilt. "Blow out that candle." His voice sounded rough.

"But the dark—"

"Snuff out the candle. I like the dark. Blackness is a friend."

She did as he bade her. "Where—?"

"I thought you'd be sleeping, dear Cailin."

"I waited for you."

"You shouldn't." He stepped close and pulled her into his arms. With his lips on her hair, he whispered, "I fell in love with you on our wedding night. So, despite what others may tell you, know that I love you, my beautiful, sweet wife. No matter what happens, always remember I love you."

Anger slipped away as if it had never been.

He wrapped her in his arms and carried her to their bed.

She nestled against him, her ear just above his racing heart.

He loved her. Tonight, that was enough.

She wanted more of that incredible love. Yet, she would question him. When the time was right. She was his wife and had every right to know about his disappearances.

6

But the following night Avondale did not come to bed at all.

Cailin spent the next day busying herself with tasks around the castle, counting every moment until nightfall.

As the sun was setting, the door to the bedchamber creaked open. She turned from her dressing table, yelped, jumped up, ran across the room, and plunged into Avondale's strong, open arms. He'd come early.

"Ah. I see you've changed for dinner, sweet. You look smashing." He nuzzled her bare neck with warm lips, and deposited a kiss just where it sent a tingle straight to her heart. "You are truly a jewel. That deep blue silk matches your incredible eyes."

Leaning back in his embrace, she smiled into his warm brown gaze. Why did she doubt Avondale? Could not a man live his life as he liked? Did a wife need to know every move a man made? A chill shivered the hairs on the nape of her neck. But a wife should know something of the man she married. Still, she refused to nag. "Did you bag a fox today?"

"Alas, no."

Avondale's clothes felt damp against her silk dinner dress, and his lean cheek cool as he pressed it against hers. He smelled of fresh outdoors and warm horseflesh as he cuddled her. Then he kissed her forehead, the tip of her nose, and lingered on her mouth.

The warm pressure of his full lips sent shivers along her spine, but he raised his mouth long before she had enough.

She wrapped her arms around his neck and kissed him until some of the loneliness in her heart drained away.

His eyes looked so kind. His arms were so tender. He seemed every inch the devoted husband.

Contentment filled all the places inside her that had lain empty. After being so rigidly tense all day, her muscles relaxed as if submerged in a warm, swirling pool.

"Cailin, you are a precious gift." He tilted her chin up and brushed his knuckles over her cheek. His eyes looked moist and his breath came in puffs. "God has been most gracious granting me such a lovely wife."

Her own breath came in small pants as if she had run up a hill on the moor. "As a staunch member of the Church of England, you must believe marriages are made in heaven. Do you not?"

"This one is."

Though his clothes felt damp and smelled slightly woolish, he looked impeccable. And his face had a ruddy outdoor appearance that she loved. The sparkle in his eyes set her heart aglow.

She kneaded her fingers through his thick brown hair and lifted her smiling face to his. Though he'd been away, she felt certain she pleased her new husband. Perhaps tonight they would talk. She would not press him, though. She could not risk his fleeing her arms.

He buried his straight nose in her hair and held

her in the circle of his arms. "The storm soon halted our hunt. It's good to see you, sweet wife." Coming from his strong lips, the words promised he cherished her.

She leaned back in his embrace and gazed into his patrician face. "I love your square chin." She wouldn't ask why he hadn't stayed home. Though every inch of her being cried out to know, she wouldn't. With the tips of her fingers she traced the outline of his chin, cleft in the center and slightly bristly to her touch. "It keeps your face from looking too perfect." She would not become a nagging wife only days after the wedding.

He was accustomed to his bachelorhood with no need to be accountable.

"That's too bad, sweetling. Nothing keeps your face from being perfect." He cupped her chin in his hand and smiled into her eyes.

She twined her hands around his neck. "I was concerned. Where have you been? The others returned hours ago." Her body went rigid. Blast, she'd done it. Started nagging. If she had no better control of her emotions, he'd think her a shrew.

He dropped his hand from her cheek, jutted his jaw, and stepped in the direction of the door. "You'll think me tiresome, but I fell asleep in the gatekeeper's little house at the far end of the estate."

"You went so far? Alone?"

"Blighter that I am, I got lost. Had a most difficult time finding my direction back to the castle. I followed your lights when I drew near enough to see them. You had candles in the window for me, as it were."

His contrite smile took her breath away. She had no heart to questions him further. They had so little time together, she feared to spoil it. "I'm so sorry, Avondale. You're chilled and wet. You must get out of those riding breeches. "I laid out your evening clothes on the bed. Mums will ring the dinner bell any moment now."

He glanced down at the formal clothes, then pulled her into his arms and pressed his lips against hers in another blissful kiss that seemed both hungry and contrite.

Dinner became a distant thought. She wanted only to stay with him in the sanctity of their room where she would have him to herself.

He pulled away.

"Unless you're not hungry." She helped him out of his damp jacket, and her fingers began unbuttoning his shirt. She puckered her lips to tempt him as she was tempted.

"Starving. There you have it. Now, run downstairs and placate your mums before she gives us both a wigging. Meanwhile, I will change."

"We could stay here."

"Best if we go down. We have guests."

She sighed and kissed his warm, strong lips again. "I could watch you change."

"Not this time, sweet."

Why ever not? Yet he looked so stern, she nodded and did as he bid. At the doorway, she sent him a flirtatious smile over her nearly bare shoulder and blew him another kiss. "You have all my love."

Once outside the closed door, she pressed her ear to hear his movements. But he must have returned to the dressing room because she heard nothing. The man possessed an uncanny ability to move with stealth.

Downstairs, she fluttered among the guests still

lingering from the wedding, hummed a happy tune, and turned often to watch the stairs, scarcely able to wait until he showed his handsome face.

She glimpsed him at the top of the stairs and lost her breath. Dressed in black velvet with a stark white cravat and black waistcoat, his tall, distinguished figure could not be more regal…or handsome. And he was her very own husband.

Thank You, Lord.

When he descended, his courtly friends immediately clustered around him. Although he offered her his arm and escorted her into the dining room, his change of clothes seemed to have transformed him into a different man. A cool aristocrat who showed neither tenderness, nor love in his attitude towards her.

Was he ashamed of her in front of his peers?

Though she smiled her sweetest, knowing her dimples showed, and patted his waiting chair after he seated her, he remained distant.

He turned his complete attention to his fellow English nobles. Snobbish as only an English lord could be, a thin line denting the usually smooth place between his brows, he barely acknowledged her presence.

The turtle soup became paste in her mouth.

It was as if Avondale were two different men. She loved the private one. The one only she saw in their bedchamber. She covered her mouth with her napkin, dropped her head so no one would see, blinked back tears, and dabbed at a rivulet that escaped.

She didn't even like the public man.

And it appeared that the public Lord Geoffrey Mountebank, Fifth Duke of Avondale, didn't fancy her any more than she cared for him.

Despite her best resolve, was she doomed to have a marriage that mirrored her parents'?

****

Megan stood at the dining room door.

Had there not been so many guests at the table, Cailin would have jumped up and hugged her. "Megan. Welcome."

When Brody strode in behind her, Cailin breathed a deep sigh. She beamed at them both. How gloriously good to see them.

And what a surprise! She'd never have believed Brody could transform from a Highland warrior into looking so dashing and distinguished. Where had the poor Scot gotten those clothes?

An image of the Earl of Mabry's cruel expression flashed into her mind. Truly Megan made an excellent choice to flee. Now she was married, and Papa could do nothing.

Cailin grasped her stemmed glass with both hands. She wanted so to clap her hands in glee. Then she began to shake. She blinked rapidly. She who had tried so to honor Mums and Papa…felt so terribly confused. She let her hands flutter to her lap.

Why was her marriage so different from what she'd expected while Megan looked so happy?

Megan led Brody to the head of the table. "Papa, this is Brody Alexander MacCauley-MacMurry, my husband."

Silence descended over the room.

Face scarlet, veins popping in his forehead, Papa jerked from his chair and ordered Megan and Brody to the library.

As soon as the three hurried from the room, conversation rose to a roar.

All the while Papa kept Megan and Brody in the library, she barely tasted her food, fiddling instead with her silverware.

Questions and conversation continued around her, but she barely joined in.

Of course, Papa was livid with Megan. That was to be expected, after she ran off to escape marrying the nasty Earl Mabry and wed Brody instead.

But Cailin couldn't concentrate on what might be occurring in Papa's library with Megan and Brody. One thought spiraled around and around in her mind.

Her duke publicly snubbed her.

Avondale seemed in high spirits, cordial and jovial with everyone. He even greeted Brody, after he and Megan returned to the table. Even Mums received one of Avondale's you-are-the-most-important-person-in-my-life smiles. Every guest at the entire table garnered his personal attention.

Except her.

When her leg accidentally brushed Avondale's under cover of the tablecloth, he moved his muscular thigh away. She leaned next to him and laid her hand on the soft velvet of his right sleeve.

But he turned his face to the Earl of Argyle and began a lengthy discussion concerning some silly intrigue at court.

Why had he changed so completely? She dropped her napkin over her uneaten food. Inside their chamber he'd been so loving. He'd been a different man, attentive and charming. He'd made her feel like a queen. He'd seemed genuinely happy to see her and had again expressed his joy in her. And their few nights together had been unbelievable.

Why had he changed? She traced the gold rim of her goblet with her finger and glanced across the table.

Brody's encouraging smile went straight to her torn heart. Such a gallant gentleman. Mayhap she could ask his opinion of the bizarre quandary in which she'd found herself.

No. Brody knew less of the ways of courtly men than she. She'd have to risk Avondale's displeasure and question him herself. She would not be hesitant. She would pour all her love into her marriage and overcome Avondale's absences and his snobbishness. She lifted her chin and smiled at her husband.

He didn't notice.

She pulled in a deep, calming breath. Nothing would stand in the way of her creating a marriage filled with love. Surely, since she'd been obedient God would bless her marriage. Bad things didn't happen to His obedient children.

She was strong and filled with love. Regardless of her hostile feelings against the public duke, she would smooth away this bump in the carriage path.

7

Avondale sauntered from the smoking room after deliberately losing a game of whist to his father-in-law, and, as was now his habit, headed for Loch Drummond.

His nightly trek to the loch gave him time to reflect. Two weeks had passed since he made his vows, and surely God had abandoned him.

He opened the back castle door. A burst of cool night air washed over him. He lifted his chin and pulled in a deep breath filled with the taste of bracing, country air. How could he face his beautiful bride? Each night brought more torture.

But tonight he *would* return to Cailin, otherwise the woman wouldn't sleep. And he *would* again permit the sweet innocent to read the Bible to him, but he would sit across the room in the shadows.

At first he'd been angry when he discovered the strength of Cailin's faith, and then he'd felt indulgent. Why not allow her this pleasure when he must deny her so many others? He lengthened his stride until his boots thundered over the marshy moor.

Her faith had yet to be tried, so, of course, she held to her naive belief.

He fisted his hands. But reading the Bible couldn't help him. Nothing and no one could. His frown softened.

Yet her turquoise eyes sparkled and her creamy

complexion glowed when she defended the faith he questioned. And he'd grown to appreciate the intelligence behind the beauty of her angelic face. He beat one fist against the other. Why could he not be like other men?

She knew exactly who she was. She was bright and shining, inside and out. Sure of herself. Secure in her world, whether inside the castle or out with the common folk.

He heaved a sigh. Would that he had that ability. He growled deep in his throat. Since he'd wed, the darkness had grown worse. How much longer could he hide his past from Cailin?

He'd silenced her questions with anger he barely controlled. And turned a stony face from her hurt.

He'd hoped being away from court and living inside the MacMurry castle would help. Of course it hadn't. He walked a tightrope. One wrong step and he'd tumble to his death. And he'd take sweet Cailin with him. He should never have married.

Yet he must produce a legal male heir.

Living with her family was proving even more difficult then he'd expected. Only during his nights alone with his sweet wife did he feel truly free. She was his rock. Yet the more time he spent with her, the less he wanted to confess. He hated to dim the love shining in her face.

She claimed his life lay in the hand of God. Hah! What man could understand God's will? He stumbled to his knees and buried his face in his hands. When he searched to decipher God, God's lack of concern stared him boldly in the face. He divined no heavenly design in his life. Not unless God planned for him to experience hell on earth.

God had forgotten him. What did the dark future hold? He pressed his forehead against his fists. With his tiny mustard seed of faith, he prayed he would not ruin Cailin's life. How much longer could he hide the truth from her?

He'd keep his dark side away from Castle Drummond and Cailin. Perhaps she need never know. His knowledge of horseflesh, his fluency in French and their subtle deceits, and his ability to play a fair game of chess stood him in good stead with the rest of the family. With Cailin he could only skulk in the shadows. He rose and rubbed the back of his aching neck.

Her father was responding to Brody's almost constant company with grudging respect. The older man yearned for a son.

Avondale groaned. He had wished to gain his father-in-law's respect, as well. But how? He'd never known his own father. Yet he must remain distant with Lord MacMurry. He wished to bring no trouble to the family and his lovely Cailin.

He walked to the edge of the loch, pulled off his jacket, tossed it to the ground, and listened to the whisper of soft waves lapping the shore.

Nothing he did during the long days tired him enough to let him sleep at night. Only Cailin with her soft, even breath lulled him into sleep just before dawn broke. Then when the first ray of sunlight filtered through the window hangings, he woke, fully alert, with the need to be away from the sweet innocence of her eyes.

Fully clothed, he plunged beneath the still black surface. The icy water closed over his head. He'd do what he could to protect Cailin. His heavy boots pulled him down, down into the black depths.

He watched Cailin from afar when she was unaware. Her wonderful eyes and her generous service to the common people revealed how much she cared, especially about the little people, the ones he barely noticed, the servants, the working people from the village, and the hordes of people who begged at her kitchen door. She deserved every bit of love he had for her…and ever so much more.

Many men died—because of him. His boots dragged him down, down. The water rushed beside his ears. Eyes wide open, he could see nothing. How easy to let himself sink to the bottom. He shook his head, trying to clear his mind of the black burden. No. He had responsibilities—to Cailin, to his royal mother, to his estates, and all the people who looked to him for livelihood and protection. There was no easy way for him.

He kicked his feet and turned his face upward to the surface where moonlight flickered a path through the dark, still water. He would not shirk his responsibility again. Not ever again.

His head broke surface and he filled his lungs with sweet, fresh air.

He loved the warmth in her eyes when she didn't think he saw her. Sometimes he let himself hope. Sometimes he dreamed of a normal life with her. When her tinkling laugh rang out, he believed the impossible.

He loved her laugh—though he heard from a distance, when she sat with Megan and Brody's sister, Fiona, who'd come with her brother to live inside the castle.

Or when Cailin played with one of the kittens that scurried around the castle. He loved the creamy curve of her cheek as it rounded when she smiled. And the graceful line of her neck. And the way her long lashes framed her beautiful eyes.

His stomach churned.

He even liked the way she wrinkled her nose when she didn't like something. And he loved the full blown beauty of her lips. Could scarce tear his gaze from them when they talked together. He loved her spirit, flashing through at unexpected times.

Last night, when she'd revealed her plan, his heart thumped fast.

"I have a mission for you." Her sweet voice made his blood surge.

"You have plans for me?" His words emerged in staccatos like drum beats.

"Yes." Those lake blue eyes sparkled like sun on the flashing waters of the sea. "I need you to help me start a home for the Highland widows and orphans left by the battle."

He hid the disappointment crinkling his soul. True, an orphanage would be a good thing, but he'd be no help. He'd never be able to face the children whose fathers he'd put into the grave.

He shook his head and water sprayed all around him.

He wanted to forget he was a murderer.

8

"Cailin, I've something important to tell you." Megan whispered and tugged at Cailin's sleeve. "Take a walk with me, please."

Cailin stopped pacing the library floor and laid the book she had attempted, but totally failed to read on a corner table. "You have a secret?"

"Shush. Just come with me." Megan rushed through the castle rooms as if they were on fire. At the back door, she pulled several capes from hooks on the wall and threw one.

After catching the cape with one hand, Cailin snugged the warm wool around her shoulders, and followed Megan out the door and down the flagstone path. Cool air blew through her hair.

Megan pushed her hand through the crook of Cailin's arm, and they huddled together against the unseasonably cool wind as they walked. She glanced around.

Cailin followed Megan's gaze and saw no servant, no member of the family, nor any of the remaining guests in sight. Apparently this was Megan's plan.

"Brody and I ventured out last night and rescued a number of other wounded warriors from the cave where they all hid from the English soldiers tracking them down to kill them."

Cailin sucked in a breath.

They passed through the portcullis and walked

down the faint path that led to the broch.

"Don't worry. We weren't seen. We hid the men inside the broch for now, until they recover from their wounds, and then Brody can whisk them to a safer place."

Cailin planted her boots on the grass. "But it is dangerous for our family to harbor wanted men."

"Those men are Brody's close friends. I can't stand by and let the redcoats find and hang them. Besides, they are badly wounded. They would die if we left them inside that cave."

"But—"

"Of course, it is dangerous. But Aunty Moira, Fiona, and several of the servants are caring for them."

"But—"

Megan thrust a chilled finger against Cailin's lips. "I am well aware of all the buts! This is something we must do. Papa turns a blind eye, though I am certain he knows the men are hidden inside the broch."

"If Papa knows, then—"

"He does." Megan gave a saucy smile. "Aunty Moira has taken a fancy to one of them."

Cailin's thoughts scrambled. If Papa and Aunty Moira thought their giving a safe haven to wounded Highlanders acceptable, perhaps Brody and Megan were not so addled as they appeared.

She gazed across the cloud-shadowed moor to the three-story round building no longer protected by crumbling rock walls, but tucked against a hill, and barely discernible to a gaze not searching for the ancient fortress. Gaping holes punctured the sagging brick walls, giving the impression the building verged on collapse.

"You condone Fiona nursing wounded men?"

"She's nursed her brothers for years, and she's acquainted with the men. They were all neighbors in the Highlands. And they are her brother's best friends."

"But she's a young lady."

Megan grinned. "Yes, and very mature for her age." She put a hand on Cailin's arm. "We should not go to the broch. I think it best that the fewer people who visit the better. There might be an English soldier lurking about, and we don't want to raise his suspicions." She turned to face the distant castle. "Let's go back inside. I just wanted to tell you without any listening ears. One of our English guests might hurry to tell the Duke of Cumberland. Then where would we all land?"

"Inside the Tower of London." Cailin shuddered and started walking home. "My family is all insane," she muttered.

****

Barely two weeks had passed since Megan told Cailin of the wounded men hiding inside their broch.

No redcoats had set foot on their land.

"Come up into the attic with me, Cailin," Aunty Moira urged, tying an apron over her navy day dress.

Cailin knotted the bow on her own apron, and followed her Aunt's clattering footsteps up the wooden stairs.

"Aunty Moira, why did you lure me into the attic? I know this searching for an old painting of Mums is a pretense." Cailin dropped to her knees to kneel beside her aunt in front of a dusty chest.

Aunty unfastened the hinge and lifted the lid.

Cailin sneezed.

Aunty put her warm hand over Cailin's. "I'm in love."

Cailin's mouth dropped. "With one of the English gentry?"

Aunty's cheeks were stained a pretty pink, and her eyes glistened with unshed tears. "His name is Ian MacDonald. He is one of the men Brody rescued, and he is recovering from his wounds inside the broch. I have been nursing him, and we have fallen in love."

For a few seconds Cailin couldn't speak. Then she managed to whisper, "I…I'm so very happy for you."

"I knew God gave me His blessing when I caught your bridal bouquet. I had only to wait and see who He brought into my life." Her face glowed. "Ian is one of the finest men I have ever met."

Cailin gathered her wits. "But he has a price on his head."

Aunty sighed. "Yes. God does not make life easy for His children."

"What will you do?"

"I would love for you to attend our wedding."

How could she throw cold water on her aunt's beautiful dream? She couldn't. "But, how will you manage?"

"Brody is passing as a Lowland Scot. With the right clothes, so can Ian. And your Mums promised to handle your Papa. She said I should move out of my rooms into an apartment on the third floor where Ian and I shall have privacy."

Her smile was the happiest Cailin had ever seen.

"And Ian will stay out of sight."

When had Mums become so tolerant? Of course, her mother wanted her youngest sister to be happy.

But marriage to another Highlander? Cailin's stomach fluttered. Dear Aunty Moira certainly would have no other opportunity to wed. Perhaps she was right to grasp what happiness she could find.

War changed life so drastically. For everyone. Long erected barriers fell. Society's taboos changed. Perhaps these were the only good results of war.

She leaned over and hugged Aunty Moira. "I love you, and I will so enjoy your wedding. When will you marry?"

"Today. I have but to change my frock. We are meeting Pastor Fergus in our own little chapel."

"Oh my. Oh my. Oh my. Why so quickly?"

"Ian and I do not know if soldiers will continue to search for him. Or if he will be detected as a Highlander. And neither of us is growing any younger." Aunty Moira's broad smile belied her age. She looked no older than a young girl being presented to the Queen. And her lovely gray eyes danced.

Cailin dropped the lid of the chest, creating a cloud of dust. Both sneezed. "Let us hurry. I cannot wait tò meet my new uncle."

Their high-heeled boots clattered on the wooden steps, and then on marble as they sped, each to her room.

"Jenny!"Cailin called.

The rusty-haired Irish maid seemed already to know how the wind blew, and she had Cailin's pink silk dinner gown spread on the massive bed.

The wedding was lovely. Sunlight glowed through the stained glass windows of the small chapel, bringing peace and joy with its soft rays.

Because Ian was a hunted man, he and Aunty Moira simply clasped hands in the outdated Scottish way and pledged their vows in front of a beaming Pastor Fergus.

And she, Mums, and Megan witnessed their troth.

****

Cailin's mind drifted like a wisp of smoke, uncertain she had really awakened. She turned on her side in the luxurious bed, and cupped her cheek in her hand. Her dream had recalled Aunty Moira's and Ian's sweet expressions as they had gazed into each other's eyes during their wedding.

She sat bolt upright in the huge, empty bed staring into the darkness. "Aunty Moira and Ian are so very happy that their happiness wraps around each person near them. Their love is palpable." A sigh worked up from the depths of her chest. "Why cannot I find that happiness?" She caressed the empty sheet where Avondale should be lying. "Love is not just what one feels, it is how one acts," she whispered. "We've been married over three months, and I still know so very little of you, my husband."

Fumbling noises emerged from their small drawing room. The normally open door was shut, and candlelight gleamed above the threshold. Bumping sounded as though someone dragged a huge chest across the floor.

Oh, Father, not again. Please, not again.

Something crashed to the floor.

She slid out of bed and cringed as her bare feet landed on cold granite. She pulled on her dressing gown, and the cool fabric against her bare skin drove away the last vestiges of sleep.

Tiptoeing to the door, she placed her hand on the

latch, and then hesitated. She wasn't afraid.

Avondale had never hurtfully laid a hand on her, but occasionally during the last few days his eyes had looked so wild she scarcely recognized him. Caught between his distance and his wildness, he seemed to be two men.

She folded her arms gently across her stomach. Now she had the baby to think of.

In the adjoining room, Avondale's voice reverberated around the walls. His footsteps paced the length of the chamber and back. He stumbled, and she heard the thud of flesh against iron. A shiver crept up her spine.

Love meant taking care of the loved one. Love decreed taking action when her husband needed her. Love entailed more than feeling warm and cherished. Love gave. And gave. And kept on giving. Even when the giver had no idea how to help.

She pressed her ear against the sitting room door. Silence. Certainly Avondale needed her. She pushed down on the hard iron latch and shoved. The inlaid door opened barely an inch.

The stench of something burning bit into her nostrils.

She shoved her shoulder against the door, but it budged only a few more inches. She squeezed through.

By the light of the silver moon beaming through the many half-curtained windows, she saw her husband sprawled across the Turkish carpet, his head next to the enormous fireplace and irons. An overturned candle burned into the thick fibers of the red carpet not inches from his limp hand.

She rushed to his side, dropped to her knees, and smothered a velvet pillow over the spreading flame.

The odor of scorch billowed up with a sooty cloud of smoke, but the fire died.

"Avondale, Geoffrey, speak to me." She shook his inert shoulder.

Where was the promise of all that strength? He looked so helpless. His jacket was hanging open, his clothes rumpled.

He stirred and turned a lax face in her direction. Opening one dark eye he drawled, "I'm in a bit of a fuzz." He put a hand to his forehead. "But I see you are the sprite who brings the breath of angel wings." He grimaced. "Guardian angel. Dash it all. Keep out that bully. Lock the doors against him. He and his horsemen. They're after me."

She turned away, unable to bear seeing the fright distorting his face. What did he think he saw?

She glanced around the room. Avondale had blocked the door to the hall with his huge clothing press. He had moved the fainting couch to obstruct the door to their bedchamber. She'd only just been able to force her way inside.

She touched his high, intelligent forehead. Her fingers discovered a large bump growing thicker.

Grabbing her hand, he shakily pulled himself into a sitting position, wound his arms around her, and buried his head in her bosom. For the time being he was quiet.

She must get him into their bed and perhaps give him a small dose of laudanum.

When he woke, mayhap he would have forgotten his nightmare and would become his sweet, gentle self…or the haughty, cold shadow of himself.

She shivered.

Either way, she must help him find refuge from

his demons. How did he cope during the day when he disappeared? Did his duties worry him so that he went a little wild at night?

As if Avondale was a small, frightened child, she kissed the angry knot on his forehead and held him against her breast and rocked him, humming a soothing tune.

For a few minutes he was quiet.

Then he freed himself and jumped up. "Billy the Butcher! Look out the window! I'm certain he's arrived. Twas only a matter of time." His normally pleasing baritone voice sounded high-pitched…and fearful.

Avondale paced the large chamber, running his strong fingers through his brown hair and leaving the thick mass standing on end. His elegant breeches wore patches of mud, and his waistcoat was half unbuttoned. Limping on one stockinged foot, and one boot, her handsome husband looked wild-eyed and totally unlike his usual debonair self.

Throwing the half-opened curtains all the way back, he pressed his nose to the glass, and then stalked from window to window. The candle sconces lighting the walls wavered, dimmed, and almost blew out from his momentum.

"Avondale, whatever is the matter?" Following him, she gazed out the window he had just left. Nothing to see outside or down below, but empty walks and driving rain. "I'm certain no one has arrived. Neither the dogs nor the servants announced visitors." She put a hand on his arm. "Please calm down. No one is anywhere nearby."

"Yes, yes. He's outside. See the blood dripping from his hands. He's calling me. Don't… don't let him inside." His brown eyes looked dark and glazed, and Avondale stared through her.

She grasped his strong shoulders. "There's no one outside, my darling."

She must discover what haunted him. She'd heard of men returned from battle who suffered still from what they'd experienced. And certainly Avondale looked like a man who'd experienced horror. Had he fought at Culloden?

She took her husband's clenched hand, but he pulled free and again paced from window to window, staring out of each one.

"Listen! Listen! Can't you hear Bloody Billy calling me?" He cupped a hand over his ear.

She held her breath and listened. The wind howled almost like an angry voice. She pressed her ear to the thick window glass, but only the hissing sleet driving against the unyielding stones of the castle reached her ears. "There's no one there. It's all right. No one is outside."

Lurching from side to side, her husband continued to pace, his single boot thudding on the thick carpet.

Doors creaked open in the upstairs hall.

She could imagine guests, nightcaps askew, peeking out.

Again she tried to calm him. "Come to bed, my dearest."

He shook off her hand and strode to the doorway to the hall. "He shall not get you. You must hide. I shall lead him away." Shoving aside the heavy furniture as if each piece was a toy, he flung the door open, clattered out, sped down the long hall, and took the stairs at a run. Soon, the back castle door slammed open and shut.

She rushed to the window. He dashed through the downpour and slopped through puddles on the path to the stables. Would he injure himself? Already his soaked jacket and bedraggled shirt clung to his body.

Soon a horse galloped out the stable door. Avondale rode bareback in a line to the open moor, his wet clothes clinging to his body. He would catch his death of consumption.

Someone coughed behind her.

She turned. "Hennings?"

Avondale's muscular valet stood just inside the open door.

She pulled her robe closed. Her hand trembled. "Please send someone to fetch His Grace back to the castle."

"Yes, Milady." Hennings backed out the door. "I shall go myself." He rushed down the hall, his nightclothes flapping about his bare ankles.

She followed.

Heads were indeed peeking from bedchamber doors.

"I'm so sorry, we awakened you. Everything is fine. His Grace had to see to an emergency. Please go return to your beds."

Yawns, nods, and a few curious looks met her gaze. Then one by one, each returned to his room and closed his door.

Mums bustled down the hall. "Is everything well?"

"I don't know." She tried to smile.

Mums looked so worried.

"However, I believe I shall entail Rafe to accompany Avondale, should he be called out again in the middle of the night."

"Rafe?"

"The brawny Scot who shoes the horses."

"Whatever for?"

"To keep my dear husband safe."

Mums eyes widened. Her mouth thinned. "To be his guard, you mean." She frowned. "Isn't his valet enough?"

So Mums had not missed Avondale's valet's real mission. How many others understood as well? If only the too long lingering wedding guests would return to court or to their own homes. Perhaps they enjoyed the Scottish country air more than the more polluted atmosphere of London. Certainly the hunting here was superior to that in England.

Or perhaps Mums's fine cook kept them too happy.

And Papa would never be rude to such high born gentry by asking them when they planned to return to their homes.

Cailin shook her head. "Apparently Avondale's valet sleeps at night. I must see that Rafe does not."

"Oh my dear, whatever can be wrong with His Grace?" Tears glistened in Mums aqua eyes.

"I wish I knew. I'll call for his royal mother. Perhaps she'll know what to do."

"Oh, heavens."

"I wouldn't send for her if I was not just a bit desperate." Cailin bit her lip.

9

Cailin watched Avondale stir, open his dark chocolate eyes, and stretch. Her heart ached at the loving expression in their warm depth.

"Ah, my dearest wife. I've just enjoyed the soundest sleep. I say, what time is it?"

"Almost daylight. Are you still feeling ill?"

"Ill?" Avondale's face puckered into a puzzled expression. "I'm quite refreshed." He opened his arms, and smiled. "Come in to bed, dear Cailin."

She hesitated. Did he have no memory of last night? Had the laudanum his valet administered after Avondale entered the castle following his wild midnight ride erased the terror from her husband's mind? What awful nightmare haunted him? Who was Billy the Butcher? If she questioned Avondale, would she cause him to slip into another spell? She must be cautious with what she said.

"I sent word to Stirling to invite your royal mother to visit us again."

"Smashing. But whatever for?" He patted the silk sheets lying smoothly next to him. "Come to me."

"I…I thought she might like to be among the first to know that we are expecting a baby." She could not bring herself to tell him the real reason she'd summoned his mother.

His eyes widened and sparkled. A huge boyish grin transformed his handsome face. His broad, bare shoulders straightened. "Fine! Fine!" He caressed her arm. "And how are you feeling?"

"Physically, I've never felt better. No morning sickness."

"And emotionally?" His proud grin had turned tender.

Tentatively she touched his lips. "I have ups and downs." She was so worried about him.

He smiled and stroked his bare chest. "That's very normal, I think. Though I'm not so sure I believe in prayer, this is definitely an answer." His warm hand cupped hers. "Having a son will take a heavy burden from my shoulders." A frown puckered his fine forehead. "You must take care of yourself. I think no horse riding until the baby arrives." With his free hand, he stroked her hair. "Now come, my sweet little kitten. I'm glad the royal mother is visiting, but you're the one I really want to see."

The familiar warm, loving feeling gathered inside her heart.

Perhaps the scene last night had been caused by taut nerves.

Avondale had returned over soon from the boar hunt in order to be in time for the masquerade Mums and Megan had planned for Fiona.

Papa had been grumpy as well, when the men had reappeared empty-handed.

Yet Avondale had seemed on edge during dinner. Had something else happened to her husband between dinner and when she found him so agitated in the bedchamber? Were affairs of his estates causing him concern? Was Bloody Billy a hired assassin?

Father, whatever Avondale's problem, please do not let him become so unsettled again. Help me make him happy.

Help me share his burdens. Help me to be a good wife. Give me wisdom.

She slid into bed next to her husband.

10

Cailin and Avondale spent a happy hour reading the Bible together and discussing the various passages before going to bed.

Once the single candle he permitted was doused, he held her in his strong arms. His full, warm lips pressed sweet love onto her neck and lips. "I fear so for the child, my bride. I would not put his life into any danger. Having a son is not to be taken lightly." He stroked her hair and cradled her against his muscle-ridged chest.

She heard the rock-solid beat of his heart. "But I'm a strong, healthy woman. We should have no fear—"

"You look as delicate as a fine china cup." Avondale's eyes, shining in the moonlight, held shadows that darkened them to onyx. "You are my treasure, and I will not risk putting you or our child in the slightest danger."

For the next several nights she contented herself with enjoying his presence and explaining the meaning of various passages in Scripture. One passage in Colossians seemed to particularly attract his attention.

Who hath delivered us from the power of darkness and hath translated us into the kingdom of his dear Son: In Whom we have redemption through his blood, even the forgiveness of sins.

Yet, each morning his side of the bed was empty.

After taking breakfast with the family, Cailin

found herself walking in the garden savoring the freshness of the morning, listening to the songs of birds, and inhaling the scent of roses.

More often than not, Brody measured footsteps with her.

"Where is Megan?"

"Ach. She seems taken with some of the English gentry. I think yer ma has given me wife the chore of entertaining the ladies." He walked, hands clasped behind his broad back, a frown between his straight brows.

"I see." Cailin avoided brushing her morning dress on the roses thrusting their thorny branches over the paved path.

They walked together in silence, each trapped inside their own thoughts until they reached the sty over the hedgerow that marked the end of the garden. He reached out a huge hand and helped her over, though she'd easily scampered over the sty since she was a child.

"I wrote a new tune for Megan. Would ye hear me before I play it for her?"

Perhaps if she went with him, she would dredge up the courage to ask him what he thought about Avondale's odd behavior. "You have your bagpipes hidden?"

Of course he did. The English forbade the playing of bagpipes and confiscated any they found, imprisoning the owner inside the Tower of London.

"Aye. They are hidden inside the mews. If ye have the time we could trot over there and I could play for ye. Ye could tell me if ye thought Megan would like her song."

Already their feet were pointed in that direction.

"And do ye think that His Grace will turn me in to the Duke of Cumberland?"

And so it went, each day falling into a pattern.

She, asking simple questions which might help her form a picture of why her husband acted so strange that he needed a bodyguard, and Brody looking lost while the woman he loved with all his heart spent her days with others.

****

Aunty Moira shared the drawing room with Cailin and the one or two wedding guests who seemed to have decided to set up residence inside the castle.

Ian often stopped in for tea as well. He seldom spoke, but his adoring looks and hovering tenderness, so at odds with his large stature and clumsy feet, proclaimed to even the most jaded English lady that the two were very much in love.

Aunty Moira blossomed in his presence, her hazel eyes shining, and her complexion glowing like a lass's. They sat close, knees touching, on the settee facing the low table holding the tea things.

One glance at Ian's proud face and Cailin guessed their secret.

"You are in the family way, are you now?" She wagged a buttered cake at her aunt.

A becoming pink flushed Moira's face. Her lips tilted at the corners. "Whatever makes you think so?"

"You have that almost holy look of expectation." Cailin touched her own rounding stomach.

A grin split Ian's homely face. "That we are," he burst out, his chest swelling and his blue eyes alight.

Several of the ladies covered their mouths. One

choked.

Cailin leaned forward and took Moira's hand. "I'm so very happy for the two of you."

Moira tilted her head and smiled. "I did catch your bridal bouquet."

"Good heavens! Surely you don't believe that superstition." Aunt Aley shifted her portly body on the sofa. She had grown grumpier each day in proportion to Aunty Moira's happiness.

"No, of course not. But I do believe in God's abundant blessing." Moira gazed around the clusters of people taking tea and cakes. "The Scriptures say there is no difference between Jew and Greek—the same Lord is Lord of all, and richly blesses all who call on Him."

Cailin nodded. Yes. Scot or English. Fugitive or gentry.

God was no respecter of persons. He doled out blessings for all.

Still, she would be happier if Avondale sat beside her in this cozy room rather than being out somewhere attending to whatever business kept him away so often.

His demons seemed tamed. But for how long?

11

The evening of the masquerade arrived.

Cailin was elated. During the past two days Avondale had remained wonderfully attentive at night and had been somewhat less snobbish during the small amount of time he was home during the day. And he'd had no more strange spells.

Perhaps she had called needlessly for his royal mother. Certainly she wasn't looking forward to the dowager's visit. And yet she feared not to ask her counsel. What if Avondale had another episode? Certainly the woman could enlighten her in regard to Avondale's actions.

"Are you ready to go down, Cailin?" Wearing a shepherdess gown and carrying a curved staff, Fiona looked as fresh and lovely as an angel. Her long auburn locks were bound with a thick yellow ribbon that matched the yellow grosgrain of her gown. She possessed the same good looks as her brother, only hers were far more delicate. She no more resembled a real shepherdess than a horse resembled a mouse. She was exquisite. Her red curls fell unbound to her waist. Her azure eyes sparkled. Her cheeks were pink above her pretty bow of a mouth.

She and Fiona met Megan in the hallway. Megan looked ethereal in her green Queen-of-the-Fairies dress with its gauzy wings. All of them glided down the stairs together.

Once again, the ballroom looked festive. Tall centerpieces of late June flowers graced the tables above every type of finger food and crystal bowls of punch. Not even the haggis that must be served at all occasions caused the slightest sickness in her stomach.

She held the stick high until the gold mask covered her eyes.

Avondale should arrive soon. He'd been detained by some matter about one of his estates, but sent word he would arrive as soon as he solved the problem.

She gazed through the eye slits at the effervescent crowd. Many of these people had attended her wedding. All wore elaborate costumes.

She and Avondale dressed as the Queen and King of England. The gold crown circling her head was a bit heavy, yet she loved it, and the gold gauze over her silk dress was fashioned after what King George's queen would have worn, had the German had a queen.

Mums and Papa came as the Queen and King of Hearts. Her seamstress had sewn a large white heart that covered most of the front and back of Mums's red satin bodice that could easily be removed so her expensive dress could be worn for other occasions. Were not her family and most Scots known for being frugal?

The joyous music lifted Cailin's heart, and she tapped her toes. Life could not be more wonderful. Her husband loved her, and she was carrying his child.

And Rafe shadowed Avondale at night while Hennings hovered over him during the day. And her husband had not even caught a sniffle from his wet ride.

Tonight was Fiona's welcome to Scottish society, with some English sprinkled in as future courters for

Fiona. The engraved invitations had mentioned Fiona's introduction to society—not her debut, which Mums planned to hostess at a later date. Mums adored throwing parties, and this ball helped compensate for her disappointment at missing Megan's wedding.

As Cailin expected, but Fiona had doubted, multiple suitors surrounded Fiona from the moment she shyly entered the ballroom. Young English and Scottish lords had been instructed by their parents to look over the new lass in anticipation of her having a large dowry. Even had there been no dowry, Cailin was certain Fiona would never lack suitors.

When Aunty Moira and Mums came by to greet her, Cailin hugged them.

Papa bent and kissed her cheek. His square face and rugged features appeared happier tonight than he'd looked since Megan brought Brody home. Perhaps her parents were accepting the Highland fugitive.

A sense of rightness filled her.

Brody and Megan were also doing well. No outsiders suspected Megan's delightful husband was really a Highlander with a price on his head.

Cailin smiled.

And never had Fiona look so happy…or so beautiful. Taller than the English lasses, she moved with the in-born grace of a ballerina.

As guests arrived for the party, Papa stood at the entrance to the ballroom, leaned on his elegant hand-carved ebony cane, and shook hands with Scots and English alike.

When most had gathered in the ballroom, Papa walked to the raised dais, stood in front of the seated musicians and banged the floor with his cane. After he had secured all the guests' attention, he signaled the orchestra. The strings and piano broke into a fanfare. Papa motioned to Fiona.

Pink flooded her face. Looking elated and flushed, Brody's sister took her place of honor at the dais.

Papa held up her hand. "This is my son-in-law's sister. I think she is something like a cousin twice-removed. She has come to live in our castle and is a part of our family, and I trust you will treat her as such."

The guests clapped.

The young gentlemen, invited for just this purpose, clapped mightily and sported grins. Most wore satins, powdered wigs, knee breeches, buckled shoes, and black masks. Others, Fiona's costume having leaked out via the servants, dressed as simple shepherds. They strutted about the room vying for Fiona's attention.

Fiona kissed Papa's cheek and thanked him prettily, her burr hidden with the strict English lessons Megan had been giving. She blushed even pinker at the toasts and well wishes many of the guests voiced.

Cailin toasted her, and then ran forward to hug Fiona, who already seemed like a younger sister.

The butler announced Avondale's arrival. He looked magnificent. Gold became his brown hair and chocolate eyes. The crown circling his high forehead fit as if he was born to royalty. The tailored swallow-tailed jacket showed off his broad shoulders and tall stature. He hadn't bothered to mask his handsome face and his eyes danced. So, his estate problem must be solved. He appeared relaxed and in a fine mood. He raised his stemmed glass and spoke to Fiona. "We are happy and proud to have you living in Castle

Drummond."

As the party ran its course, Avondale, less haughty than usual, danced with his strong arms around her, causing her heart to soar to the vaulted ceiling. His white teeth showed in a smile as he whispered, "Motherhood becomes you."

She loved whirling around the floor in his arms with his eyes staring into hers.

"You will not overexert, will you my darling?"

"I shall be very careful. Our child is precious to me." Yes, God was in His heaven and He loved her. That was apparent from all these blessings. She smiled and gazed around. She must share her feelings with Megan and Fiona.

But where were they? Both had disappeared. She had little time to think of their absence since Avondale whirled her back onto the dance floor.

At least three dances later, Fiona reappeared, her cheeks pink and her blazing blue eyes huge. She looked even more beautiful. Certainly the girl was catching the eye of every available titled bachelor present. Then Fiona dropped gracefully into one of the chairs situated artfully in clusters around the room. She motioned to the lord of the moment that she wanted a drink.

"Cailin, you must rest now. Think of your condition." Avondale's jaw jutted, so she decided he might be right.

She took leave of him and slid into the one available chair by Fiona's side before the gallant who obviously planned to do so was able to sit.

A frowning Lord Winslett bowed and reluctantly left.

They rested together, plying their fans to warm

faces.

"Brody is back. He's wounded. But all is well. Megan and I made him comfortable," Fiona whispered behind her fan.

"Praise God." Megan had worried about Brody disappearing from the boar hunt, but Avondale and Papa had not known the reason.

Cailin heaved a sigh. She was certain Brody had gone to rescue more fugitive Highlanders, but she'd kept her thoughts to herself. No need to worry Megan. She smiled. Brody was back and all was well! Perhaps she and Megan would have babies at the same time.

How sweet for the cousins to grow up together. What fun to have new life in the castle. How wonderful that Avondale provided the protection they all needed to live safely in the aftermath of that horrible battle.

Without Avondale, Brody would be outlawed, sold into slavery, or dead. And because of their location so near the battlefield, both they and their castle would be vulnerable to attack by both English and Scottish soldiers. Everyone living inside this castle owed their thanks to Avondale, from Papa down to the youngest child of the poorest serf.

And Fiona's life had changed drastically. She now stood a chance to marry well and live happily in the Lowlands, where before she would have only become wife of a highland clan leader…or worse, to a renegade. It was so good to see her clear blue eyes shine. She obviously loved life inside the castle with all its opportunities.

Papa approached and bowed. "Aye, my sweet colleen, will ye take a turn on the dance floor with me?"

"Delighted, Papa."

He swung her into a jolly reel. His dancing was not so elegant and protective as Avondale's, but he was enthusiastic. He smelled of new material, smoke, and even slightly of horses. At the dance end, he patted her cheek. "Yer a lovely lass, ye are, Cailin. Ye have done your old papa proud."

He would be elated when she told him her news.

But Avondale wanted her to wait until the first dangerous months passed for her to unveil her secret.

She smiled. "Thank you, Papa." When she turned from his big form dressed in red satin, a breath of fear shivered the nape of her neck. She gazed over the entire room full of dancing, laughing people.

Just as some sixth sense had warned her, Avondale had disappeared. Where was he? In the flurry of dances, she'd lost sight of her husband.

And now, where was Fiona? She scanned the room, but saw no lovely apparition in a yellow dress with auburn curls cascading to her waist. Saw no smiling face with a light sprinkling of freckles. Saw no long queue of gentlemen awaiting a dance.

Fear churned inside her breast. Had she gone somewhere with Avondale? Impossible. Fiona avoided Avondale.

Since the Battle of Culloden, when the redcoats slaughtered all her family except her widowed mother, herself, and Brody, the Highland lass had little taste for Englishmen. But she carried this too far. Avondale was an upright, just man, and Fiona had no right to condemn him simply for being born English.

Cailin had not judged Brody for being a Highlander. For bringing danger to their castle by his very presence. She blinked rapidly.

Brody was lying wounded from his attempts to help other Highlanders. Hidden somewhere inside the castle. Were there other hunted men now hidden in the old broch? How long could they continue to help the Highland warriors without being caught?

She stilled the worry churning her stomach. Not even the king would dare enter the castle looking for fugitives. The family all owed a great debt to Avondale.

But he feared someone. Who? Why?

Almost everyone had removed their masks. There was no athletic figure dressed in gold. No enchantress dressed in yellow. Had Avondale gone for a cigar? Had Fiona hurried back to check on her brother? Had she gone to the garden to take a walk with one of the lads so eager to spend time with her?

Ghostly fingers traveled down Cailin's backbone until her hands grew icy. What if Avondale had another spell? This one during a public event? Surely not, he'd been so relaxed.

Still, she gazed around the gaily decorated ballroom for Rafe, glad she'd elevated the burly blacksmith to his new position of bodyguard. Happier still that she'd given the tall Scott strict orders that he must not, under any circumstances, let Avondale out of his sight.

Some warmth returned to her hands. She could see nothing of Rafe, either. Apparently the bodyguard remained with Avondale.

Oh, God, please keep Avondale out of trouble.

She had tried to talk Mums out of holding this masquerade, but Mums had her heart set.

Cailin sighed. She'd felt it was too early for Avondale, but absolutely could not give her reason to

Mums. Avondale was a private man and wouldn't want anyone but her and Rafe, and maybe Hennings, to know of his problems.

The band struck up a lively waltz.

Aunty Moira, her auburn hair shining as brightly as her green eyes, glided out onto the dance floor. A limping man, dressed as a Bard, held her hand and swung her into a waltz.

Cailin gulped.

Was it safe for the wounded Highlander to be here? The two must think so. Except for Ian's pronounced limp, the two looked elegant, serene, and so very happy as they swayed to the rhythm of the waltz.

Cailin smiled as memories flooded in.

Brody had freed the fugitive Highlander from the cave where Ian and a number of other wounded warriors had been hiding from murdering English soldiers. Aunty Moira had nursed, and then fallen in love, then married Ian. Without Avondale's protection that love would never have blossomed. Ian, as well as the other men, would be dead.

She could see God's hand working. Her husband had saved so many lives.

But was her family taking too big a risk tonight? She would have advised following a more cautious route and keeping everyone in hiding, perhaps even Fiona. Her family certainly had great confidence in Avondale.

But they didn't know what she knew. She must keep his secret. With so many people depending upon him, no wonder Avondale felt the pressure.

As her blushing aunt looked over Ian's stalwart shoulder, she blew Aunty Moira a kiss.

Mums and Papa swung out onto the dance floor and circled Aunty Moira and Ian.

She and Avondale were expected to join the four dancers next.

Then Megan and Brody.

What should she do? Oh, there was Fiona. She hurried over towards the double doors, making her way through a number of eager shepherds clustered around Fiona. With her fan, she tapped the lass's bare shoulder. "Please take my place on the dance floor. I'm feeling woozy."

Fiona's beautiful smile lit her heart-shaped face. "I shall be happy to." Her carefully spoken words showed not a hint of her Highland brogue. She extended her bare hand to the tall and handsome young Earl of Sussex. The lad blushed and bumbled, then grabbed Fiona's fingers as if he feared the slender shepherdess would disappear, and led her proudly onto the dance floor.

Cailin moved to speak to Lorna. "Please continue the general dancing. I'm feeling unwell."

Lorna made a large O with her pretty mouth, smiled, and tapped young Viscount Wickham with her furled fan. They moved to the dance floor.

Amid a flurry of graceful dresses and unusual costumes, other dancers followed.

With that task successfully undertaken and since no one seemed to notice Avondale's absence, she felt free to track him.

Surely the armed bodyguard knew Avondale's whereabouts and wouldn't be far from her husband.

She must find them both.

12

Fiona felt certain she could smile no more. Her lips felt wooden. Speaking proper English and dancing with English gentry curdled her stomach. But not one Lowland Scottish lord caught her fancy. She stole down the stairway, away from the busy, brightly lit ballroom, and hurried through the dimly lit hall to the entry room. Though he was injured, it was such a relief to know Brody was safe. Guilt slid off her shoulders, leaving her footsteps lighter. But had English soldiers followed him?

She peeked out the tall front window.

"I say, comely lady, why are you hiding out here alone?"

She jumped.

Lord Avondale!

She'd been so busy searching the shadowy drive and carriages parked behind their patient horses, that she'd missed his footsteps.

She backed against the window, crumpling the big shepherdess bow at the back of her yellow gown. "I…I'm expecting someone."

Lord, please forgive my lie.

"You don't say!" Lord Avondale's words held all manner of nuances.

She gazed down the empty hall to the ballroom. Not even one servant in sight. Her heart tripped faster.

Then his dazzling gold-clad body moved to block

her view. "Did you hear the voices?"

Skin crawled on the back of her neck. "Voices?"

Glinting through the shadows, his brown eyes looked calm, but odd and slightly empty. "Yes, the voices told me you'd be here waiting for me."

"What?" She tried to catch her breath. "I don't know what yer speaking of." She'd forgotten her schooled English, her burr very evident.

"Oh, yes, my dear. My voices never lie. They said you were waiting for me." He reached for her hands.

She slipped away, her back pressed against the wall.

He closed the distance between them and grabbed her wrists. "You need not be afraid of me. I'll keep your little secret." He smiled.

His eyes appeared so empty she thought she could see to his soul. And it looked tortured.

"I have no secret. Leave me alone." She pulled against his tight grip. His scent had a male tang, strong and fearful. "I must return to the party. They're waiting for me. The dance—"

"No, no, little miss. You shall accompany me. I must keep Bloody Billy away from you. He's after me—but he'll gladly take you instead. A beautiful, pure maiden, a Highland lass who knows the location of many a warrior with a fat price on his head. Oh, yes…Bloody Billy will indeed snatch you. It is my duty to keep you safe."

She opened her mouth, but he jerked her against his satin-clad chest and clamped his free hand over her mouth. "You must stay quiet or he will hear you. He's very close by."

She bit his hand. Though she tasted metallic blood, he seemed impervious to pain. She hadn't even felt him wince. Amazed at his iron grip pinning her chest and arms, mashing her mouth, her knees buckled. Though her stomach shook, she kicked Lord Avondale's ankles and stepped on his feet, but he never noticed.

"The Butcher is waiting. He's impatient. I must take you to a safe place where he can never find and hurt you. If he gets his hands on you, he plans to humiliate me and show his power."

Just as the orchestra struck up a loud dance tune, Avondale lifted his hand, and forced open the front door.

She screamed.

He clamped his hand back over her mouth.

Her heart fluttered like a trapped butterfly. Her scream had been lost in the blaring music. Cool air whistled through her dress and scattered goose bumps over her skin. She lost a slipper, and as Lord Avondale dragged her down the carriage path cobblestones tore at her foot. Then he half-carried her between the hedges. Under the deeper shadows of the rowan trees, her feet squashed some of the red pomes dotting the ground.

She writhed and fought his iron hand, but she might as well have been a fairy in the clutches of a giant gargoyle. She'd never have imagined he had such strength. He dragged her deeper into the night, away from the lighted castle, away from the stable, away from the road that led to the village.

Where was he taking her? Who was Bloody Billy? This man only looked like Avondale. Surely he was an imposter. Did he have a twin? Was he mad?

The tight clench of his hand bruised her mouth. She could scarcely draw a breath. As he dragged her over a hedgerow sty, her dress tore on brambles. He was headed for the total darkness of the forest and the river.

And there was absolutely nothing she could do. Chills spidered her entire body until she shook all over. Why had she not worn her dagger?

She lost her other shoe. Dew wet her shredded hose, and brambles tore her arms and dress. Behind her, the music and lights diminished until they were only a memory of safety. Ice all but paralyzed her breathing. She had no doubt Avondale would accomplish whatever he had in mind.

Oh God, protect me!

She needed help. Desperately.

"Yes, yes, yes." Lord Avondale called out as if in answer to someone. "I will save her."

Her heart beat harder. She gasped for breath as he half-carried, half-dragged her over the rough ground. Sobs choked inside her chest, held down by his iron grip.

Clouds shrouded what moonlight was left. Ahead lay the dark stillness of the forest. The rushing of the river over rocks sent shudders over her body.

He dragged her beneath the trees, deep into the forest until the moonlight twinkled out, leaving them in intense darkness. The rocky, cold ground tore her bare feet. Bushes reached out and scratched her, grabbing pieces of her gown. If Avondale didn't slow, she'd soon be indecently clad. The roar of the river grew louder.

"Bloody Billy wants this pure, little lass. He wants the information she carries inside her head. He will hurt her to get it." Lord Avondale stumbled on a rock, dragging her down with him. In the tarry darkness, he rolled on top of her, crushing the breath from her lungs.

13

Fiona's chest hurt. As Lord Avondale sprawled on top of her, the hard muscle encased inside the cold satin sleeve slipped inches below her chest, and his hand loosened its death grip on her mouth. But she couldn't draw a breath.

Lord Avondale's patterned red satin jacket spun before her gaze as her head whirled in dizzy circles. Had she been able to breathe, she would have screamed.

But no one could have heard. They were quite alone in the dark forest.

Lord Avondale stirred, but his bruising weight didn't lift. Beneath her, sharp edges of stones pricked her arms and legs. Would she die here squashed flatter than a bedbug?

A long minute passed.

Then she found her lungs working again. She gasped in a deep painful breath, and the pungent odor of wet grass assailed her. She pulled in another breath in preparation for a scream.

Lord Avondale's hand tightened over her mouth.

She could only moan. But she who had killed an English soldier while freeing wounded Highlanders had more spunk than to give up. If only she could work her arm free to pick up a rock. She brought both elbows up hard against his chest and fought, wiggling and kicking, to free herself.

"Mmumph." He shifted his weight, keeping her pinned.

Her nose, buried in the palm of his hand, felt smashed. She moaned again.

He released her mouth. As she gasped in another breath of life-giving air, he grabbed her wrists, and pulled her to a sitting position on his lap. He hugged her so tight she thought he'd crush her ribs. Her wrists burned from his rough treatment.

A moment passed, but Lord Avondale didn't stir.

She wriggled around, craning her neck until she could glimpse his expression. What was his plan?

An errant shaft of moonlight floated across his face, granting her enough light to see lifted brows, and that a quizzical expression had replaced his frowning determination.

Surprise? No longer hard-chiseled obstinacy? All but mesmerized, she watched his countenance melt into consternation.

Lord Avondale's raised brows and open mouth were not hidden by even a grain of self-restraint. He seemed amazed at seeing her. "Fiona! I say, what the blooming night are you doing sitting atop my lap?" He released her wrists and scooted back on the rock, leaving enough space between them that the cool wind made her shiver in her shredded dress.

"What am I…?" She almost blurted out the situation before common sense stampeded to her rescue.

Everyone inside the castle knew Lord Avondale on occasion behaved in a strange manner. But this was beyond the pale. Did the man not know what he had done? Dare she remind him? No. Perhaps he'd free her if she pretended nothing out of the ordinary had occurred.

"Why, Lord Avondale, don't you recall? We decided to take a short walk. In the darkness, we stumbled on this rock."

His handsome face continued to look blank, and then crumpled into confusion. "But Fiona, your pretty gown is torn." He reached to reattach the ruined sleeve of her dress onto her bare shoulder. "Surely you should not be out in this strong wind with no cloak."

He stumbled to his feet, looking unsteady, totally unsure of the situation, and his part in it. A deep line creased his forehead. He shook his head and rocked back and forth.

She drew a long breath. Avondale appeared to be as sane as a man could look. Yet, at the same time, the big man seemed as lost as a child.

Despite her earlier fear, her heart compressed with pity.

Moving like a person awakened from a dream, he helped her to her feet, unbuttoned his fitted coat, and slid the smooth satin around her shoulders.

"Oh, I must have torn my dress when we fell. Think nothing of it, Lord Avondale. But, yes, I am cold. I shall return to the castle with all haste."

He stood exposed in that shaft of icy moonlight, with his forehead furrowed, and his expression woebegone.

New pain slashed her heart.

His shoulders slumped. "I…I didn't…you're not injured, are you?"

So, this wasn't the first time Cailin's husband found himself wakening to an unreal situation. Would he remain in his right mind until she could escape?

"No. Thank ye, I'm fine. But I must leave. We've

been gone overlong. I must return to the party. Ye see, Lady MacMurry counts on me." She stepped backwards.

He reached out and grasped her shoulder.

Her feet rooted in the wet bracken. A long branch scratched her back.

"But your shoes. You're barefoot." His hand tightened. "I shall carry you back. It's far too cold for you to walk about without slippers."

She shrank back. "Nay. I'm fine."

He released her arm.

"I love the feel of moss on my feet. Ye must try it sometime." She wanted to turn and run, but he might slip back into his spell, and continue with whatever plan he'd been about to carry out.

And shades of haggis, who was Bloody Billy? Why was Avondale so fearful the man would hurt her? The duke had the solid protection of the king. Few men dared touch him or his. Who could possibly frighten him? If there was danger, why didn't he tell the authorities?

After thrusting her goose-bumped arms inside the sleeves of his jacket, she remained a step or two in front of him as she all but ran back to the beckoning lights of the castle. When the lilting sounds of music wafted through the misty air, she did begin running.

He took her cold hand in his hot one, and raced with her.

The hair on the back of her neck prickled. She dare not remove her hand or do anything else that might send Cailin's husband back over the brink. Her tattered dress fluttered in the wind, exposing ankles and legs a brother-in-law should never see.

Somehow she'd have to detour far enough to enter

near the back staircase. She'd not like to be seen by anyone in her present state—especially not alone with Lord Avondale.

The same thought seemed to have occurred to him.

"Um, Fiona. The back staircase, don't you think?"

She nodded, gasping for air.

He wasn't even breathless. Physically, the man was in better condition than she could have guessed. Mentally, she feared he would again exit the world of the sane at any second.

"Aye. The back entrance." Certainly she'd never heard of Bloody Billy, nor of any attempt to take her by force from the castle.

She rushed under the back porte-cochere and winced as one of her wet feet slipped on the rounded cobblestones, bruising her instep.

His strong hand holding hers kept her from falling.

A hysterical laugh worked up into her throat. Now her kidnapper helped her. What would he do next? Had he really thought he was saving her?

A wave of compassion for Cailin smothered the nervous laugh. Cailin had wed a madman. And God allowed it. Cailin, who trusted God so totally and completely. Fiona shook her head. She would never understand God's ways.

Just as they reached the wooden door, heavy, uneven footsteps echoed through the mist.

Fiona glanced over her shoulder.

Hennings stumbled over to them. Obviously the big valet had been deep into his cups. Still, he lurched their way with obvious intent to intercept them.

Lord Avondale stopped. "Oh, I say, Hennings,

you're just the fellow I need. Fiona has taken a nasty tumble. Will you be so kind as to see to her welfare?"

The burly valet skidded to a halt inches from Lord Avondale's outstretched hand. The alcoholic stench of the servant's breath scalded her nose. Lurching like a sailboat luffing under a badly trimmed sail, the tall man managed an awkward bow.

"Not so, Milord. The dowager gave strict orders I was not to let you out of my sight. Nor will I."

He'd arrived a trifle late for that.

Fiona clamped her lips to shut off harsh words. She jerked her hand free from Lord Avondale's. So, Avondale's ma had assigned the valet as a bodyguard for her son. Did the old woman fear for his safety or was she concerned about what her son might do to someone else? Did she know he recalled nothing of his actions?

Either way, she agreed with the dowager. Lord Avondale needed a watchdog. His Grace had to be kept on a leash. Or better yet, a chain. The man was surprisingly strong.

"Lovely, Hennings. Do stay on top of your duty." Fiona hoped the edge in her voice made its way through the man's alcoholic fog. The odor of Scotch on his breath churned her stomach. Still, she could not have been happier to see the man. "I turn Lord Avondale over to your care."

She just wanted to escape.

She unlatched the heavy door. She'd have a private chat with Cailin. Who knew what other secrets her sister-in-law kept? She hesitated. She certainly didn't want Lord Avondale climbing the dark staircase with her. His black mood might return. And Hennings was drunk. She had no desire to walk the back hallways with two such unstable men.

She suppressed a shiver.

Englishmen. Why had God made so many of them? Of what use were they?

"Um, Hennings, I suggest you take Lord Avondale up the side staircase. It's not seemly for the two of us to be seen together when we're in such a state."

Hennings' mouth dropped as he apparently noticed that beneath Lord Avondale's coat, her gown was torn.

"Yes, Milady." He swung his gaze back and forth between Lord Avondale and her, looking so much like a bewildered bull that she wanted to shake the man.

"See to your duty." She didn't relish standing with these two men, her back to the dark, misty forest, and her bare feet on the cold step to the dark rear entrance to the castle. She didn't trust either of them. She put a tart edge to her voice. "Immediately, Hennings."

"Yes, Milady." The broad-shouldered man smacked a hand against the small of Lord Avondale's waist-coated back. The servant and the still bewildered, but compliant, lord lumbered down the cobblestones to the side entrance.

Avondale's voice carried clearly through the darkness. "I've had responsibility drilled into me from birth. A boy trained to be a duke does not cry for any reason. Not when he is beaten, not for love. He does not play with children of common rank, no matter how lonely. He must excel at studies and never shirk duty. Never complain, never apologize, and must take upon himself an arranged marriage. He must only choose companions from the select. He must learn detachment and obedience rather than rebellion. It's all so accursedly cursed." He groaned. "Somehow I think I failed my duty just now."

Strange, what things haunted the duke. She would never have guessed.

The mumble of male voices and footsteps grew faint as the two disappeared around the corner of a turret.

She pulled in a deep breath and shivered.

Thank you, my Father, for protecting me.

She hugged chilled arms to her chest.

Hennings wasn't known as a gossip, but what he'd witnessed might start his tongue wagging if she didn't take steps to prevent it. She sighed.

With the danger past, her legs were watery porridge, and she shook all over. Stiffening her knees, she pushed open the heavy, iron-bound door.

She'd carry her dagger from now on. And she'd have to tell Cailin.

14

Cailin tossed her golden mask onto the beverage table, picked up a stemmed glass of punch, gulped it, and slammed the empty glass back on the white tablecloth. She felt like screaming. Instead, hands clenched, she gazed around the lofty, tastefully decorated ballroom. Everyone else danced gaily with a partner.

Where was Avondale? How was she to hold this marriage together if he continued to disappear?

She had asked God to keep Avondale by her side through the festivities. And He had failed her. Fighting off a sense of despair, she forced herself to smile at the many nobles bowing and acknowledging her presence as they escorted their partners to the food and beverage table. Why had God denied her when she had obeyed Him and her parents with this marriage? God blessed obedience, didn't He? If so, why had He given her such a difficult husband?

Here she stood, wearing the most fabulous gown she'd ever owned, its billowing gold hooped skirts caught halfway up with large velvet bows above scalloped lace, and her golden curls falling in ringlets almost to her waist. In the place of prominence as befitted her husband's rank, she, amidst all the couples, stood alone.

She unfurled her fan and used its folds to hide her trembling lips. She would not cry. Tears closed her throat and pricked behind her eyes. She blinked rapidly and performed a curtsy to the Marquess and Marchioness of Tullibardine. As the couple danced beyond her hearing, they put their heads together and whispered. She cared not a fig about their gossip. She simply wanted her husband by her side. Proving his love. Showing his protection.

She wanted Avondale out of trouble, normal, and resplendent as only he could be. She wanted a kind, sensitive husband, a loving father for their child. She wanted him as attentive in public as he was in private. Was that too much to ask?

Her shoulders shook. A sob worked up through her laced bodice to the ruffles cupping her shoulders. No, this would not do. She sniffed and straightened her shoulders.

Every other person in the room looked so happy, dancing in the circle of a loved one's arms or paired together, chatting intimately. Why not she? The headache that had threatened grew into full-blown misery. Sidestepping into the shadow of a white pillar, she massaged her temples.

Why didn't God answer her prayer? He seemed deaf to her pleading. She believed in Him with all her heart and obeyed Him in every way she knew. She gave money to the poor beggars who showed their licenses at the castle's kitchen. She loved her fellow men and God with all her heart.

So, why didn't God love her back? Surely He knew that for the first time in her life, she wavered in her solid faith? Why didn't He answer her prayers? What had she done to deserve His silence?

Aware of her many noble guests, she smoothed her expression, warmed her smile, and forced herself to remain cordial.

For what seemed hours she played the part as best she could, upholding the gaiety of the party and honoring Fiona's debut. She set her mind to focus on Fiona's happiness, but the lass had also disappeared. Anxiety built inside Cailin's chest. She had to find Avondale.

Finally, she said her farewells to those guests close enough to the castle to return to their own homes.

Then she, Mums, and Aunty Moira escorted those guests who were staying overnight to their suites. At last, her duty accomplished, she hugged Mums and Aunty Moira, not wanting to share with them her anxiety, and went in search of Avondale.

She prayed the burly servant, Rafe, would prove to be an excellent bodyguard. She'd chosen the big Scot because the man had muscle and barely spoke. She didn't want Rafe bandying her dirty linen to public view and felt certain he would not.

But perhaps Avondale had escaped Rafe's supervision. Otherwise, Rafe certainly would have herded her wandering husband back into the ballroom to attend to his guests.

How could Avondale, so handsome and desirable, be so unreliable? When he was present, he looked the pillar of strength and stability.

She left the ballroom and stood at the front door where the final guests were taking their leave.

A young man in a shepherd's simple costume approached.

"I say, Duchess. Your little cousin Fiona is a bit of all right. Where have you hidden the young lady? I wanted to make my adieus personally."

She smiled with real warmth. "Ah, Lord Montrose.

Fiona is around somewhere. Surely, you're more acquainted with her movements than I." She had a warm spot for the young Marquess.

His mums and hers were great friends, and she and Megan had grown up playing with Charles and his older siblings. She sighed. Too bad Charles hadn't been old enough to wed her.

But he'd make a fine husband for Fiona. And from his disappointed expression at missing her, he appeared to think so as well.

She fanned her hot face at the disloyal thought of preferring to have wed someone else. At times Avondale embodied everything she'd ever dreamed of in a husband. She bit her lip. But those times proved precious few.

"Well, yes. I had my eyes on Fiona all evening. That is, until Lady Megan needed to speak to her so urgently. I've not seen a spot of her since. That was..." The young man pulled an elegant gold pocket watch from behind his shepherd's pelt, "...almost an hour past."

"Ah, well. Fiona's quite young. She and Megan have probably gone to rest." So, Megan had taken Fiona somewhere. What was Megan up to this time? Had she taken Fiona to nurse Brody?

Disappointment clouded the young lord's pleasant face. "My parents insist the hour is late and we leave at once. Pray give the Lady Fiona my farewell."

"I shall, Charles. And I'll extend an open invitation to you and your family to visit us often. Mistress Fiona dotes on your company."

The young man straightened his shoulders and fairly glowed. He tripped over his feet as he bowed over her outstretched hand. "Thank you, Duchess. My family and I gladly accept your kind invitation." His large hazel eyes gazed at her above her hand which he still pressed to his lips. Then he raised his head. "I shall come often."

"I fear there will be a regular parade of young noblemen to our door." She touched his pelt-covered arm. "There seems to be a new breed of catnip here that brings all the noble Toms in the countryside."

"Catnip indeed! But Mistress Fiona did ask you to invite me specifically, did she not?" Young Charles's face hovered between hopefulness and chagrin.

"She did." The lie flowed easily from her tongue. Was a white lie acceptable to God? She didn't know. But at the moment, she felt far from happy with God, anyway. The thought amazed her. Never before in her life had she been unhappy with God.

Forgive me, Father.

Nevertheless, her usual calm trust didn't return. Would she spend her life at social events covering for her husband? Was her marriage to echo her parents' relationship despite her best efforts? Would she and Avondale become truly distant and hateful to one another? Now that she stood likely to give him an heir, would he take a mistress and move to one of his other estates?

She tapped her foot as she waited for Charles to join the last of the departing guests, and then rushed to the servants' part of the castle.

The kitchen where the help congregated fermented in an uproar. Glasses, filled and empty, showed the servants had celebrated and were yet frolicking. Some wore make-shift costumes. Many looked red-faced and were acting free with one another, obviously well into their cups.

When she entered, the cavernous kitchen grew quiet. The bevy of servants snapped to attention.

"I'm seeking Hennings."

"Ah, Your Grace, Hennings was here up until…?" His brows arched, the head butler gazed at the other servants.

"Hennings left about an hour past, Milady." The big cook dipped her cheerful face respectfully. "He seemed in a bit of a hurry, he was."

A cold chill shot down Cailin's backbone. Her voice quivered. "And how long did he tarry in the kitchen before he left?"

The dusting maid dropped a slight curtsy. "Your Grace, Hennings, he stayed here in the kitchen for the best part of the evening. Then Rafe rushed in and hurried him out."

Cold certainty spread to Cailin's chest. "Hennings remained here during the masquerade? But not Rafe?"

"Aye, Your Grace. Rafe scooted Hennings out of here like he was a bad little boy."

All the servants stared at her. She must not show her distress. She hid her shivers beneath the billowing silk costume. She'd asked both men to watch over Avondale during the masquerade. Obviously, Hennings believed he needn't take orders from her. The dowager paid his wages. Thank God Rafe was on the job. "Thank you, Celeste. Where are the men now?"

Celeste lifted her apron to half hide her face. "That what be so funny. Hennings, he heard the tall clock chime, and he took off like a hare chased by a dog. That scared he looked. He didn't even need Rafe's hand on the back of his neck."

"I see. Thank you." She worked to keep her shoulders from slumping and walked stiffly from the cheery kitchen. She well knew the buzz of conversation following her departure meant she hadn't handled her search at all well. Nor had she managed to hide her dismay.

She cared little of what the servants thought, except for the need to keep them from gossip. And she'd given them fodder. She clinched her clammy hands. She must find Avondale before he hurt himself.

And what if Bloody Billy was really after him? What if the man really was a threat? What if her husband lay wounded or dead somewhere on the grounds? Once again, the castle would be without protection…and she would be without a husband. Their baby would be without a father.

She hurried back to the ballroom, but found it empty except for the musicians packing their instruments in cases. The silent room with its drooping decorations mirrored her wilting heart. Alone and used. Cold fear pulsed its way to her hands and feet, turning them into blocks of ice.

Where was Avondale? What had he done this time? Would she be able to fix the problems he'd created? Was he safe? She'd have to assign Rafe to stay by Avondale's side day and night. She could trust the big Scot. But the man did have to sleep.

Was Avondale becoming a threat? Who knew what he would do if he had another spell? What terrible demons drove him? She must summon her courage to find out. She wrapped her arms around the precious child in her womb. Was his inheritance in jeopardy? He had a legitimate claim to the title and lands.

She feared, not only for Avondale, but for herself and for their child.

Her slippers thumped as she ascended the main staircase. Absently she touched the round golden balls that held the sequined masks looped to the banister. Since her wedding night, she'd fancied Avondale wore just such a mask.

Now she must unmask him. Discover his secrets.

Alone together, he seemed kind, sweet, and attentive to her every desire. He made her feel cherished and loved beyond what she'd ever dreamed.

But when he left the sanctuary of their bedchamber, he metamorphosed into a different man. He was not one man, but many. When in company with his courtly attendants, he grew haughty towards her. With his mother, he simply ignored her. With Papa and Brody, he seemed one of the family, though he seldom included her in the circle. While on the hunt, whether fox or boar, friends mentioned he was highly competitive.

She'd taken to spying on him when he withdrew to the library. He'd pace, book laxly held in one hand, and talk to himself. Almost as if he spoke to someone else.

That frightened her so the hair on her head stood up.

She reached the top of the staircase and paused, looking over the balcony, down the curve of the stairs, and into the enormous entry room with its stuffed stag and great, heavy paintings of her forebears. Now shadowed with low burnt candles, the place looked as haunted as she felt.

She'd never before thought such things of her home. Had Avondale brought this eerie atmosphere to her castle? Living with the duke shook her faith. She fingered the heavy diamond necklace hanging from her throat. She wouldn't find her answers standing in the hallway. She turned, strode down the corridor to her suite of rooms, and placed her hand on the long, burnished door handle.

Since she'd been unable to find Avondale, she'd wait for him, and no longer be put aside by his wonderful lovemaking. Tonight, she'd discover what drove him.

But if he were hurt or dead, life would become empty, without texture or substance.

A light tap on her arm startled her from her thoughts. She spun to face Rafe.

The burly blacksmith-turned-guard bowed, most of his muscles hidden by the satin suit that gleamed in the candlelight. "Lady Cailin, might I have a word with you?"

"Of course, Rafe." She caught her breath. "For such a big man, you do move quietly. I didn't hear you approach."

"Aye, Milady." He moved closer. "We found the duke near the forest. Hennings took him to yer rooms. He'd had another spell. This one looked verra bad."

"Oh, dear. I must go to him." She turned and took a step, but Rafe's strong hand grasped her arm.

"He hurt the Lady Fiona."

Cailin drooped. Her body felt old and heavy. "Where is she? Is she hurt badly?"

"I think she went to her rooms. Nay, she was more scared than hurt." His eyes glinted and his mouth looked grim.

"Did anyone see what happened?"

"Nay, Milady. She were alone when the duke grabbed her."

Cailin gasped. "Avondale grabbed her?"

"Aye, Milady. Ye know I will do anything for ye. Anything. I serve ye with me whole self. I hold nothing back."

She could barely hear Rafe's words over the hammering of her heart. She leaned towards him. "What are you suggesting?"

The candle cast dark shadows over his rugged face. "The duke is dangerous, Milady. He could hurt ye." His gaze slid from her face to her waist. "Or yer babe."

Would Avondale hurt her? Surely not. And yet, he had grabbed Fiona and dragged her to the woods. For what purpose? She could not fathom his motives. But, she would never allow him to hurt their child. And yet, he was so very strong.

"Perhaps the duke could meet with an accident."

15

"Avondale."

He looked up, his eyes heavy lidded. "Cailin, love. Where have you been?"

His gold satin trousers looked wet, dirty, and stained from the knee down. He wore no coat. His waistcoat was missing and his silk shirt hung carelessly open at the neck. The splotches of grass stain that had bled into his shirt and trousers told her he'd been outside.

Rafe spoke the truth.

"Why did you disappear from the masquerade?"

Arm on the cushion of his chair, he propped his chin in his hand. "I say, love, I've been right here in our bedchamber waiting for you."

"No, Avondale, you haven't."

He looked like a small boy caught with his finger in the pigeon pie. His wonderful lips thinned. "But I must have been here."

She saw no point in arguing. While she reinforced her courage, she struck flint to steel and lit the candles, stirred up a fire in the chill room, and sat stiffly in a straight chair close to where he slouched in his wingback.

She swallowed and took a deep breath. "Please talk to me. Tell me what is going on."

A stubborn expression pulled at his face. But he leaned close to her, and began to lightly stroke her arm.

She moved away. Tonight she would not be distracted.

He sat straighter, his chocolate eyes dark. "Yes, let's talk." Then he appeared to change his mind, drew her closer, and began to nuzzle her hair.

Gently she pushed him away. "No, Avondale. Tell me the truth."

His eyebrows rose. "Come, Cailin. I've a need to more than talk with you." Suddenly he stood, swept her into his arms, and strode to their bed. As if nothing else in the world mattered, he placed her in the middle, pulled off her slipper, and massaged her right instep.

Though her heart ached, he looked so boyish and eager, she couldn't help but smile.

He unbuttoned his stained shirt.

She stopped his hand. "Tell me. Where did you disappear to tonight?"

His loving expression changed. He dropped his hand from his mostly unbuttoned shirt. "Your guard dog didn't follow me did he? I managed to elude him." His smile suddenly looked odd and off-kilter.

The slight comfort she'd taken in his earlier actions faded.

"You see, you cannot control me. I may live from the good bounty of your father, but you cannot command me."

She shrank back into the cushions. The flash of anger in his eyes surprised her. Though he'd fathered the child nestled inside her womb, how little she knew Avondale. "I do not desire to master you. I merely want to know where you went. You've been outside. You might get hurt…alone in the dark."

He turned on her and gripped her wrist so that it burned. Heat penetrated deep within the ring of his fingers. "Have I not been the best of husbands to you? Have I not fulfilled my husbandly duty and given you what you wanted, an heir?" He dropped her wrist, and paced the room. "Or is it I who wanted the heir?" He scowled. "And yet you must know where I am at all times. You are not my mother." He stopped and glared. "Call off your watch dog. I will not be treated like a child."

She fell against the pillows, confusion swirling inside her brain. This was a side of Avondale she hadn't expected. She must instruct Rafe to be discreet. Perhaps he should move into the adjoining apartment. Protect her and her unborn child if Avondale became violent.

His voice rose. "I gave you my title and my protection. For no fault of my own, I married below my station. Now I live in this awkward, back country castle. What more do you want from me!" His face grew red.

Her heart slid to her stomach. Disappointment swept her smile away. Not only was he unstable, she…she hadn't pleased him. A cold fog settled inside her breast.

He rattled on. "I do all this so the royal mother can keep her estates and her reputation. Dash it all, what do I get in return? You order a big brute of a man to guard me. I will not become a prisoner in this castle." His leashed strength, clearly visible in his bunched muscles, waited to break free.

She sat upright and braced her arms back against the pillows. "Avondale, Rafe follows you to keep you safe. I don't understand your behavior."

His anger crumpled. "You don't understand? You don't understand! What about me?"

Fear evaporated at the expression of pain on his face.

He clenched his upraised fists. "How would you like to wake up in a place you don't comprehend how you got to? You have no inkling why you are there. You find yourself with a blighter you don't even know, or with someone you're afraid you may have injured." He knelt beside her in the bed, his knees pressing her thigh.

She reached out and pulled him into her arms. Perhaps, after all, she didn't want to know what was wrong with him. His problems were too deep. His feelings too intense.

He buried his face in her neck. "I don't know what happens." His deep, baritone broke, scraping the edge off his voice. "One minute everything seems fine. The next I find myself in an unusual place…with no memory of how I got there…and no memory of why I'm there." He jerked upright, grabbed his hair with both hands, and gazed wide-eyed. "And no memory of what I've done."

She tried to simply breathe. One breath in, one breath out. "We'll conquer this, darling. Together, we'll find a solution." She brushed his perspiration damp hair back from his forehead and kissed the top of his thick brown hair. Chills raced through her heart. Avondale's problems were so hurtfully knotty.

"No. This isn't something we can work out. When I was a child, the royal mother chased the voices away."

"Voices?"

Oh God, what kind of man did you let me marry?

He swallowed, clamped his lips, and his eyes grew hooded. "Perhaps we should discuss this in the morning." His face changed as he thought better of sharing his secretive revelation. Then he blurted, "When I was younger, I felt certain everyone else heard my voices. Then the royal mother decreed that wasn't so. She said I must keep quiet about the voices. She forbade me to tell anyone. Said if I were declared incompetent, we'd lose everything—title, lands, money."

She scooted slightly away from his muscular body. She didn't want to hear about the voices, either. They caused goose bumps to dot her arms and fear to clutch her heart. Yet, she'd been shielded all her life. It was time now to face her responsibility. She must help her husband. She pressed a hand against the side of her mouth. "When do you hear these voices?"

"Not often. Not for a long time. That is, before I married you, I hadn't heard them for a number of months. Then the royal mother ordered me to marry you."

Though she'd always known the circumstances of her marriage, to hear them spoken so openly made her cringe inside. She hid her feelings. His problem needed solving, not hers. Every titled lady faced her identical situation. She should have been immune to being treated as property.

A faint smile played over his lips. "I'm glad the royal mother chose you and not Lady Isobel. You are so beautiful. So sweet. So giving. I had no wish to marry. But you are a gift." He took her tense hand in his warm, gentle one. "And I love you."

She pushed the vision of Lady Isobel, the rich, skinny, pouting spinster, to the back of her mind. She'd known from babyhood she'd been destined to enter an arranged marriage. She'd believed her love could overcome any barrier. She pulled her hand away. Now she wasn't so certain. Avondale had seemed a perfect match. And she'd been happy, at least when they were alone. And somehow, she'd thought together they would overcome this problem, and she could make him content. Thought she would have a good marriage. Thought she would make a loving, joyous, normal home for their child. Now, she was not certain happiness could ever be theirs.

Why had Avondale's voices returned?

"You're not pleased with me, Avondale. Is that why the voices came back?"

Crystal pools of sorrow filled his brown, puppy eyes. "Oh, no, Cailin." He traced a finger over her face. "You surpass all my expectations."

"Then why did the voices return?"

He buried his head in her breast. She barely heard his teeth-grinding grunt.

"I'm shamed."

She lifted his face so that he must look at her. "But why? I know of no nobility who hasn't entered an arranged marriage."

"Dear heart, our marriage is not the problem. The tragedy happened before we wed." He shut his eyes. "The voices returned because of what I did."

She urged and urged, but he would say no more.

Fully clothed, sprawled in the bed beside her, he turned on his side away from her, and closed his eyes.

What awful thing could he have done that stood to ruin their marriage? That made her doubt her ability to make him happy? Was she destined to have a masquerade of a marriage rather than a true blending of soul, heart, and body?

Could she live that way? What other option did

she have? She would never accept Rafe's suggestion of an arranged accident happening to Avondale.

Not unless her child was in danger.

16

Cailin gathered her skirts and plopped down beside Megan in the nook beneath the budding roses woven over the arbor. She yearned to enjoy this first bright June day since Megan's final trip last night to rescue the last of the wounded Highlanders. Cailin pulled in a breath of sweet spring air. "I think Fiona's party yesterday was quite successful."

The cold rocks of Castle Drummond loomed behind her. In front stretched their fertile farmlands, dotted with the crofts Papa provided for his tenants. She couldn't see the broch on the back side of the castle where Megan and Brody hid the men, but it seldom left her thoughts. Megan and Brody had the survivors safe in the broch now, so she could delicately bring up her problem.

"Yes, and I expect Fiona will have a steady influx of male callers soon." Megan gazed out at the paddock and the horses.

Cailin bent to pick up her tapestry bag of knitting. She'd brought Megan to the arbor to talk with her about Avondale's strange behavior. She'd seen too little of her sister since Megan spent her time rescuing the wounded men, but she wanted to seek her counsel.

Avondale's behavior was driving her to the end of her wits. And she had to admit, anger caught her by the throat when she thought of his antics. She'd tried her best to soothe, heal, and coax her husband into confiding in her. Today, she'd even stooped to ordering her maid to spy on him. But she'd not spoken to Avondale since he'd turned from her last night. Nor had she seen Fiona.

But she was having a hard time talking to Megan about Avondale. She gazed at the land spread before her. Spirited horses frolicked in their paddocks as happy to see spring as she. Newly foaled babies on spindly legs nursed, and yearlings raced, brown hides shining, heads held high, and short manes flowing. How she adored this estate.

And when Papa died, all the land and possessions would pass to Avondale as eldest son-in-law. But, if he were proven incompetent, and she had no male heir, the crown could step in and seize their entire estate and all its holdings. She caressed her stomach. So much depended on the little one nestled inside her womb. Such a responsibility for a baby.

"Are you happy with your husband?" Cailin lowered her head, letting her unbound hair hide her hot cheeks. She plucked a rosebud, inspected it for bees, held the sweet fragrance to her nose, and inhaled deeply. Anyone with eyes could see Megan bloomed like the red rosebud Cailin held.

"Humph. And is doing your duty to family a lighthearted thing for you?" Megan frowned.

Why did Megan not answer the simple question? Brody was such a fine man.

"I'm not speaking of duty. I'm speaking of love." Cailin picked a dainty piece of half-finished blue garment and tiny needles from her knitting bag. Last night she'd lacked courage to insist her husband tell her what happened. She was not at all sure she possessed the strength to hear his answers.

"Love?" Megan gazed across the lawn at Papa, draped over the front of the horse paddock.

Cailin frowned, her attention caught by Avondale cantering smartly towards the stable. Surprise, he was home!

He jumped off with a flourish and handed his horse's bridle to a stable boy. Taller than Papa, he was not as broad, but far more athletic. Her husband's brown hair and mahogany eyes presented quite a pleasing picture. Unlike last night, this morning he appeared calm, arrogant, and totally in control of himself and his surroundings.

How looks could deceive. He'd been out of his head last night. Why would he not confide in her? Was it because he sensed that part of her did not want to know? Did not want to wrestle with such insurmountable difficulties?

"Seems your husband has many errands away from the castle." Megan frowned and tossed her bud to the gravel path. "He knows Brody's a Highlander, doesn't he?"

Cailin gazed intently at her knitting. "Yes, Avondale is absent much of the time." She pressed her lips together, and then looked up. "Though we haven't spoken of Brody, I'm certain Avondale knows he's a Highlander."

She gazed at her husband's features, as handsome in his aristocratic way as Megan's husband's more rugged face. And Avondale's regal presence was as strong as the Highlander's more earthy one. Both men were outstanding specimens of manhood.

But Brody was so much easier to talk with. While Avondale disappeared each day, she had often found herself in Brody's presence. She'd look up from whatever she was doing and there he was trailing after her. Their conversations always turned to Megan.

Cailin smiled. She'd never seen a man more in love with his wife.

"Lord Avondale must have a touch of Welsh to have his coloring."

"Yes." Cailin stared at Avondale and Papa standing together, watching the horses running loose in the paddock. "Avondale doesn't show it in public, but he's kind and good-hearted." She enjoyed looking at her husband during his rare daytime appearances. A smile played over her lips. If only he didn't have his awful spells.

"Bosh! I think him cold and stuffy."

She stiffened. "Careful Megan. You're speaking of the man I love."

"But you scarcely know him."

"We've been wed more than three months. The same as you and Brody. Don't tell me you two turtledoves didn't enjoy those long evenings in your room where you two scamper so soon after dinner," she teased.

How well she knew about long evenings alone with a husband. Those times with Avondale were her only means of not losing her own mind. When they were alone, Avondale's brown velvet eyes gazed into hers with warmth and appreciation. The man changed into an entirely different person when the sun rose.

Megan plucked a rose and used the bud to hide the blush coloring her face. The few occasions she blushed, she turned beet-red, and she looked neither dainty, nor ladylike. "You're everything a woman should be. While I, myself—" Megan shrugged. "I'm only the second daughter, not the son Papa prayed for.

He's never forgiven me for being a lass. Nor for wedding—"

Cailin put a hand on her sister's lips. "I'm with child, Megan." She'd heard these laments before, and today had more urgent things to discuss. "I had no show these three months, and I feel so full here." She pressed her bodice. Her cheeks burned.

Megan squealed and grabbed her hands. "I'm so happy for you." She lifted her fingers and counted out nine. "The baby will be born in January. A New Year's child. I'll be an auntie. We'll have lovely baby sounds and sweet smells and laughter filling the castle."

"Yes. I'm so very pleased and yet, I need to ask you—"

"And you'll be too preoccupied with the baby to spend so much time with Brody after he mends."

Cailin gasped. True, she and Brody had been together a lot, but—"I'm so sorry, I had no idea you didn't want me to spend time with Brody. I've not seen him since he's been wounded. Before that, it was just that Avondale's gone so much, and you seemed—"

"Of course I don't really mind all the time you two spent together. I'm not keeping charge of his schedule." Her sister didn't look her in the eyes.

"Perhaps you'll be a mother soon, as well." Cailin squeezed her hand. "Our babies can grow up together. Play together. Learn together. Be as close as you and I."

Megan frowned. "Blatherskites. You're the golden lass who has grown into a golden woman. And now you'll be the golden mother. I've been so preoccupied worrying about Brody, I missed noting your happiness and bursting beauty."

Cailin forced a smile. Golden only to those who didn't know her real situation. She felt shriveled inside.

And lonely. In public Avondale barely spoke to her. Even those rare times they dined together, he never spoke. Nor did he so much as smile at her as the men left for cigars and whist.

She hated being snubbed. She so wanted to confront him, but she feared that would send him into more nightmares and ravings. She wouldn't be a nagging wife. His nightmares made him so upset, she didn't know if he might become violent. Last night for the first time, she'd feared him. So, today she'd seen to it that only a door separated their room from Rafe's, because Avondale was so strong that with one swipe of his large fist, he could kill or injure their unborn baby.

And she'd had to invite his mother to return to give her advice on how to handle her husband. He was so very odd. Would her baby be odd also? Why was her marriage in such a tangle?

"Then there's Aunty Moira, so excited after I introduced her to Brody's friend, Ian. They were immediately attracted to one another. That was a marriage conceived in heaven. Or, more exactly, conceived by me. Your marriage and Aunty's are so happy." Megan's bright hair hid her downcast face.

Cailin tried to keep her mouth from dropping open. "Are you saying yours is not?"

"I like Brody. Even admire him. But since our marriage, his enormous pride stands between us like a stone wall."

Cailin twirled the prickly stem of a rose in her fingers. "You can forgive him that."

But the cold silence Avondale gave her. That she didn't know how to overcome. With his frosty dark eyes, his broad shoulders and his look of haughty wealth, in public he was so very intimidating. Yet he was so very loving in private. The private one she admired and loved with all her heart. The public one she could so easily let herself despise. Then there was the third man, the haunted one who suffered nightmares. The man she now feared.

Nor was she anxious to feel the weight of the wrath Rafe told her about. Avondale was a man of impassioned temper. Goose bumps crawled on her arms. And the voices he'd mentioned. The very thought sent cramps to her stomach that made the baby kick.

She'd prayed about her marriage situation, but God hadn't spoken. Why, with the very things she deemed most important, did God choose to remain silent? Perhaps God was testing her. His word said He loved her. She believed His word. "Do you think God tests those He loves?"

Megan smiled. "I think all of life is a test. And yes, God truly tests those He loves. Why?"

Cailin had tried to soften Avondale's heart, but he gave her such withering looks in public, that in private she had not the heart to bring up the prickly subject of his public behavior. So she'd spent time with Brody and taken to visiting the broch and seeing to the feeding of the wounded men hiding there.

The surgeon visited daily, and the men, strong and healthy save for their wounds, were recovering nicely. Soon, Brody would take them to a different hiding place. He'd said they must keep moving, most likely back to a spot the English had already searched.

Difficult though it was, she must talk with Megan about her marriage. "Don't you think it's wonderful, what happens when a married man and woman are alone together?" She picked up the blue knitting she'd dropped on her lap, and her needles began to flash. She would ease into the subject of Avondale's odd behavior.

Megan buried her nose in her rosebud.

When Megan didn't answer, she asked, "Aren't you happy with Brody? He loves you so much. I've never seen a man who has a harder time keeping his hands off his wife."

"Humph." Megan fished around in her tapestry bag, and pulled out some knitting. "Perhaps if Papa approved of Brody as much as he does Lord Avondale, I'd be more content."

"How can you say that, Megan? Papa all but grovels over Brody. Your husband's charmed our Papa until I scarcely recognize him."

Megan shrugged. "I noticed the change in Papa."

"Papa's put Brody in charge of all our horse breeding. He loves the idea of the new thoroughbred horse Brody wants to breed from our English mares and our imported Arabians."

Megan tossed her fiery hair. "I didn't know about Brody's new responsibilities, nor his innovative ideas. But I see how Papa values Brody's opinion."

Cailin dropped a stitch. "I'm surprised you didn't know. I confess I feel guilty I've gotten to know Brody so well. He's a really nice fellow. But, truly, all he speaks of is you."

Megan tilted her head. "Really?" She raised her brows.

Cailin sighed.

Megan seemed to need reassurance about her marriage, too.

Perhaps Avondale's silence was her fault. She'd just have to change. She peeked through her eyelashes at the handsome man talking with her father. He seemed to be getting on famously with Papa. In fact, Avondale got on well with everyone…except her. And she would soon be the mother of his child.

Her child, who would be confused by the different ways his father treated her. But then, her son would see only his father's indifference. No, though she dreaded what the man might tell her about voices and finding himself in unknown places, she would have it out with Avondale. She would not permit him to treat her coldly in front of their child.

She wrinkled her nose. How had Avondale captivated Papa when she'd seen so little of him? The way the wind riffled his brown hair over his high forehead all but took her breath away. His looks and fitness called out to her. His strong intellect when he questioned the words she read to him each night from the Bible appealed to her. She was so pleased with the way his questions appeared less defensive, and his interest in what God had to say had grown.

Still, the man wore a mantle of protectiveness about him so strong it seemed to be his definitive trait. He'd been born to power and trained not to show weakness. Need appeared foreign to his make-up. Perhaps a public showing of love had also been bred out of him? She would not think of the voices again until he told her more. Perhaps she had misunderstood.

She studied the broad shoulders of the man who kept his distance in the daylight hours, but when moonlight filled the bedchamber he made an abrupt about-face and switched into the man of her dreams.

Except last night had been such an awful exception. No, she would not think of that now on this beautiful, sunlit day. Nor would she think of the nights he'd awakened with bad dreams.

Her heart twisted.

She glanced at Megan, who was staring at her with a strange, quizzical expression. Then comprehension sparked in her eyes. "You are afraid to birth your baby."

"Well, having a baby is rather a frightening prospect."

Megan shook her head so vigorously that pins fell out of her shining copper curls. She dropped her tangled knitting to pin them back in. "Papa will bring in the best surgeons."

"Yes, of course, he will. But there is always so much danger." For now, she'd not share her concerns about Avondale with Megan. Somehow, speaking about the baby made it far too difficult to talk about Avondale's oddities. She would find another time.

Her sister fidgeted on the woven reed seat. "Now that you've gotten to know your husband better, do you think Lord Avondale will betray Brody to the Duke of Cumberland? I hear even some Lowland men who weren't anywhere near the battlefield have been hauled off to prison." Megan ran fingers through her long hair and flipped the breeze-teased tresses over her shoulder. "As of yesterday, there's a reward of a hundred pounds on the head of each of Bonny Prince Charlie's fugitive soldiers."

"Good heavens, Megan. Is that what's been bothering you? Why didn't you say so? You've been mooning around the castle all week. I thought you and Brody had a spat." Cailin shook out her knitting. "My answer remains as I told you the day after you wed. I doubt Avondale would turn Brody in. He respects

Brody." But how well did she know her husband with his strange personality quirks? Now that Avondale's aides had returned to court, what did Avondale think? She must watch and see. She would warn Brody if she caught even a hint of Avondale's alerting the English soldiers.

Papa clapped his hand on Avondale's broad shoulder and left it there.

"Papa's never treated me with that openly fond look, no matter what I've done to try to earn his love," Megan whispered.

Cailin breathed in the sweet fragrance of the roses twined overhead. How had Avondale managed? She dropped a stitch. The same masterful way he clouded her thoughts. The sun turned his brown eyes into spicy cinnamon. She shook her head. Just looking at him made her stomach flutter. How could she be so foolish when he harbored such a problem?

Avondale turned to the arbor as if he could feel her gaze. Oh, she so well appreciated his bold, clean features, and his proud carriage. She sighed. Avondale was indeed courtly. His aristocratic presence could fill any area. When he entered a room the atmosphere changed. She didn't have to turn to see him. She found herself unbearably aware of him. If only he would acknowledge her.

He didn't.

Pain stabbed her heart. This constant upset couldn't be good for the baby. She must focus on her sister's problem and calm herself.

She leaned closer to Megan. "You have such dark circles under your eyes. Are you and Brody having difficulties? He hasn't said anything."

"Of course not."

"I'm so glad."

Her sister wasn't telling the truth. Perhaps later Megan would confide in her. If she wasn't ready yet, nothing would convince her to speak. Cailin wrinkled her brow. Since Avondale was never at home, when she was at loose ends, she and Brody just coincidentally met. "Brody's so obviously in love with you."

"Is he now?"

"He is. But marriage does take a good bit of understanding and flexibility." She gazed at Avondale. If only she could puzzle out the mystery of his different personalities. How could a man be so complex?

Megan shivered hard enough to vibrate the arbor. "Since you love Avondale so, mayhap I'm mistaken in my interpretation of your husband's attitude. He seems a bit fearsome to me."

Suddenly Cailin felt totally out of sorts. "I never saw happiness in Mums and Papa. Not even affection. Perhaps your marriage is one in a million." She stuck her finger with her knitting needle. "Brody is so attentive to you." She hesitated. "And you're so cool in return. You must make an effort."

"And, what of you? The servants told me of Lord Avondale's wild episode."

Cailin sighed. So, news about Avondale's misadventure had gotten around. Finally the subject had been broached. "Dear Megan. I'm glad you know. Marriages aren't all joy and happiness. We marry for better, or for worse. Perhaps, wedding vows might be better worded, that we marry for better *and* worse. No one is perfect, but the Bible tells us that love covers a multitude of sins. For his sake, we must keep the matter quiet."

She bit her lip. Had Megan spoken of where Avondale was last night…or had she referred to one of his earlier episodes?

She didn't want to know the details of where her husband had been last night.

17

The three carriages turned from the main road into Castle Drummond's long drive.

Cailin pushed open the window of her bedchamber and leaned out. Guests already half-filled their twenty guest rooms. Evidently titled English gentry thought nothing of overstaying their welcome. But surely her mother-in-law would not need three carriages for a brief over-night visit. Was this gloom she couldn't overcome good for the baby? Probably not.

Clattering and crunching on the gravel, creaking of the carriages, and shouts of "whoa" filled the air.

Servants ran to service the newcomers.

She pulled her head back inside, smoothed her day gown, and tucked errant curls into the brown velvet band around her head. She sighed deeply, straightened her shoulders, and forced her low-heeled slippers to move in the direction of the door.

She had invited the dowager. Now she must get some answers.

Slowly she descended the main staircase and pasted on a smile.

The servants were still ushering the visitors into the drawing room. She entered directly behind them.

"Milady, where should we take all these trunks?"

"George, take the dowager's trunks to the large, yellow guest room. I shall have to sort out what else goes where later." She laid a hand on the tiny flutter in her stomach. Had breakfast disagreed with her?

Five elegant ladies gazed at her. She walked directly to the dowager who was already ensconced on the wine velvet settee at the center of a cluster of chairs in the comfortable room. She curtsied and took Avondale's mother's extended ring-covered hand. "I'm so pleased you could come."

The dowager smiled a genuine and very kind smile.

A spray of joy radiated through Cailin. She motioned to the other ladies. "Please do be seated." And she sat on the edge of a chair facing her mother-in-law.

"May I introduce Lady Jane, Lady Sarah, Lady Marie, and Lady Anne?" the dowager nodded to each lady in turn. Each of the much younger ladies nodded, smiled, and settled straight-backed and poised into their chairs.

"My friends did not wish me to travel alone."

"Of course not. And you all are most welcome. I do recognize each of you from my wedding and I'm so pleased you could come." She glanced at her butler standing just inside the door. "Please serve low tea. I'm sure the ladies would like some refreshment."

Each woman nodded and murmured appropriate answers.

"And, George, please put the ladies' trunks in the room they used during the wedding week."

George hastened off. His low voice issuing orders floated back into the drawing room.

The dowager perched her pince-nez on the bridge of her nose and peered at her as if she was a prize mare. "Dear Cailin. We shall only be staying the night.

We are on our journey back to court. The king has summoned us, and we shall not want to keep him waiting." She smiled and patted Cailin's hand with her wrinkled, warm one as if they had been close friends for years.

Cailin stifled a gasp. Was this the same woman who had been so snobbish? This was a woman she could take into her heart and perhaps even confide in. Did opposite personalities residing in one body run in the duke's family? Why hadn't this woman been as gracious and accepting at the wedding? "Certainly you don't want to keep the king waiting, but you are welcome to stay as long as visiting here suits you." She offered a heart-felt smile. "You are a part of my family now, and I love having you here with us."

The dowager beamed. Her entire face radiated warmth. "My dear, I was so very pleased when you wrote you carried Avondale's heir." Her ample chest expanded. "I am elated." She brushed at a tear caught in a wrinkle at the corner of her hazel eye. "You are an exemplary wife. I am quite proud of you."

Warmth heated Cailin's cheeks and rushed all the way down to her neckline. So, that was why the woman had changed.

"You are so delicate appearing, I feared you might have problems getting in the family way." She glanced at her ladies. "I took the liberty of bringing my own mid-wife. She has delivered a healthy babe during a difficult birth even when the mother so unfortunately passed."

Cailin swallowed.

Obviously in a choice of saving either the mother or the child, the mid-wife had been instructed to save the oh-so-valuable heir. A son could not be replaced, but a wife so easily could.

Her stomach fluttered again. She forced a smile. If lives were in danger, she too would make that same choice and save her child. Already her love for her unborn baby was paramount in her life. Not because he was an heir, but simply because she loved him.

"Thank you, Dowager Duchess. I am happy you are so very thoughtful. I'm more than grateful you brought her." She clasped cold hands together and gazed at the four ladies staring at her.

The one with the steely glint in her eye held up a stern finger. "I have had much experience in birthing."

"Ah, Lady Anne. I believe I have heard rumors to that effect."

"Yes, my skill is well-known. I shall be staying throughout your confinement and shall oversee your delivery."

"I'm grateful. But, of course, my father is also bringing in our family surgeon. I'm certain he will be glad of your help." Why did she feel as if a net was being drawn around her?

"You will find I can assist greatly in your day-to-day care." Lady Anne's smile, the way she sat with her shoulders back and hands clasping her fan, and her school-master expression showed she would allow no objections to her ministrations.

Cailin's neck tensed.

The most robust of the four ladies nodded. "And I am quite well-known in court as the most capable person in England to oversee a wet nurse. I shall be taking over the heir's care as soon as Lady Anne delivers him."

Cailin's mouth dropped. She failed to hide her involuntary shudder. "Thank you so much, Lady

Sarah, but I am perfectly capable of nursing my own child. And I shall be responsible for his care myself."

"*Tsk tsk,* Cailin. No duchess takes on those onerous duties." Her mother-in-law patted Cailin's hand. "My dear, you will be so happy to have the help I'm providing. You will find birthing a baby is exhausting, and my ladies are the best in England." She rose, and warm, flabby arms embraced Cailin's shoulders. "My ladies will oversee your diet and make certain you do not overtax yourself. I myself shall return after the king's Christmas ball in time to be included in the heir's birth." She smiled around the room. "And, of course, Cailin will move into a separate bedchamber. Sometime men forget how delicate a mother-to-be's condition is, and insist on her wifely duty." She beamed. "We shall have none of that inside this castle."

Cailin gasped. She could not force out a word.

"I'm overtired after my trip. I shall forego tea and go directly to my room." The royal mother's jeweled hand squeezed Cailin's arm. "And you, my daughter, look a bit pale. I strongly suggest you take to your bed."

Were her feet rooted to the carpet? Was her tongue stuck to the roof of her mouth? She wanted answers to save her marriage. Instead a tyrant had moved into the castle.

George brought in the tea things. The scent of jasmine tea sent her stomach into a roil. She'd not had the morning sickness. And definitely not in mid-afternoon, but she must hurry to find a chamber pot.

****

As morning sun shone through the long hall

windows, Cailin rapped her knuckles on the dowager's door.

"My maid has finished packing. You may come inside and take my trunk to my carriage," the dowager called through the closed door.

"It's Cailin. May I have a private word with you before you take your leave?"

Faint rustling floated through the carved wood, and then the door burst open. "Of course, my dear. Come inside." A look of implacable determination tightened her mother-in-law's face.

Cailin walked inside and the woman motioned her to take a chair. She perched on the edge and opened her mouth.

"You do look better this morning. Lady Anne and Lady Sarah are seeing to your welfare, I trust."

"Yes." Cailin cleared her throat. "Actually they are—"

"You will become accustomed to their help. I suggest you relax and leave everything in their capable hands." The dowager strode to the window and gazed out. "Where is that servant of yours? I'm sure you don't let your people get away with incompetence. I really must be on my way."

"He will be here shortly. I—"

"The horses and carriage are waiting."

"Yes, but I really must have a word with you." Cailin rose and joined her mother-in-law at the window.

Below them the horses were indeed pawing the gravel with impatience.

She put a hand on the older woman's arm. "Avondale is behaving in quite a strange fashion. I hope you can advise me."

The woman sighed, plodded over to a chair and dropped into it as if she had the weight of the world on her shoulders. "What strange behavior?"

Cailin sat on a chair facing her. She straightened her shoulders, gazed into the troubled hazel eyes opposite her, and related everything about Avondale that puzzled and upset her. "Has he ever had strange dreams and fears?"

The dowager reached out and took her hand. "I'm so sorry, my dear." She lowered her head and peeled off her gloves. "Geoffrey showed signs of being a bit odd as a young man. Still, almost until he reached his majority he was fairly normal." She sighed. "Then he had spells where he seemed a different person." She shook her head. "I think the problems started with the accident on his horse. He and a group of his friends were following the hounds chasing a fox. His big hunter refused a hedge and Geoffrey sailed over his head and landed on the other side. He was still unconscious when they brought him back to the estate."

"I'm so sorry."

"He was ill for some time. Occasionally acted as if he didn't know where he was." Her eyes took on a far-away look. "We hid his problem, and the bouts of darkness and hearing of voices seldom occurred. Then this war with the Highlanders erupted. Geoffrey was at court, and then taking his turn in the House of Lords. When he returned home his spells had increased and so had his ravings. Something weighed on his conscience and troubled him greatly."

Cailin nodded. "And?"

"I could no longer keep his odd behavior secret, and his betrothed, the daughter of Count Spencer, broke their engagement."

Cailin gulped and gazed down at her folded hands.

"His actions grew so strange that rumors abounded." Her fingers trembled as she took Cailin's hand. "He gambled away most of our money." Tears filled her eyes. "Before his injury, my son was not interested in gambling dens. I'm still not certain that's where the money went, but it is gone." She swiped at her face with her balled gloves. "We still have our lands, our estates, and our houses in London. There's no worries for Geoffrey's heir, but thanks to his reputation for madness, he was quite ruined. No titled English lady would have him." She wrung her hands. "And if he doesn't produce a male heir, and the crown declares him incompetent, my nephew will inherit everything. Including Geoffrey's title."

She leaned forward. "I love my son. I could not have him rendered penniless, so I was desperate to have him appear normal at his wedding. That's why I spent every minute with him. I couldn't chance letting him out of my sight."

"Why didn't you tell me?"

"Would you have married him?"

Cailin shook her head.

"You were my last hope." The royal mother smiled through her tears. "And you are expecting the heir. You've done so well, my dear. I will never forget your service and will help you and the duke apparent in every way I can."

Cailin had never felt more like a piece of chattel. Still, the woman meant well. And perhaps Avondale could yet be healed. "How long ago did he fall?"

"It's been four years now. But his behavior grows

worse each passing year."

And she was the sacrificial lamb. "So I can never expect a normal marriage with a man in his right mind?"

"Never is a very long time."

A hard knock sounded at the door. "I've come for your trunks, Milady."

Her mother-in-law jumped to her feet and turned towards the door.

Cailin grasped her arm and pulled her to a halt. "How can I help him?"

"Laudanum when he grows out of control. I've ordered Hennings to act as his body-guard. He's a good man."

"But the nightmares. The demons he fears? How can I help him?"

"My dear, Geoffrey is a stalwart, loving man. His problems grew much worse after The Jacobite Rising. I think he suffered an additional trauma because of that Highland problem. The massacre at Culloden seemed to send him over the edge. Perhaps having this heir will bring him back to his senses."

Her mouth tightened. "Your duty is to keep Geoffrey's escapades secret and protect your child. You must not let my son touch you until this heir is born. Everything depends on this child. Had I not been ordered to court in Geoffrey's stead, I would remain here and guard your health myself." She nodded. "Good day. I shall return at Christmastide." Her wrinkled lips kissed Cailin's cheek. "If his behavior gets out of hand, you must lock him away." She walked out of the room and down the stairs.

Cailin watched from the window as the dowager's weight on the steps bowed the coach.

The other two coaches followed, one carrying Lady Jane and the other Lady Marie.

Cailin dropped on the settee and covered her face. Her poor, dear, wounded husband. Surely she could do more for him than drug him, keep him under guard, and lock him inside the castle.

Whatever she did, she would certainly not move out of Avondale's bedchamber.

18

Bright sunlight filled the corridor as Cailin tiptoed past the nursery.

Megan had left the door ajar and rustled about inside.

Cailin hesitated outside the door. As soon as she finished the task at hand, she would hasten back, and have another chat with Megan. Cailin gently rubbed her stomach. Her sister would likely spend a good portion of the morning seeing to preparations for the coming baby. And the nursery offered them a private place to talk.

When would she feel the first stirrings of life? Even with the grim venture she faced, Cailin tingled all over at the thought of a new life invigorating the castle. She couldn't keep from smiling.

But she couldn't think of her baby now. She must complete the task. Her velvet slippers noiseless on the thick carpet, she rushed to the far end of the long corridor before she could change her mind. How long since she'd visited the armory? Months? Years? She didn't like weapons, so she'd had precious little need to enter the locked room.

The heavy key dragged down the pocket hanging around her waist beneath her day dress. No one had questioned Mikey when he'd gotten the key for her.

Fiona had promised to delay all the women in the tapestry room by inking out an ancient Scottish design of thistle and heather that all the ladies were eager to work into a quilt for Cailin's very own first born. The design, which promised to bring good fortune and health, intrigued the ladies. They had avidly set to work with their sewing.

Having begged off with morning sickness, none had questioned her absence. She hurried down the narrow back staircase, her low-heeled shoes making almost no sound, and paused to check the lower hall.

No one in sight.

She scurried down the hall until she stopped at the far end, her heart beating fast. The wooden door, banded with iron and secured with a great iron lock, distinguished it from the other closed doors lining the corridor.

Gazing up and down the hall, she listened intently. Outside this furthermost room from the family's living quarters, she felt isolated. Through the ceiling-high, thick window panes extending across the end of the hallway, the faint banging of pots and pans, chatter, and laughter drifted over from the kitchen directly across the open-air, cobbled atrium.

The scullery maids and parlor maids had finished their daily routine, so they wouldn't disturb her.

Papa had long since departed on one of his quick, secret trips to England.

Megan worked in the nursery, and all the other ladies of the household were sewing in the tapestry room far from earshot.

Unfortunately, once again, she had no idea where Avondale was. Carefully she fitted the giant iron key into the heavy lock. It glided in easily, and then wouldn't budge. She strained with both hands.

Grudging as an old man disturbed from his

slumber, the key creaked until the lock clicked. She pushed open the door and slipped inside.

Wrinkling her nose, she blinked against the stale, dank odor. Apparently she was not the only one who seldom visited this room. Very little light illuminated her way. The few windows loomed far above her head, high, round, thick, and heavily glazed. Outside the windows, a forest of green trees partially obscured the sun, shrouding the huge room in a sort of gloaming dimness.

The walls wore no tapestries to warm the thick stone, enveloping the room with unusual coolness. She hugged her arms close to her body. She'd take what she needed and quickly leave.

After striking the flint, she lit the candle, raised it high, and appraised the large space. Dressed wooden rafters crisscrossed the vaulted ceiling. A huge stone fireplace stood at either end of the massive room, looking quite like empty black mouths, open to cry about their unused state, or perhaps her illicit entrance.

No carpet shielded her thin slippers from the granite floor. Cold seeped through the velvet soles. Her candle's flame didn't illuminate the dark corners. The flickering light merely shot massive wicked shadows from the stacked and hanging arms up the distant walls.

She shivered. Nasty place.

Tall pikes, great swords, Lochaber axes, heavy shields, and torges lined the walls. Papa kept pistols and muskets locked in the tall cabinets. Obviously, the key she held was far too large to fit these closets. Papa must keep the cabinet keys somewhere else.

She stood gaping, as if she'd never before seen the massive room. A realization dawned. Small wonder

Papa had wanted a son.

She had entered a man's world, a whole domain enclosed in this one room. Papa had told her stories of when he was young, accompanying his father to this room. The two of them had oiled and cleaned each weapon. Papa had spent many hours with his father, honing his skills with these guns and swords. Before he died, Grandpapa had taken Papa on numerous boar hunts, fox chases, and such. The two of them had used many of the weapons.

Much as she disliked this room, Papa loved it.

These arms spoke eloquently of his care, all polished, and smelling of gun oil and other strange odors. Ancient coats of mail posed in different spots as if a knight still stood protected inside.

Enough weapons lined this room to equip a small army. A shiver spidered her spine and raised bumps on her arms. Perhaps the ghosts of that army still haunted this room. Silly. But the room did have a mysterious, hard, killing ambiance.

On her last visit, Papa had held her hand and ushered her to this long table. A fire had burned inside the hearth then and illuminated myriad maps that still lay spread across the length and width of the table, overlapping each other. She'd been barely tall enough to see the interesting colored lines that she'd wanted to explore. The memory brought warmth to her heart. She shook her head. She must get to the job. Where should she start?

Tall as she was, even when she stood on tiptoe she couldn't reach the weapons. A double bladed knife in its carved sheath hung just above her fingertips. She needed a stool.

But there was no stool.

This room had been designed for men. Tall, heavy-muscled, lithe men like Avondale and Brody. She but visited here. A stranger in her own castle.

Papa had been right. He needed a son. He deserved a son. Perhaps she would give him a grandson. She touched her abdomen. Yes, there was a small bulge.

No matter how hard she tried, she could never learn to wield these weapons, even had she wanted to.

With a flash of insight which brought a stab of pain, she realized that Papa had expected something different from her than he would have from a son. And she had not disappointed him. But he had so disappointed her.

Pain shot through her heart. Papa betrayed her trust. She'd obeyed his express will and wed the Duke of Avondale. And he was a madman. What was she to do? Perhaps he hadn't known of Avondale's strange fits. But surely he must have wondered at a duke wedding a mere daughter of a Baron.

The weight of his betrayal struck her so she could barely draw a breath. Papa must have known of Avondale's disability. In order to protect the castle, he'd knowingly chained her forever to a lunatic. And she had no way out.

She fell to her knees on the cold stone and buried her face in her hands. "Oh, Papa. How can I forgive you?"

As she knelt, another thought, like a sledge hammer to her heart, struck her to the core. Her throat closed. She scrunched her eyes against tears creating hot pools behind her eyelids.

Father, God. In my anger against Papa, am I disobeying You? Will you punish me by making my son mad as well?

Or will you punish me by giving me a daughter?

She tried to still the painful anger racking her heart. *Father, God. Please forgive my sins. Help me forgive Papa. Show me what to do about my marriage. About the sometimes wonderful, sometimes horrifying man I married. What shall I do?*

Cailin listened. She yearned to hear the still, small voice of her Shepherd. Her knees ached, yet she waited. In the stillness, with the unfamiliar odor and sight of weapons of war gleaming around her, peace crept into her heart. A verse she had memorized during her childhood rose to the surface of her mind.

My sheep hear My voice and they follow Me. They will never follow a stranger.

The anguish in her heart lessoned to a dull pain. Yes, God would tell her what to do. He would protect her and her baby. She could trust God. He would not betray her. She rose to her feet. Perhaps bad things did happen to people committed to God. Perhaps God had a reason for permitting hardship and heartache in a person's life.

Avondale had never come close to threatening her. Her presence seemed to calm him. So she had no need of a weapon with which to fight him off. God would be her fortress and her shield. Nor would she use a weapon when she embarked on her new mission. God was her fortress and defender.

Father, though I find a beautiful, loving side to Avondale, I also find a dark, fearful, and mad side to him. He is two men caught inside the body of one. He is good and evil. He is light and darkness. He is my husband. We are one flesh. I love him and I fear him.

And he is so tormented. How can I help him?

"Surely I won't have to lock him away."

Silence echoed back from the huge, shadowy room, glinting with weapons of war.

19

The nursery door still stood ajar, but no sound came from within.

Cailin hesitated. Normally she would have rushed inside, eager to talk with Megan. But her time alone in the armory with God made her more sensitive. She tilted her chin high. It was way past time she begin to think of others' needs above her own.

Megan had questioned the time she spent alone with Brody. She needed to explain herself more fully. She fingered the small, gold cross she wore every day above her engagement diamond. And so she would.

She knocked gently.

"Who's there?" Megan's voice floated from behind the closed door.

Her voice sounded muffled, followed by a series of sniffs, and then a delicate blowing of Megan's nose. Was her always-confident sister crying?

"It's Cailin."

"Oh. Just one minute, please." Rustling inside showed that Megan was preparing herself. "Come in."

Cailin pushed open the door into the bright, cheery room. Megan sat in a cushioned rocker.

Wooden toys, carved boats with canvas sails, miniature furniture, and toy horsemen lay scattered around her feet. She hugged a baby-blue knit blanket to her chest, and Megan's dewy-eyed gaze didn't quite meet hers.

"Am I intruding?"

Megan's brows lifted. Surprise lightened her sad face. "No, come in and sit with me. I'm glad of company."

But her sister really didn't look that happy to see her. Cailin couldn't quite put a finger on Megan's attitude. Her eyes were rimmed with red. She hid sadness behind a tight smile, and smoothed a frown from her forehead with her fingers.

Behind her sister, the clothespress gaped open, revealing dainty white and blue muslin along with fine linen baby clothes piled in uneven rows. Pink and blue bonnets, tiny white booties, pastel parasols, and a silver rattle clustered over small wicker chairs like loving promises waiting to be fulfilled.

Cailin hugged her arms. She so wanted this baby. A son to give Avondale the male heir he needed…and Papa. The realization of just how much she wanted this child swept over her, leaving her knees weak.

But if she bore a daughter, and daughters far outnumbered sons in her family, Papa being the last male in his line, knowing what she now knew of Avondale, could she ever let him touch her again? What if she carried a lass?

God, please give me a normal son.

A son. The thought brought warmth to her cheeks and love to her heart, chasing the fear into a thin vapor.

As she walked into the sun-filled gold and blue room she trailed her hand over a child's wooden table and chairs. Sweet memories nestled inside this place. When they were children, she and Megan had loved this small upper corner of the castle.

Megan sniffed again.

Cailin brushed her memories aside. "You've been

crying." She hurried to Megan's side and perched on the footstool beside her rocker. She took one of her sister's slender, cool hands, which dangled forlornly from the rocker's arms.

"Yes."

"You're unhappy with Brody?"

Megan lifted a tear-streaked face. "He's always with you!"

Cailin's throat caught.

Had Brody spent that much time with her? He did seem to seek her out most days.

She touched Megan's hand. "I'm so sorry. I didn't realize I was monopolizing him. He saw I was lonely when Avondale was always away."

"And what of me? When I was lonely?" Megan swiped a sleeve over her cheeks.

"You never seemed so." Cailin clasped her arms around her knees. "Brody's a brother. A shoulder to lean on. A sympathetic ear."

"Brody's always been in love with you."

"What?" Guilt knifed between her ribs. The hours spent talking, jesting in private with Brody. How must they have looked? Oh, she was so very selfish. "You're so wrong, Megan. Brody adores you. The way he gazes at you with his heart in his eyes. The tender way he speaks your name. The songs he writes about you."

"Then why does he spend so much time with you? And is that baby you carry really that cold, stuck-up Avondale's?" Megan's mossy eyes sparkled with unshed tears.

Cailin wrapped her arms around Megan's trembling shoulders. "Of course this is his baby." She pulled Megan closer. "Brody treats me as a sister. As a woman in pain. He knows Avondale and I are having problems. He seeks only to help." She dropped her arms. "Brody's a fine man, Megan. He would never betray you. Never." She gently pulled her sister's chin around to force Megan to look into her eyes. "Nor would I. And Brody would die for you."

Slowly the shadows left Megan's deep green eyes turning then softer, until they seemed like pools of clear water with sun sparkling through. "Thank you." She turned her head slightly away. "But please don't spend so much time with him. People are talking."

"Of course, now that you've pointed out the problem, I surely won't." A twinge of sadness curled through her heart. She'd miss his company.

Megan sat straighter. A frown marred her forehead. "So, why are *you* in pain? You're going to have a lovely baby. You'll bring laughter and happiness into the castle. Though your husband is snooty, you've still got the very best of everything. Our parents' love, your new title, an entire castle filled with people who chit-chat with the king." Megan lowered her head until her red hair hid her face. "You obeyed Papa, and you've found happiness."

Cailin drew in a shuddering breath. She could trust Megan. Perhaps a new pair of eyes could help her discover what was wrong with her husband and what she could do about her problem. "I fear Avondale's not of sound mind." She caressed her stomach.

Megan's face said she couldn't agree more. "I'm not surprised. Before you wed, I tried to warn you. What's wrong?"

"You're aware, of course, that my husband treats me badly in the daytime." She couldn't hide a tender smile. "But when we are alone he is wonderful." A deep sigh worked up from the bottom of her soul.

"Except for when he's experiencing one of his spells. I do love him, you know. But I'm at my wit's end as to what to do with him." She sighed. "His mother tells me he's been peculiar from young manhood." Much as she wanted to, she couldn't tell Megan most of Avondale's other behavior. It seemed too much like betrayal.

Megan squeezed her hand. "Yes, that's no secret." Green eyes blinked. "He's wonderful in the bedroom?"

"Marvelous." Her cheeks grew hot. "I'm so confused. Why does Avondale treat me so badly in the daylight and so beautifully in the dark?"

Megan picked up a stuffed doll and toyed with its wigged hair. "In public he treats you as if you're below his lofty station." She frowned. "But in private, he's really good to you?" She stiffened her shoulders. "We're intelligent women. Between us, we can figure the answer to this problem."

Cailin threaded her fingers together until her knuckles turned white. She nodded.

"Brody kept secrets from me. And I was insanely jealous each time he disappeared with you. But I accept now there was no reason for my feelings." Megan cupped her hand over Cailin's. "Several nights ago I experienced great fear over Brody's welfare when he failed to reappear after a midnight rescue mission he took with Fiona. Then came blessed relief when I found him badly wounded, but more or less safe. The man is a knight, putting himself in danger to save his fellow Highlanders. It takes all my strength to keep him alive."

"Yes, and now after the broch's been empty less than five days, there are three more wounded Highlanders hidden there from English soldiers." Cailin rose from her stool and began to pace. "And

Fiona feels deeply for one of the hunted Highlanders."

"Does she now? We mustn't let a romance blossom between the two. Those men could be discovered any day and shot, hanged, or taken to the Tower of London." Megan frowned. "We mustn't let her miss the opportunities she has of a fine marriage with one of the English gentry."

"You're right. We must keep Fiona and the fugitive apart. We don't want Fiona's heart broken." Cailin picked up a soft, blue knit baby blanket and held it to her cheek.

"Speaking of broken hearts, you're not getting away that easily. Tell me more of you and Avondale."

"His behavior is so strange. He refuses to allow more than one small candle lit in our chamber." Cailin hugged the blue blanket as if it shielded her from a spear. "And, no matter how early I wake in the morning, he is always gone."

Megan rubbed her chin with the doll's hair. "Hmm. He acts as if he likes darkness."

"Exactly." Cailin nodded, frowning. "In the daytime he avoids me and surrounds himself with his friends or goes hunting or disappears altogether. At first I thought he liked being with Brody. But not for some time now. He also avoids Brody."

"Yes, he and Brody did seem to get along somewhat at first. Umm…Cailin, do you suppose Lord Avondale's jealous of the time you and Brody spend with one another?" Megan pushed her red hair away from her face, her mossy eyes again full of questions.

Cailin gave a nervous giggle. "How could he be? He's gone long before Brody and I—" She stopped and frowned. "I'll insist that Brody play his chanter and sing with you." She lay down the soft blanket. "I see now it was selfish of me to take up so much of Brody's time."

Megan shook her head emphatically. Then she bit her lip. "I won't gloss over the truth. That's exactly what I'd love for you to do. The time you spent with Brody irritated me quite a bit more than I like to admit."

"I doubt I will hurt Brody's feelings when I refuse to spend time with him." Drat. Why was she still burnishing the truth? She had to confess Avondale's behavior. She would have nothing come between Megan and herself. Nothing. Betrayal or not, perhaps Megan could help. She pulled in a deep breath. "Actually—"

Fiona stuck her bright head inside the door. "Cailin, do you have a minute?"

"Come in."

Megan rose and strode to the nursery door. "Yes, come in. I was just leaving." She glanced back over her shoulder. "Thank you so very much, Cailin. I expect you to keep your word."

Fiona walked inside. Her brows rose. "What was that about?"

"We just had a sisterly chat. Cleared the air of something." She smiled and pointed to the rocker Megan had just vacated. "Sit down. What's on your mind?"

Fiona lowered herself into the rocker and leaned forward. "I…I have to tell ye something." She cleared her throat. "Something rather awful. I wouldn't bother you with it, but I don't know what to do."

Cailin put a hand to her fluttering heart. She didn't want to hear this. "It concerns Avondale?"

Fiona gave a faint smile. "Yes." She heaved a deep

sigh. “Ye know I love ye like a sister?”

“Thank you. And I you.” She took up her needles in case the revelation to come proved too difficult, and she wouldn’t be able to meet Fiona’s young gaze. She must find out the details sooner or later. “What has happened?”

“The night of the masquerade…”

Cailin’s temples throbbed. She began taking slow purls with her needles.

“His Grace…” Fiona clutched her hands together. “I think he lost his bearings somewhat.”

She knitted faster. “And?”

“He dragged me out of the castle and into the forest.”

Cailin dropped her knitting. “I know. Rafe told me.” Dread clutched her with the implacable hand of doom. “This had to have happened when Rafe went to the kitchen to fetch Hennings.” She didn’t want to hear, but Fiona needed to unburden her heart. “What was Avondale like?”

“He didn’t seem himself at all. It was as if someone else was inside the duke’s body.” Fiona shivered. “I never have seen anything quite like his eyes.” Her mouth trembled. “He looked so elegant in his costume, and yet he wasn’t himself at all. I don’t know how to explain it.”

“Yes, I’ve seen that look. Like a man sleepwalking.” Cailin picked up her knitting. “Or a man lost, out of control, wandering in darkness.” What could have caused him to have such demons? The dowager said The Rising, especially after the Battle of Culloden, had made Avondale ever so much worse. Tears welled in her eyes and she kept them focused on the tiny blue coat she was knitting. “Go on.”

"We'd just gotten inside the cover of the trees when he abruptly sat down on a grassy bank and pulled me into his lap."

Oh Father, no!

Her needles flashed through her knitting. Purls, knits, she had no idea what type of stitch she made.

"But suddenly he grew very still. He looked at me with the most puzzled expression on his face. Like he had no idea why he was sitting on the ground or why I was on his lap."

"He didn't hurt you?" Cailin dropped the knitting in a soft heap onto her lap and touched Fiona's arm.

"No. The dragging to the woods tore my costume and scared the daylights out of me, though."

"Then?"

"Then Hennings came running up, walked us back to the castle, and took the duke away." Fiona pulled in a deep breath. "I think I saw Rafe running towards us in the darkness, but I didn't stop to see for certain."

"Oh, Fiona, I'm so sorry you had to go through that." Cailin gazed into the wide, green eyes. "But you must promise to keep this a secret. It is of the utmost importance we keep Avondale's problems a secret. The title, the inheritance, the power, you understand?"

"Of course I do. They must be kept for your baby. I won't breathe a word."

Cailin knew she would not. The family was keeping their own secrets about Brody and his sister hiding inside the castle. "No, of course you won't. We are sisters now."

"Is the duke a threat to our family?"

"I don't know, dear. Rafe and Hennings are never to leave his side. One by night and the other by day. And no one but the four of us must ever know what happened."

"Not even Brody or Megan?"

"No, Fiona. They have their own problems. We must not burden them with ours." She scooted to her knees in front of the girl and hugged her. "We must never speak of this again. I am only happy Avondale didn't hurt you."

Fiona hugged her and whispered, "Who is Billy the Butcher?"

"I don't know." But she would find out. And she must decide what to do about her husband.

Rafe's plan of a hunting accident could only be used in the most terrible of circumstances. Used only if her baby was in danger. Her fingers twined around the gold cross at her throat.

Oh God, there must be other options. Will Avondale need to suffer an accident?

20

Cailin rose from her knees and lowered herself into the nursery rocker facing Fiona. She took a deep breath. Was her husband losing all control? Had she indeed married a madman? If Avondale was a lunatic, would her baby be born with his father's weakness? Would she have to lock away the man she loved for his entire life, visiting him only in the dark of night so he wouldn't shy away from her? Or would she have to take even more drastic measures?

She sat up straight and dropped her face into her hands. Was that Avondale's secret?

Was there something about her that frightened him? Was that why he avoided her in the daylight? Certainty deep inside signaled yes. Her dear husband was not snubbing her, he was afraid to be around her. She rubbed her eyes.

But only in the light of day did he keep his distance. In the sheltering darkness the man was impossibly perfect. She loved his touch. The words he whispered in her ear. The concern he had for how she spent her day. The pride in his manner as he spoke of their child. And she loved listening to his stories of his estates and events that happened during his childhood, and how much he abhorred court life.

So, she'd been interpreting his actions entirely the wrong way. He was not ashamed of her—heavens, he was ashamed of himself. Tears welled and spilled in warm rivulets down her cheeks. For no fault of his own, her dear husband had periods of blackouts—times when he could remember nothing. He'd had an injury and suffered through some awful experience and so sometimes lost his way.

Oh heavens, he blamed himself and had been too ashamed to face her in daylight. But he showered his love over her when hidden by darkness. Oh, she knew she was right. She caressed her abdomen. How soothing the balm of truth to her heart. Now she need not fear asking him for his explanation. And she would. Then, perhaps he could see she would never, never be ashamed of him.

Fiona touched her arm. "I'm so sorry my story made you weep."

Perhaps when he faced his shame, Avondale would begin to heal.

"No. It's best you told me. I must know what happens with Avondale. I must learn to deal with the problem and help him. Thank you for telling me." She smiled and wiped a handkerchief across her wet cheeks. "I just pray that you are all right."

"Yes. No harm was done." The sparkle returned to Fiona's aqua eyes. "I believe the man has so much integrity that even when he's not himself, he wouldna harm a lady." She smiled. "Ye see somehow he groped his way back to reality."

"Thank you for thinking so highly of my husband." Cailin squeezed her hand. Then she sat up, took a deep breath, and picked her knitting from her tapestry bag. "But you must practice your English at all times, even when alone with family." She jabbed a needle into the blue yarn. "Now we must plan."

"Aye. I mean yes."

"I wasn't able to get into the gun cabinets. Papa keeps the keys. Nor could I even reach one of the broad swords Papa has hanging on the walls. I'll have to get Mikey to help us."

Fiona's lake blue eyes clouded. "I'm no'…not so certain we should take weapons. I've seen far too much bloodshed."

"But two unarmed women, alone in the Highlands?"

"We'll have the closed carriage crested with the duke's emblem, and Mikey will be with us."

Fiona picked up a tiny china doll and played with its silk dress.

"It's dangerous. Perhaps we should take Aunty Moira?" Cailin frowned in concentration, stroking her cheek and rubbing her chin. "We could all wear our best dresses and give the excuse that we are visiting a dressmaker. The soldiers would realize we're not Highland women."

"Mayhap ye…you had better stay in the castle and keep yer wee one out of danger."

"True." She stroked her stomach. "But the others are in danger. How can I stay?" She sighed. She would have to alert Rafe to keep Avondale close to the castle on strict surveillance while she was gone. "I think we should take Aunty Moira."

"Didna ye…didn't you notice, yer Aunt's still sickly in the mornings, though she's already showing her condition?"

Cailin's stomach fluttered. "Yes, Aunty Moira being older and expecting a first child could be difficult for her. Aunty must take special precautions." Their two children could play as they grew up. What a joy to have small feet pattering about inside the castle.

Perhaps soon, Megan would be in the family way as well. "So, then, due to her delicate health, we shall leave Aunty Moira to her chore of tending the wounded men already hidden in the broch."

Father, guide me in this marriage situation. I think of Avondale constantly. How can I help him over his nightmare? Guide me, please. And please keep him away from the broch. Somehow, I think his problems are connected with The Rising. I'm certain discovering the wounded soldiers sheltered there would do him no good.

She swallowed down her feeling of abject failure. She had no idea how to help Avondale, and yet he depended on her. "Then it will be you, me, and Mikey. Aunty Moira's new husband, Ian…his brogue is too heavy. And he's the very picture of a Highlander."

"I will visit the men Mikey and his wife have been nursing in the broch, and beg one of their *sgian-dhus* for each of us."

"*Sgian-dhus*?"

"Aye…I mean yes. That's the short, razor-sharp dagger a Highlander wears strapped to his calf just beneath the top of his high hose." Fiona winked. "And we can strap ours above the top of our hose, much higher on our thighs."

"Oh." This lass, barely entering into womanhood, yet talking so knowledgeably of daggers, was always full of surprises.

"Aye...yes. And there are other weapons a woman may wield." Fiona gave another knowing wink.

Cailin put her hand to her mouth to cover a cough. This lass understood far more than any Lowland gentlewoman would.

"I can see what yer thinking. In a one room cottage a lass does learn the private facts of life early." Fiona giggled. "No'…not that I am closely acquainted with them, dear sister-in-law."

Cailin's fertile imagination painted a clear picture of husband and wife, children, and babies all crowded into one room. And the intimate things that happened between a husband and wife open to the eyes of the surrounding family.

How would Avondale, with his obsessive fear of light, react in a situation of that nature? Before they wed, he'd never shared so much as a room. Fortunately, her husband would never have to face such a situation.

Even as her cheeks burned, she ached to ask Fiona more about her encounter with Avondale. But the lass had seemed so eager not to talk about the near tragedy. Perhaps later Cailin would find an appropriate time.

She must make this daring rescue and, in the meantime, map out a plan to keep Avondale locked up safely. He often tried to slip away from Hennings and Rafe to venture out on his own. Since the episode with Fiona, she could not allow Avondale his freedom, but she had no wish to frustrate him.

The bodyguards must learn to enter into Avondale's plans and become companions rather than shadow and restrain him.

"The rain crows have been cooing all day. It's set to rain tomorrow. The redcoats donna…do not like to be abroad in a heavy drench."

"You're right. They'll more likely be lounging inside ale houses and barracks rather than patrolling the roads. We'll leave directly after breakfast." She patted Fiona's shoulder. "You're doing a fine job of working on your speech. You've improved your brogue so much. Soon no one will even suspect you are a Highland lass."

"Thank you. And it might be best if you do not tell the duke yer plans."

"Of course not. I don't wish to upset him. And Brody must continue to rest and regain his strength after that terrible wound. But he'll soon have to move the men out of the broch."

"Aye. When Megan found him at the bottom of the back staircase bleeding and almost unconscious the night of the masquerade, I thought surely he would die." Fiona laid aside the china doll and started to briskly fold a pile of baby blankets. "But the three men he rescued are still safe inside the broch." She smiled a secret smile. "And I see Grady each day."

"You and Megan patched Brody up. A few weeks from now he'll be good as new."

"By the look of him, gaining his strength may well take a verra…very long time. He lost a lot of blood. Do ye…you ken if we can get him up those great stairs from the store room to his own room?"

"Yes. As soon as he is well enough to stand, Rafe and Mikey will take him upstairs."

Megan spent her days nursing Brody, while Cailin spent her hours wondering what awful deed Avondale might pull next. A trill of loneliness curled her stomach. She missed the warmth of Avondale's presence of an evening.

He arrived in their bedchamber later and later each night.

Always she felt acutely aware of his virile presence. He was not a man to be ignored. And, like a blood-sucking leech, a nagging sense of emptiness clung to her each morning as she climbed alone out of her bed.

She waited and waited later each night so he could sit in the shadows of their room and listen while she read the Bible, but he made fewer and fewer comments.

Though he tenderly met with her in the darkness each night, no matter how early she awakened, Avondale was always gone. She longed to see his face smiling at her from his pillow, but it was always empty.

Prayer hadn't dispersed her concern, but seemed to intensify her sense of helplessness. She couldn't share this with Fiona. Her sister-in-law already thought Avondale was a monster.

"Our tale that Brody's out boar hunting won't hold water if Molly or one of the other servants finds him lying injured in Megan's bed." Cailin nodded decidedly. "Yes. Brody's better left hidden in the storage room until he mends." She tucked her knitting in the tapestry bag, rose, gathered her skirts in her hand, and took a step towards the nursery door. "Between you, me, Megan, and Mikey, we can continue to sneak food to Brody until he can limp around. Then we can circulate the story that a boar gored him." With her hand on the doorknob, she called over her shoulder, "In the meantime, we two will embark on our grand adventure on the morrow."

"Ye…you think the boar hunting story is holding? I heard the servants ask when the hunting party is expected."

"Yes."

"If yer sure you won't change yer mind about this dangerous plan, I'll see ye…you in the morning, then."

21

"Ready, Fiona?"

"Right behind ye, Cailin."

A rooster crowed, announcing the pale lilac dawn that barely colored dense overhanging clouds.

Cailin lifted her skirts and led Fiona at a fast walk to the carriage house. Dew from the morning air sparkled on her skin, and the clucking of the fowls sounded so peaceful, she wondered for the hundredth time why men waged war.

Why did men think it necessary to destroy one another, leaving their wives and children to fend for themselves in a hard-scrabble existence? She shook her head.

One thing she knew for certain, men and women looked at life quite differently. Several stray curls escaped from her bonnet so she brushed them back from her face. Would she ever understand men?

Pleasantly breathless and quite ready for adventure, she slid down onto the leather seat across from Fiona's slender body and lovely, shining face. Her blonde coloring and azure eyes mirrored Brody's, but were sculpted with a far more delicate hand.

The carriage jounced forward and Cailin balanced on the cushions to settle in for their long trip. "Are you ready for this?"

"Aye…I mean yes. More than ready, I'm that homesick."

"I'm so sorry. I thought you and your mums had settled into the castle quite happily."

"Och, Cailin, donna…don't get me wrong." She'd slipped into her native brogue. "Ma and I are verra happy. 'Tis just I miss the young'uns so."

"And your sisters-in-law too, I wager."

"A—yes. Both Duncan and Collin built such nice wee homes within shouting distance of Da's place. And Jenny and Mary oft as not, walked across the meadow to cook with Ma and me. And the mothers never left the wee ones behind."

"Jenny and Mary are your sisters-in-law?"

"Yes. Cailin, with you, Megan, and Jenny and Mary, I am that blessed to have the best in-laws in Scotland. I so hope we can find them."

Cailin squeezed Fiona's small gloved hand. "I feel equally as blessed to have you as my sister." Warmth flowed into the lonely places in her heart. She did love Fiona. Who wouldn't?

The lass was sweet, funny, kind, and extremely thoughtful. How fortunate for the entire family that Brody had brought his sister and mother to live with him and Megan inside the castle. Fiona carried sunshine into each room she entered.

Cailin turned her head and gazed out the window at the scenery flashing past. If only Avondale hadn't frightened Fiona so. What caused him to fall into one of his black spells? She must discover the answer. She fisted her gloved hands. She simply must.

The carriage rocked past the outer paddocks. Inside the lush green meadow, the spindly legged spring foals romped beside their sleek-coated mothers, setting her mind on Brody.

He'd offered sage advice on the breeding of next

spring's brood. The man had an uncanny fine way with horses.

If only Avondale wouldn't disappear each day. Surely a duke knew more about horses and the care of the estate than a piper like Brody.

Just thinking of Avondale at home, tending to the estate, seeing to the horses and sheep, and spending time with her, brought a melting softness to her insides.

Watching their foals nurse from their mothers sent a wave of weepiness over her. In five more months, Lord willing, she would carry a babe in her arms. A child of her own. She would never be lonely again. And she wouldn't hand him over to a wet nurse, no matter how militant her mother-in-law grew.

She shivered and hugged her arms. What if her son shared the same malady as his father? She lifted her chin. Whatever her child turned out to be, she would love him, adore him, protect him, and make his life happy. She folded gloved hands over her stomach.

And if she bore a lass, she would spoil her, adore her, and dress her in pretty satins and lace. She stiffened her shoulders. She'd make very certain her daughter would wed a man she loved. She gave a tiny, hopeless sigh. And that the bridegroom would be as normal a man as she could find, title or not.

She pressed her nose against the glass carriage window and watched the heather and bracken rush past. Beside the road, the burn twinkled through the glen. She couldn't hear its roar because of the crunch of the coach's wheels on the rutted road, the drumming of the horses' hooves, the squeaking of the harnesses, and the carriage creaking as it swayed along. But she knew the sound was there.

Below them, rushing beside the carriage road, the speed of the river exploding over smooth rocks reminded her of her vow to make her marriage a happy one. She would not let any rocks jutting through the surface of her marriage keep love and happiness from bursting through.

Regardless of the dark cloud that hung over Avondale, she would raise her bairns in a loving atmosphere with a father close by to give the children a model to look up to.

Would Avondale be as gentle with the children as he was with her? Or would he frighten his children with his strange moods and dangerous behavior? Would they wonder why Hennings and Rafe never left their father's side? She pressed a hand over her fluttering heart. She must stop worrying or risk bearing a nervous babe.

She yawned. Of late, she'd gotten precious little sleep.

Avondale would get well. She'd told herself so numerous times…and managed to half-convince herself. But what turned his tender expressions dark? And what haunted his dreams? She must make him tell her. If only he didn't come to bed so very late.

"Are you scared, Cailin? Yer so quiet."

Fiona's hand on her arm pulled her thoughts back to today's mission. "Of course not. Why should anyone threaten us? We're but two ladies on a mission of mercy."

"But ye've not seen what the soldiers do to harmless ladies." Fiona's eyes looked large and glossy. "While I've hidden behind bushes, I've seen them strip my friends, have their way with them, and then run them through with a bayonet."

Cailin clenched both fists. No one would harm her unborn child. "We've the carriage, and we've Mikey. And more than that, we've got our guardian angels hovering over, protecting us. Remember, we're not defenseless Highland women, we're Lowland Ladies backed by the crown on a mission of mercy."

"The soldiers may not take well to our mission. They want naught to do with saving Highland bairns. The Duke of Cumberland wants to burn us all out of our crofts and lands."

"Even the Duke of Cumberland wouldn't dare mistreat the Duke of Avondale's wife. If they ignore the crest on the carriage, they will respect the diamonds we wear." She fingered the necklace she seldom wore and the baubles dangling over her gloved wrist. "These and the ones you are wearing will set them back on their heels."

Fiona gave a little shiver. "Mayhap we should have brought His Grace with us for our safekeeping."

As the carriage tilted on the rutted road, Cailin braced herself with the carriage strap. "You are more frightened of the soldiers than of my husband? I know you avoid being alone with Avondale." She braced her other hand on the cushion between them. "But be charitable to him. You saw that he's…he's not quite right in his head." She closed her eyes. "And, mayhap not in his heart, either."

"Oh, Cailin, you deserve so much better in a husband. You—"

Cailin put a gloved finger over Fiona's lips.

The lass's eyes gradually lost their look of sympathy laced with fear.

Cailin could pinpoint the exact time Fiona's agile mind leapt to a different topic altogether. She'd seen that curious gleam in her sky-blue eyes too often to miss.

"Well, then, and are you happy with His Grace? You seem in a deep study this morning. And I wonder if you need protection during the nights."

"Please don't fret yourself about me. Avondale is everything a husband should be when we are alone together." Except for his nightmares and pacing. And the tormented expression that always followed when she could stand his nightmares no longer and shook him awake.

"I'm more than glad to hear that from you."

Cailin couldn't repress her sigh. She must change the subject or risk making the child growing inside into a melancholic. "And what of Brody? Is he mending well?"

"Yes, his spirits remain good. Megan stays by his side most times. I spell her at scheduled intervals. No one is the wiser that the king's soldiers almost killed him as he rescued three more Highlanders." Fiona's eyes, so like Brody's direct unflinching gaze, met hers, and she set her full lips into a stubborn line. "That's nay…not what I asked. And are you happy with Avondale?"

Did all her confused feelings lay open upon her face for the lass to read? "To be sure, Avondale satisfies me."

"You donna…don't fear him at all?"

"Never." Avondale pleased her. Not only while she was in his bed, but friendship with him was blossoming. During their nights reading the Bible, he'd grown into a shoulder to lean upon, an ear to talk into, a heart to share her dreams with, and she hoped soon, a faith to pray with. But that was before his last episode. And he still refused to tell her his secret.

"I had been wondering. What, with Megan not being in the family way. None of my brothers were wed this long without…."

"Fiona!"

Fiona's face became a picture of remorse. "I'm that sorry, Cailin, if I've embarrassed you. Don't you Lowland women talk so freely among yerselves?"

"Well, well, yes. Sometimes. With someone we know quite well."

"Are we nay…not sisters?" Fiona tried to conceal her hurt expression.

"I'm sorry. Yes. That is, if there is something to discuss. Megan has not divulged any problems to me."

"Well, you see, Brody being so…I thought mayhap Megan had some…problems."

"You thought I spent too much time alone with him." Cailin gazed outside, only half seeing the woods that had already begun to thin into clumps of birch and hazel, and the fenced meadow filled with brown Highland coos with their shaggy coats, enormous long horns, and cuddly appearances. "I admit I was lonely. I thought Megan was completely occupied with the wounded men." Cailin made a pretext of untying and retying the ribbons on her bonnet. "I was selfish. I shall not be spending time alone with Brody again."

"No, Cailin, don't quit entirely. But it would please me if you took along a chaperone."

"After today I expect my time will be needed elsewhere." She smiled to show Fiona she wasn't angry and reached for her hand. "I hope we two shall always be able to talk freely with one another."

Fiona's wide azure eyes cleared. "We shall be great friends as well as sisters."

As the coach began its upward climb and the meadow beside the road transformed into moorland scrub and bare rock, gravity pushed Cailin against the cushions. No turning back now, even had she wanted to. With the road too narrow to reverse the coach, they were committed to reaching the Highlands.

All the while, she gazed at the passing scenery, her thoughts concentrated on Fiona's troubling conversation. Did the entire household think she'd spent too much time alone with Brody? Did everyone think Avondale was dangerous? What would they think if they knew of the men hidden inside the broch? What would they think when the carriage returned home this evening? If the carriage returned home.

She avoided looking at Fiona, not yet old enough to pin up her hair, who knew too much about the relationship between a husband and wife. Perhaps Mums and she should think more quickly about a suitable husband for Fiona.

Hot blood rose to Cailin's cheeks. She'd heard that lasses in the Highlands wed at quite an early age. And Fiona expected Megan to be in the family way because her brothers had evidently been extremely virile. The lass was smart far beyond her years. She must see about procuring a suitable husband for Fiona. Or send her safely off to boarding school.

But today had a different purpose entirely. "Do you have many nieces and nephews?"

"Yes. Our homestead 'twill be our first stop, though it's farthest away. I'm aunty to one niece and nine nephews."

"Ten!"

"A—yes. But you have met the two oldest lads."

"Of course. The two seven-year-olds that Megan

and you brought to the castle a few weeks past."

"Yes, and your papa sent them right off to boarding school."

"Of course, you miss them, but the castle wasn't safe for two very tall, lively boys. Soldiers ride up and visit on occasion, and they aren't able to hide their accents. And they do need to be in school. Papa did what he thought best." She smiled. "And I do agree with him."

"Will he send these off as well?"

Cailin frowned. "I wish I knew." She gripped Fiona's gloved hand. "Wherever they end up, they'll be better off."

Fiona nodded, though a glaze of sadness dimmed her eyes. "Duncan was married eight years and had five bairns. Collin wed six months after Duncan and had five bairns as well."

"Were they in a race?"

Fiona giggled. "Yes. Always they competed. But Duncan had all lads, and Collin had all lads save baby Fiona." Her dimples played in her cheeks as she gave a delighted smile. "And Duncan was that jealous of the little lass."

"You had another brother as well?"

Fiona's smile dissolved. Her chin trembled. "Angus." Tears sprang to her eyes, making them look like crystal-blue lakes.

"Angus had no children?"

"Angus couldna settle on just one lass. Every lass in the Highlands set her bonnet for him." Fiona's forehead crumpled, and tears overflowed, trickling down her flushed cheeks. "Angus, he left many a broken heart when he didna return from Culloden." She pulled out a crumpled handkerchief and wiped her wet cheeks.

Cailin wiped at wetness on her own cheeks. "And Brody? Did all the lasses set their bonnets for him as well?"

Fiona nodded and a smile peeked through her tears. "But Brody never noticed. Always, from the age of fifteen, his heart and soul belonged to Megan." Fiona gazed down at her gloved hands as if she'd said something she shouldn't. As if she might have a secret love herself.

Cailin sighed. Did Avondale love her like Brody did Megan? She sat upright, swaying with the movement of the carriage, and offered a shadow of a smile. A stone jammed in her throat until it settled with a thud inside her chest. With his sickness, was he really capable of love?

Fiona giggled.

Cailin decided the lass's breathy laughter erupted more from excitement than joy. Dimples etched Fiona's sweet innocent expression. Fiona was fifteen. Did she already fancy herself in love? Perhaps with one of the earls she'd met at the masquerade? Surely not one of the fugitive Highlanders who survived that horrible battlefield in Culloden? One who still hid in the caves and bracken? She'd mentioned someone named Grady. Oh, yes, Cailin must take thought to Fiona's future.

Fiona smiled fondly. "Such a comfort to know that Da, Duncan, Collin, and Angus, they are all biding in heaven with our Savior."

Cailin nodded. "I'm so sorry for the great losses you've suffered."

The carriage lurched, and Fiona grabbed Cailin's hand to steady her balance.

Cailin smiled encouragement.

Fiona's expression grew solemn, and her brow wrinkled. Then she smiled and gave a knowing toss of her bright curls. "Highland men are like that ye know." Her blue-eyed gaze held a question deep inside its clear, honest depths. "Highland men are faithful to their wives until the day they die. Our men are as feisty as Highland bulls, but they are faithful. English men are not so, are they?"

Cailin shifted on the cushions and stretched her legs. "We should arrive soon."

The question in Fiona's gaze all but jumped out and bit Cailin.

She would not acknowledge it. The stone inside her chest made it hard to breathe. English men, especially gentry and those at court, often took mistresses. Their marriages were business matches between powerful houses forged to retain the power and the money.

Her own marriage legally bound Avondale to protect the MacMurry castle, land and tenants. In exchange, he received a fruitful wife and a very large dowry.

And now she knew why he'd had to lower his standards to wed a lowly daughter of a baron. Her heart twisted. Nevertheless, she would stand by him at any cost. And she *would* make this marriage a happy one. No matter how many black times he experienced when he could not account for his time. If only he would let her help him. Her mind returned to the conversation with Fiona.

"Ah, you sly lass. You are wise beyond your years. Please don't tell me you are in love with a fugitive Highlander."

"And so I won't."

Cailin sighed. She had asked the question the wrong way. She turned her irritation at herself to the coachman and banged her parasol against the carriage roof. "Mikey, can we not drive faster?"

Mikey's voice floated down from the driver's seat. "Nay, Milady. The horses be pulling hard. I donna want to wind them."

"Is something wrong, Cailin?"

"No, of course not." She must discover if Fiona was bewitched by a Highland fugitive. The gleam in Fiona's eyes worried her, but Cailin dredged up a smile, sprinkled it with sugar, and smoothed her gloves over her wrists like she wished she could smooth her concern. "I packed all the herbs, unguents, and poultices I could find into the boot, along with several pots of good beef stew and some yeast biscuit dough."

Fiona smiled. "I think a batch of haggis, and some tatties and neeps would be appreciated as well."

"I asked cook if she could supply those. She sniffed and said she didn't know how to fix them. She made a face and asked, did I think she was a Highlander?"

Fiona's sunny disposition bubbled into laughter. "The bairns will love the stew. We can set the biscuit dough into the frying pan, tighten down the lid, and make an oven over the coals in the fireplace. The bairns will have a lunch fit for a king."

"And tonight when we get them safe to the broch, Mikey's wife has promised to prepare a dinner of cold chicken, scones and bannocks, new cheese, and tea."

"But, do we have room inside this coach for all eight bairns and my sisters-in-law as well?"

Cailin eyed the interior and tried to imagine fitting

all the MacCaulays into the expansive space. "This carriage easily accommodates six adults. You and I can hold the youngest two on our laps, and their mums can each hold one. With the extra shirts and trews we brought, they will fool the soldiers."

"The soldiers might decide to kill them."

"Women and children? Surely not."

"Ye do not ken the English."

"Well, if we are stopped, I shall do all the talking." Cailin pulled back the curtain and peeked outside. "Why are we slowing?"

The carriage swayed to a stop. The trap-door on the rooftop opened, and Mikey called down, "The road ahead be blocked with a road crew. It appears the English be widening this drive. They be spanning a bridge across yon river."

"Why do ye suppose?" Fiona tilted her head. "This road but leads to the Highlands. Nowhere else."

"I wager the king plans to build forts along this route and patrol the roads day and night. The fat German king be sending the Black Watch to make certain the Highlanders donna carry weapons or play the pipes. Hold on. 'Twill be rough as we go around." Mikey slammed the trap shut.

As the carriage slowly jerked over rocks and rough ground, Cailin gazed out at the laboring men. She opened the curtain wide as they crept past, so the musket-toting redcoats might get a full view of the two well-dressed ladies bedecked in jewels sitting inside.

The muskets held locked-on bayonets.

Hair on her nape shivered. A tremor scurried down her spine. Fiona had said the lobsterbacks had their way with Highland women, and then bayoneted them. She cradled her stomach.

Metal clinked against rock. She peered past the mounted soldiers to watch the closely guarded laborers clanking along the carriage path, dragging leg irons and wielding pickaxes. The men, young and not so young, looked to be ragged and ill-fed Highland Scots. Yet they plied their picks and axes earnestly, making their ring echo across the glen as they struck rock.

As their carriage rumbled slowly past, one chained man's deep set, hopeless gaze met hers. "Do you recognize any of the prisoners?"

Fiona shrank back from the window, her face drained of color. "Aye. I know many of them. They're men from a number of different glens." She shook her head. "None of them fought at Culloden. They're herdsmen and crofters. Each has a wife and bairns." She crinkled her forehead. "What will happen to the bairns with their pas being prisoners?"

"Perhaps we can rescue some of them." Cailin glanced back at the twenty or so laboring men, their bare, sweating backs bent, their emaciated limbs extending beneath tattered trews. Their gaunt faces looked grim and set. The ring of their picks on solid rock sounded a lament.

Still, a shaft of joy filtered through her. She'd been right.

The English soldiers had barely spared a glance at their passing. Soon the clang of the picks faded beneath the louder creaking of the carriage.

For a long while, neither she nor Fiona spoke.

Her mind remained on the plight of the Highland crofters and their families. The coach rattled on through the darkly shadowed pass, and then entered a fern-rusted glen. They jolted, bounced, and rocked nearer the crest of the tall purple hill melting into grey sky.

She loved the wild solitude of the Highlands with its treeless moors, rugged cliffs, and tiny villages of five or more homes nestled into the protected glens. She loved the wind-flayed desolation of the mountains, and realized Fiona had to really miss her home. She knew the lass longed for her family.

They neared the river's source, born in the peat moors of the mountains. A fine, cold vapor drifted above the rushing water. How did people make a living in this somber expanse so high in these mist-capped mountains?

Fiona gasped. "Look!"

22

Cailin pulled in a sharp breath. Her gloved hand crept to her mouth. The recently burned out cottage and brye told its own sad story. Overgrown weeds and thistles ran riot around the ruined croft. "The place looks abandoned."

Fiona's eyes were wide, her hands clasped as if she were praying.

"Tomorrow we'll return to see if anyone still remains here. Were they friends of yours?"

"Aye. The McCoy didna send any men to Culloden. I donna expect the older lads are around. They were twelve and thirteen. Old enough the English took them."

"Surely not!"

"Ye donna ken the English." Fiona scrunched her eyes shut. The sun glinted on a single leaked tear.

Oh yes, she knew of the English. She knew of Lord Henry Mabry, and his obscene demands Megan had escaped that fateful day inside the stable. She remained forever thankful that Shamus, the groom, had run to Megan's rescue. That incident firmed Megan's resolve to escape the betrothal and run off to marry Brody.

She'd seen the dreadful wounds inflicted on the hunted men inside the broch. She'd heard the stories of how English soldiers raped and molested innocent Highland women and children. She'd heard of the horrible massacre at Culloden. "I know more of the

English than I would like." Something from her tone apparently alerted Fiona.

The lass glanced at her, all wide eyes. "But ye are—"

"Never mind! Though I wed one, the war makes me hate the English almost as much as you do."

The horses slowed. Pressed back against the cushions as the coach settled aslant at an angle heading higher up the mountain, she wondered why her Lowland Scots always sided with the English. She'd not found the Highlanders to be barbarians. Rather the opposite. Englishmen seemed to have won that title.

Fiona leaned forward and peered out her window. Anxiety and expectation fought each other on her expressive face. "I pray our cottage is no…not burned."

"So do I." Cailin drew her cape closer about her shoulders to ward off the shiver that had nothing to do with the darkening sky.

After what seemed a long pull uphill, the road petered out. The coach slowed, and then ground to a halt.

Cailin didn't wait for Mikey to come around to assist her. She pulled down the handle and pushed open the door. From her side of the coach she couldn't see the MacCaulay cottage. But the site looked hauntingly beautiful, even with black storm clouds closing in.

As she descended the two small steps, she inhaled a deep breath of liquid gold air, so sweet she wanted to simply stand and breathe in the freshness. She looked out over a gentle glen nestled in the highest nook of the mountain.

Above her, the shrill of an eagle with his wings outstretched in graceful flight, symbolized the freedom surrounding her. The gaunt majesty fairly took her breath away.

Here in the midst of this beauty and silence, Fiona had lived. This beautiful land had helped form the strength and integrity that screamed through everything she did. She had to be homesick.

Cailin drank in the singular beauty of the Highlands, full of loneliness, harmony, and strength. The land had qualities that built character and perseverance. Far below, the forest smiled with silver birch and oak, and the rushing river slowed until it joined the mirror smooth loch. Looking smaller than a robin's nest, her castle reflected gleams of light from its battlements and banners.

She rounded behind the carriage to the other side, and her dress boots sank into the peat moss. A peaceful sense of timelessness and beauty surrounded her. Awe rose in her chest as it had when she'd visited the newly rebuilt St. Paul's Cathedral in London.

She shook her head. She couldn't stand here gawking. Work awaited. She walked past the blowing horses and found Fiona already farther up the glen.

"We must walk from here." Fiona called, and held out her gloved hand.

Cailin's heels dropped deeper into peat as she leaned forward and walked up the steep incline. She took Fiona's small hand and they hiked together up a barely discernible path. The ground beneath her stylish boots felt soggy in places, although the abundance of rocks and thick tufts of grass kept her boots mostly dry.

"There's our home!" Fiona bounded ahead, her bright curls bouncing beneath the rim of her bonnet as she ran up the slope.

Cailin pulled in a deep breath. The cottage looked intact. She tilted her head and hid her mouth with her gloved hand. This was Fiona's cottage? For this she'd been homesick? Cailin gazed around.

The MacCaulay family's hut blended with the hillside. Blocked with various sizes of stone, with a roof cut from thick turf covered over with thatch, the tiny building would have fit inside Castle Drummond's entry room…with space to spare.

Fiona started dancing, her new boots tripping in a Scottish jig, her face sparkling. She pirouetted up the path and didn't stop until she stood on the humble threshold. "Come in, Cailin. Welcome to our home."

Cailin stepped across the threshold. In a few seconds her eyes adjusted to the gloom. The cottage had no windows. An aged, smoky scent that spoke of peat fires and emptiness wafted to her nostrils. She followed Fiona through the small room floored only with hard-packed earth.

A hole cut into the center of the roof probably would have let out a thin trail of smoke had a fire been laid. The walls were black from peat smoke.

She kept her expression bland, so as not to offend Fiona, and rubbed her arms where the chill penetrated her cape and the woolen sleeves of her day dress. A desolate feeling lodged in her chest. Where were all the relatives they'd come to rescue?

"I donna ken where everyone is." Fiona's crushed expression hit Cailin mid-stomach.

Neither of them had expected the cottage to be abandoned.

"I felt certain Jenny and Mary would move in here with their children…" Fiona's voice trailed off into a bewildered groan.

She stooped and with loving hands moved a peat spade aside and gathered a harp lodged in a dark corner. Made of willow, strung with long, sturdy strings of cut and dried intestines attached with carved bits of bone, the instrument looked crude to Cailin. There were few other furnishings inside the rude cottage.

"The willow makes the music magical." Fiona strummed her fingers tenderly across the strings of the small harp. "And yet this harp is out of tune." She stopped strumming and trudged around the center of the room, the movement of her long skirt causing ashes to rise from the dead fire pit. "Magic or no, nay one is home." Her slender shoulders sagged, and her lower lip trembled. She clutched the harp to her breast.

"Perhaps your sisters-in-law will return soon."

"Nay. The fire is never left to die. Something's amiss." Frowning, she ran back outside. "Oh, I hope we are not too late!"

Cailin glanced at several reed beds lining the walls and at the sturdy wooden table under which a lone stool stood on three legs. A single wooden plate and a horn spoon waited on the table top. A bench leaned against the wall. A large cauldron hung from the ceiling on a pot chain just above the fire pit. There was nothing more to see. No other cooking utensils, no clothes, no signs that anyone lived inside. A layer of dust and ash mantled the wooden table. She crossed the desolate room and joined Fiona outside.

Cailin pulled in a deep breath of fresh air, but it failed to clear the stale stench of emptiness from her lungs.

The air had grown oppressive with a storm hurrying to overtake them. Black, boiling clouds swirled lower until they all but reached the carriage top down the hill.

Fiona had disappeared somewhere behind the cottage.

Cailin picked her way through the peat and overgrown thistles to the rear of the cottage and found a brye attached to the house. After stepping over the mud-streaked wooden threshold, she discovered that only hanging skins and hides separated the barn from the abandoned cottage.

She wrinkled her nose at the pungent smell of old manure and decayed straw. In her hurry to leave the hut, she'd missed the fur-covered hides. In winter, cattle obviously stayed inside and lived close to the family. Today, the brye, too, stood empty.

Where were the children? Quickly she moved back outside.

A lone calf bawled in the glen and ambled in their direction.

Her heart turned over. How different life at the castle had to be for Fiona and Brody. What an adjustment they must still be making. How their pride must suffer. From these humble beginnings and with seemingly little effort, they'd assumed the aspect of Lowland nobility…but these independent people were now totally dependent on her family.

Could she have adjusted as well had she been transported to this lone cottage so far above the family, meadows, castle, and horses she loved? She pressed her lips together. Being honest with herself, she doubted she possessed the ability to live within such rude, uncomfortable surroundings. Fortunately she didn't have to.

She shivered and snuggled her cape closer. The air

was thinner here and the wind colder. Shadows seemed to grow longer each moment she tarried, and the empty homestead had a lonely, haunting quality that made anxious inroads into her heart. She shivered again.

More than that, the house emitted a sense of pain and loss.

Fiona's worried face appeared around the far stone corner of the cottage. "A storm is hustling this way."

Cailin tightened the ribbons to her bonnet and nodded. "Mayhap we should tumble the bairns into the carriage and feed them later." She lifted her hands, and then helplessly let them drop. "If ever we find any of your family."

Fiona's shoulders sagged beneath her elegant blue dress. "I donna ken where they have gone. Looks as if no one has been here for some time. Our poor calf's ribs are poking out. She looks half-starved."

"Where can they all be?" Mingled odors of wet earth, wood, growth, and decay surrounded Cailin. She walked to a small knoll and planted her polished shoes on a rocky outcrop. Turning slowly in a circle, she searched the rocky area but saw no signs of life. Her bright hope of helping Fiona's remaining family faded. "Are there caves nearby?" She lifted her head and straightened her shoulders. She must offer a positive slant on the outcome of their journey. "God will show us what to do."

Fiona turned and walked purposefully back to the front of the cottage. "We must tie the calf to the rear of the carriage and take her to a neighbor. Mayhap the Chattens know where my family has gone." Fiona's clever hands were busy fashioning a harness from a rope hanging near the front door. "Did ye ken, Cailin, that a soldier can pass within a foot of a Highlander hidden in hedgerows, and he sees naught, nor even hears a crackle in the thick branches? We be that good at hiding out."

"Really?" Cailin raised a skeptical brow. Not here, she felt certain. This place had definitely been deserted. Probably weeks past.

With Fiona leading the calf, they walked down to where Mikey already coaxed the horses into a tight semi-circle within the small flat area that fronted the long path up to the cottage.

He gazed down from the driver's seat. "Before we go home we'll need to water these horses, Milady."

She nodded, unable to shake her deep sense of disappointment. They'd come all this way only to find no one. She'd hoped so to bring Fiona's relatives back to the castle. She yearned to care for the mothers and protect the children, and give them a new home before sending them to be educated in Lowland schools.

"Fine, Mikey, while you water the horses, Fiona and I will search around."

She'd noticed the patches darkening the horse's sleek coats as well. The teams shifted, rattling their harnesses, snorting and blowing.

"They need a spot of rest, too. Aye, it's downhill all the way from here." Mikey swiped a hanky across the sweat beading his forehead. "'Tis a difficult descent. But donna fret, I'll hitch two teams behind the carriage to help keep us from careening down." Mikey tipped his livery hat and turned to the eight snorting horses.

Fiona bounded back up the path and rounded the corner of the brye.

Cailin followed more sedately.

Fiona found two wooden buckets and a yoke. She hooked the ancient-looking buckets to either end and heaved the long-beamed yoke across her shoulders. "Come, Cailin, I'll lead the way to the spring."

Cailin blinked.

Fiona planned to carry the water herself?

Mikey's long, running steps overtook Fiona, and he lifted the yoke from her slender shoulders and settled the beam across his own wide shoulders. "Milady, allow me."

Fiona raised her brows and grinned. "I've carried many a yoke with brimming buckets of water and milk."

"Aye, Milady. But 'twas afore ye became a great lady. Ye must think of yer hands now."

"Why, thank ye kindly, Mikey."

He plodded ahead through knee-high bracken, breaking a path for them. The sound of tinkling water led them up a hillock to a clear spring bubbling from the peaty ground. As Mikey knelt to fill the buckets, Cailin breathed in the incredible stillness of the place.

Would Avondale find a measure of peace here? Mayhap she would bring him.

She stood knee deep in a rank growth of ivy and fern bordering the gurgling spring. A single shaft of sunlight glimmered on the crystal running water, clear as a wavy mirror. A lone willow let its green, lacy branches dance in the breeze and trailed its ruffled fingers in the water.

If ever a place held peace, this one did. Yes, she would bring Avondale. She would make a clearing in the overgrowth and spread a lunch for him. But first she must lure him to this spot before he disappeared at the break of day.

Suddenly a tiny voice shrilled, "Fiona!" Not ten yards away, a small lad burst out of short bracken and weeds that Cailin swore could hide nothing larger than a water snake.

"Liam!" Fiona jumped the spring, the end of her long gown trailing into the water, and caught the lad in her arms. Her face radiant, she lifted the bairn into the air. The wind caught her skirts, and billowed them around her and the lad.

More rustling in the underbrush, then a crew of boys tumbled into sight, surrounding Fiona like kittens greeting a mother cat. Grimy, mud-clotted, tattered youngsters threw thin, dirty arms around Fiona's bright green waist, while others caught her woolen day dress in dirty fists.

Cailin's heart flip-flopped.

Dirty, smelly, thin and ragged, but blue eyes shining, the tumble of greasy-haired youngsters had appeared as if by magic out of the thick bushes. One, two, three, she counted seven barefoot, bone-thin children with what would prove to be, once they were scrubbed clean, blond hair.

Fiona swung the lad she'd called Liam to the ground and grabbed a tiny, barefoot lass who crawled shyly from the ferns. The toddler tucked a thumb into a badly soiled mouth.

"Baby Fiona!" The delighted Fiona swung around. "She's my namesake. And the only lass in the bunch."

She hugged the dirty baby, who clung to her neck with both tiny arms. Huge round tears made white streaks down the babe's thin soiled face. "Where is your ma?" Fiona soothed the small lass with hugs, kisses, and soft murmurs.

Liam's big eyes gazed up at Cailin.

"It's all right, Liam. This is Cailin. She's Brody's wife's sister. You may call her Aunt Cailin." She shot a questioning look at Cailin.

"Yes, Liam. You may call me Aunt Cailin." She had thought the children would call her Lady, but she liked aunt so much more. Besides, if soldiers came to inquire at the castle, having the children call her aunty would help protect them.

Liam's pale, freckled face lit with a grin, showing two missing front teeth. Then once again, he looked too serious and too old for his age. "The soldiers took Ma and Aunty Mary. Both of 'em."

Fiona's stance stiffened, but she kept a smile on her face for the benefit of the younger children, Cailin guessed.

"When?"

"Donna ken exactly. 'Bout a month past, I think. We been hiding since."

"Were they hurt?" Fiona asked the question carefully, as if she already knew the answer but hoped she didn't.

"The soldiers wasna verra nice to them." Liam looked up at the clouds that were fast approaching, bringing wind and chill with them. His lip trembled, but he caught it between his teeth and straightened his thin shoulders. "They dragged them inside our house and did things they shouldna." Both hands were fisted at his sides. "Ma and Aunty were screaming for a long time." Round drops coursed down his cheeks.

Naked fear widened Fiona's eyes. She had a death grip on Baby Fiona, and the skin on her face stretched tight. She looked close to panic. "Are they alive?"

"Aye. The soldiers dragged them up on their

horses. But they were bleeding and crying." Liam jutted his jaw. "I wanted to go after them, but I had the bairns to take care of."

"And it was quite a brave thing ye did too, laddie. Ye did the right thing." Fiona knelt in front of Liam and pulled him into her arms. "And all this time ye've been taking care of the wee ones." She hugged him as if she would never let him go. "I'm so proud of ye!" Tears wet her cheeks.

"Indeed, yes." Cailin swallowed the bile in her throat. She had to take control. This was no time for tears.

These bairns were cold, hungry, and mourned their mums. She'd ask Avondale what the soldiers did with the Highland women, and maybe they could be ransomed. But for now, she had to take care of the bairns. "We've room for all of them inside the carriage. The rain will soon be upon us, and that's a blessing. Any guards upon the roadway will seek shelter."

Fiona nodded. Hugging the single baby lass close to her breast, she headed towards the cottage and the waiting carriage. "Aye," she said under her breath for Cailin's ears only. "The soldiers will stay nice and dry inside their barracks. They willna be likely to venture out to stop our carriage."

"Best we leave now, Milady." Mikey lifted a small lad in each brawny arm, carrying them beneath the yoke of slopping water buckets. His long-legged trot set the pace back to the carriage.

Cailin gently took the hands of two boys who looked to be about four or five.

Liam grabbed the hand of another lad about his age and one a tad smaller. The lads easily caught up with her, and their eyes didn't stray from her. The two younger boys clutched her hands.

"Everything's all right now. We'll take you to my home where it's warm and cozy and give you lots to eat." She smiled brightly over the lump in her throat. How could soldiers be so cruel, raping the mothers and leaving the children to die?

"Are ye really Brody's wife?" Liam panted, his eyes narrow.

"No. My sister is his wife. And he would have come himself, but he is injured." She couldn't blame Liam for his disbelief. The price of her boots alone would have fed the family for a month. And Liam appeared intelligent enough to realize that.

"Brody lives inside Castle Drummond. We're going to take you and the other bairns to live with us there."

Liam stopped so suddenly, one of the younger lads fell to his knees. "Ye are?" He broke into a run to catch up with the others. Though obviously full of happy news, he didn't yell, or even raise his voice. The lad hadn't made certain the bairns stayed well hidden from possible returning soldiers without learning to hold his tongue.

The cold, small hands in hers were caked with dirt and bone thin. She could barely wait to get them inside the shelter of the carriage.

Once they all piled in, it proved a tight, uncomfortable squeeze. And the children did have an aroma.

She ignored the smell. "We're taking you to a broch not far from our castle where I'll keep you for a short time until danger from the soldiers passes. Then we'll move you all into the castle." She hoped.

Oh, if only her parents opened their hearts to these

fatherless bairns.

Eight pairs of bright blue eyes stared at her, not quite comprehending this sudden glimpse of salvation.

Mikey opened the trap and called down. "I think we best let the calf run free. She'll slow us down. She'll find food enough and mayhap another family will care for her. We best get as far down the mountain as we can so as not to get hung up in muddy ruts once the rain comes."

Eight pairs of bright eyes looked up, and eight small mouths hung open at this voice from heaven that spoke through the top of the carriage.

Cailin nodded. "Please fetch the harp from inside the cottage and store it in the boot with the food we brought. We'll stop to eat once we reach the wider road."

Mikey had just slammed the boot on the harp when the first large drops fell. From his weight jostling the carriage she knew he'd hitched himself up onto the driver's seat. He unset the brake and hailed the horses.

With a jerk that surprised the bairns, who sat round-eyed and open-mouthed, they started on their return trip.

Then the rain slammed against the windows and quickly filled the ruts in the muddy path. How could Mikey see to drive? Each time the carriage slid in the deepening mud during the descent she prayed Mikey wasn't driving too fast for the condition of the steep, rutty road.

"Ye said Uncle Brody's injured. What happened?"

She touched Liam's hand. He sat crunched beneath another lad almost as big as he, his leg pressed against her long skirt. "Brody was rescuing some Highland fugitives the soldiers were taking to the gallows, and they shot him." At Liam's startled look, she quickly added, "He will be fine. Just has to mend his wound." She smiled. "And the three men he rescued are hiding inside the broch for now."

Liam, eyes wide and gaze taking in the lush interior of the coach, heaved a sigh.

If soldiers stopped them, she trusted God and His army of angels to shelter and keep the boys. And surely Avondale's name and power would protect them.

With her chin buried in one lad's matted hair, she remembered as clearly as if it had happened yesterday how on the night of their wedding, Avondale had tenderly wrapped his arms around her. His fingers left a trail of heat when he'd touched her face. And his lips had all but melted her knees from beneath her. She did love him so.

But how would he react when she told him of the children she'd rescued?

She pictured him lying on his elegant bed, so difficult to see in the darkness because he refused to have more than one candle lit. With her arms wrapped around the lad in her lap she wondered what it might be like to see Avondale's body that she knew only by touch.

The carriage lurched over a huge boulder that the stiff wind must have loosened and sent into the road, jogging her back to the present.

She'd expected the children to be lively, squirming, and asking for trinkets and sweets like the Lowland children she'd ridden with from time to time.

Such was not the case. These children rode with eyes wide and sculpted lips closed. They might be dirty and smelled as if they hadn't bathed for longer than she cared to think, but they behaved like little gentlemen. Baby Fiona relaxed with closed eyes, her adorable face snuggled against Fiona's breast.

Even Fiona remained quiet. Her great, lake-blue eyes with their long sooty lashes gazed unseeing, filled with grief. Fiona had expected to embrace two sisters-in-law as well as her nephews and niece. The troubled expression on her young face revealed her thoughts of her sisters-in-law's fates. Unvoiced questions glimmered behind Fiona's sad gaze. Occasionally her lower lip trembled.

Cailin had no answers. Were Mary and Jenny still alive? Were they kept as slaves somewhere inside an English soldier's home, being mistreated in the worst way a woman can fare? Or had they been sold to merchants sailing to the New World? As soon as she got the bairns settled, she would investigate.

But that didn't stop her heartache. Inside the dark carriage, guilt cut into her heart like the dead weight of responsibility she carried. Her burdensome emotions stole some of her joy at finding these bairns safe. Why hadn't she come to help sooner?

"Are there any other members of your clan in hiding?"

Liam nodded. "Grandpa." He shook his head. "The soldiers," he mumbled. "I don't know where he is."

Fear curled up into her heart and wound down to her fingertips, leaving them cold and trembling. Was there no end to the evil Cumberland's soldiers would do?

The crowded carriage rocked down through the narrow, twisting gorge. Fog clung, thick and soupy, to the isolated stretch of road. Whispering globules of crystal dripped down to cascade off the tips of leaves and branches flashing by their window.

Father, You promised to be a Father to the fatherless and a Husband to widows. I'm taking You at Your Word. If Jenny and Mary are still alive, please protect them.

Steady rain fell harder. The children nodded off, rocked to sleep by the swaying carriage. The atmosphere hung heavy. Dull sounds of horses' hooves reached her ears. Metal wheels slipped and slid along the narrow pitted road. Over the thudding rain, she heard the straining of leather harnesses, the flap of reins, the rhythmic thudding of hooves, and the occasional snort.

If the soldiers stopped their carriage, she didn't want to know in advance. She lowered the curtain at her window shutting out the dark sky and slashing rain.

Fiona lowered her curtain as well.

The two older boys by the other windows roused and followed suit. Their eyes grew heavy and their chins fell to their chests. As they plunged deeper into sleep, the gaunt haunted look on their young faces softened into innocence.

Soldiers who imprisoned seven-year-old lads, enslaved their mums, and left the smaller bairns to starve wouldn't stop to ask questions of two women with a carriage filled with Highland bairns.

She scrunched her own eyes closed.

Surely God spread His sheltering arms around their lurching carriage.

23

Behind Cailin, the drawing room door slammed, making the myriad of candles waver.

Fiona ran to stand before her. "The rain has stopped. Come with me to the broch. I'm dying to see the bairns."

"But it's already dark." Cailin dropped a stitch, stuck the blue-threaded needle into the unfinished baby quilt and pushed back the quilting frame. Still wrapped in her own exciting cocoon, she gazed up. "Why are you animated? Yesterday we visited the bairns for several hours, and they settled in beautifully."

"I'm most anxious to see Grady."

"Ah. So that's what is turning your face pink." Cailin placed the thimble back on her third finger. "All right. If you like we will visit the bairns again." But she must see that Grady was moved soon. "You seem far too enamored with the lad."

"The little ones are happy under Mikey's wee wife's tender care." Fiona smiled her saucy smile.

"Wee wife? Elspeth has to be six feet if she is an inch."

"Just a manner of speaking, Cailin." Fiona dimpled. "Do ye…you ken if they are safe."

"I think so."

"Aye. For the time being. Those partially broken down, monstrous walls serve as a warm welcoming home. But I'll breathe a good deal easier after all of them move into the castle."

If.

Cailin swallowed. She must see that Mums and Papa didn't harden their hearts against the sweet bairns. But until then, the old broch, which had been built upon the site of a Norman motte and an even earlier Iron Age hillfort, would serve as their home. True, the surrounding wall had mostly tumbled down, but the round stone tower stood mostly intact.

"That ancient stone structure isn't likely to enter a searching English soldier's thoughts. But I will breathe easier when the bairns move into the castle. I must talk with Mums."

"Aye, the sooner the better."

"Have you seen Avondale?" Blood rushed to her cheeks. Had she spoken aloud? Once he saw the bairns, perhaps he would stay home more.

"Nay."

Cailin's heart stuttered. How she prayed Avondale might smile at her just once in the broad daylight. What was wrong with the man? He acted as though she held him in judgment. He had a sickness beyond her ability, yet she must help him. But he had even begun to avoid her during their times alone at night.

She heaved a deep sigh. Well, she wouldn't dwell on that. She preferred to hold her good memories close and not ruin them by trying to uncover Avondale's mystery.

"I'll carry the torch. Do ye think the bairns need us to bring them anything?"

Tonight she would face her husband and make him explain. She smiled in her secret heart. Perhaps she'd calm his nerves with her lips. When he was relaxed, she would insist he tell her what haunted him. Warmed with her plan, she rose from her chair. "No. Mikey said they are well taken care of. Let's—"

Hennings entered the drawing room, his bearing stiff and formal. He bowed. "I'm very sorry, Milady. Lord Avondale asked for you. He's in your rooms."

Her eyes teared.

Thank you, God.

"Oh, dear, Fiona. I really must rush to him. You go ahead to the broch and see to the bairns." She smiled and tripped from the room, her light footsteps tapping a pleasant tune on the granite.

Avondale wanted her.

****

Fiona had gotten but half-way across the keep when Avondale stumbled into her path.

His clothes were disheveled. Minus his suit coat, his shirt rumpled, his sable-lined vest half-unbuttoned and one bare foot, he walked with a pronounced limp on the cobblestone.

She turned to run.

Like a bear from a cage, he rushed at her. A low growl vibrated from his throat. Before she could utter his name, he grabbed her arm in his iron grip. She fought to break away. He seized her other arm.

"Let me go!" She jerked and fought and tried to kick him. "Avondale, stop!" She stumbled and turned her ankle on the cobblestones. She gazed frantically around in the dusky twilight. Where was Rafe? She writhed in Avondale's gasp. Arms aching, she exerted all her strength but couldn't pull free. Her feet slid on the damp cobblestones.

****

Cailin's feet flew down the long hallway. She took the stairs as quickly as she dared and sped in the direction of Avondale's suite of rooms. Though scores of candles lighted the passage, it remained shadowed and dark. Halfway to the double doors, she stumbled but caught herself before she fell. "What—?"

A human form lay on the floor.

She knelt beside the figure and held her candle close to his face. "Rafe!"

Rafe's body splayed full length on the hall floor, the back of his dark head dressed with a puddle of blood. He moaned.

He was alive.

The door to their suite stood open. What she could see of the small drawing room looked a mess. A chair was overturned. The heavy rug was bunched. A candelabra lay broken on the granite floor.

She rose, and then hesitated. She needed to summon one of the servants to tend Rafe, but first she must find Avondale. Goose bumps puckered her arms.

As she turned to go inside, she caught the hem of her skirt on Rafe's limp foot, and then jerked it free. A hard knot circled her heart. She hurried on, knowing she wouldn't find Avondale in his rooms, but she must make certain. Perhaps he, too, was hurt.

Did he truly not recall his actions while under the influence of his black spells?

He'd made a wreck of his strapping bodyguard and their rooms showed evidence of a massive struggle. What was Avondale up to?

Her heart fluttered crazily against her ribcage.

His spells were steadily growing worse. Would he harm her or their child? Hand on the doorknob, she hesitated. Perhaps her love was not strong enough. Perhaps she'd have to take other measures to keep her loved ones safe from her husband.

She opened the door. The bed chamber was empty.

A scream filtered through the heavy glass window. Someone outside. Fiona!

Cailin picked up her cumbersome skirts, rushed back to the hall, and passed Hennings leaning over Rafe.

"Oh, see to him, Hennings, while I find Avondale." She didn't wait to hear his reply. Clinging to the banister so she wouldn't fall and harm her unborn child, she hurried down the stairs.

Thank you, God. The candles are lit so that I can see my way.

A wild pulse beat in her temple.

Just what was Avondale's obsession with Fiona?

Her husband had so few lucid hours lately. Would she have to lock him away and remain a virtual widow the rest of her life? Her mouth went dry.

What had he done? She must pry the haunting out of him. Her stomach quaked anew. But she must now be strong and face the problem with her husband. If she could not, she must take measures to restrain him.

She tightened her lips. Or take more serious measures. She shook her head at the horrifying thought Rafe had proposed. No. No. No. She wouldn't even think of something so drastic.

Despite his ever more frequent demented spells, she loved Avondale. How could she face locking him away? Or…the other?

Leaning against the ground-floor castle wall, she paused to catch her breath. This continuing suspense couldn't be good for the baby. She followed the melee of sounds that replaced Fiona's scream.

The clamor came from outside in the keep. Voices, screams, footsteps, and vibrating above it all, Avondale's distinctive baritone, sounding wild and incoherent.

For the baby's sake she must be careful. She must not put her baby in danger.

She neared the back kitchen and called through the open archway, "Help me, please. In the keep!"

Pots and pans thudded against the wooden dry sink, and then heavy footsteps lumbered after her. Good, at least two of the cooks were following.

She pulled open the exterior door, caught a whiff of fresh evening air mingled with the scent of burning torch, and sighted two shadows struggling near the outer door of the curtain wall.

Avondale gripped Fiona by both arms and was dragging her towards the stable.

Cailin motioned to the cooks. "Hurry, help me with His Grace."

The two robust women nodded. "Ye take it easy, Milady. Ye take care of that wee one in yer womb. We'll see to His Grace."

So, all her efforts to keep Avondale's malady strictly between Hennings, Rafe, and herself had been wasted. Apparently, even the cooks knew her husband suffered a severe mental problem. A small sense of relief washed through her.

"Thank you." She turned back through the door, and scurried down the long hall in the direction of the servants' quarters. She knocked on every closed door she passed.

Soon heads peeked out, candles held high, and a bevy of voices queried, "What do ye need, Milady?"

"Come, help me with His Grace. He's having one of his spells."

She didn't wait to see who followed, but rushed back to the castle keep where she found the two cooks wrestling with Avondale.

Avondale swatted the two cooks with butting head and slashing elbows as he dragged Fiona towards the stable.

The twisting group maneuvered halfway through the curtain door.

"Hurry, please," Cailin screamed over her shoulder to the massing servants, their feet pounding towards her. "Please don't hurt His Grace."

One of the servants, a short, brawny Scot, carried a club. "I'll just give him a wee tap on the noggin, Milady," he rushed past her. "Then we can carry him to his quarters."

"Oh, do be gentle," she urged.

In a few strides across the cobblestones, the man caught up with her husband.

The wee tap the brawny Scot administered didn't appear so benign.

She groaned for her dear husband as his knees bent, and he crumpled to the cobblestones.

"Are you all right, Fiona?" The lass looked shaken and her gown was torn at one shoulder, but she nodded.

"Aye. He didna hurt naught save my arm." She rubbed her skin, and tried to stretch the tatters of her sleeve over the scratched, reddened nakedness of her arm. "I think I'll trudge upstairs to my room and enjoy a sip of tea."

Cailin nodded. "And take a hot bath."

Fiona walk slowly back towards the castle.

Cailin sighed, and her shoulders drooped. She felt as if even the babe within her womb carried the weight of the castle on his shoulders.

Avondale's lay arms outstretched, his face against the cold cobblestones.

Then, as if the man she loved weighed not an ounce, the short, strapping Scot heaved Avondale, his head lolling, onto his own broad shoulders and carried her husband back into the castle.

She followed and touched Avondale's limp hanging hand as they lumbered up the wide granite steps.

The Scot soon had Avondale ensconced in his own huge bed.

"Thank you. I would beg you to keep His Grace's illness to yourselves." Cailin waved a hand at the bevy of curious servants gathered outside Avondale's bedchamber and filling his sitting room. "T'would be unseemly to spread gossip of his ill health throughout the countryside. I would hate to have to dismiss any one who repeats ill news to the neighborhood."

"Oh, nay, Milady. We will keep this wee problem to ourselves." The short Scot who had knocked her husband unconscious faced the other servants. His polite voice took on more than a hint of authority, "Will we nay?"

"Aye. Aye, that we will," the other servants chorused.

"And I'll see to Rafe as well, Milady," the robust Scot promised. He walked back into the hallway where Hennings still knelt beside Rafe, holding a bloodied cloth to his head.

She must discover the Scot's name and raise his station among the house servants. Whoever the man turned out to be, poor Rafe was injured, and she needed a new bodyguard. Judging by the sound of his heavy burr, the unknown Scot had to be a Highlander. Perhaps he was one of the fugitives who had been nursed inside the broch. If so, what was he doing in her servants' quarters? Perhaps Brody had added more than one fugitive to her contingent of servants.

"Come, let's nay tarry. 'Tis nay a sideshow." Again the Scot took command.

The remaining servants emptied Avondale's drawing room and filed down the hall to the back stairs and their own rooms.

The two cooks left Avondale's drawing room last. "We are that sorry, Milady, if we hurt His Grace. He fought us something fierce."

"I see you have some scratches and bruises as well. Thank you for helping, ladies. I am certain you kept Mistress Fiona from harm. I'll see you are rewarded for your loyalty. Do have someone to clean your scratches."

"Thank ye, Milady." The two hefty servants bowed awkwardly. "Aye, the head housekeeper will take care of us. Donna worry yer head for our sakes." They backed out Avondale's door.

Cailin shut the door, and then leaned against the heavy wood, as all her strength seeped from her legs.

A small tap sounded on the door.

Cailin opened the door a crack.

"Cailin, what is wrong with Lord Avondale?" Fiona's pretty face looked pale, and her eyes were like huge, blue pools of clear water. She rubbed her wrists.

The fluttering in Cailin's stomach came from her babe. "I wish I knew." She pressed her hand over her heart hoping to slow its pace. She took another deep breath, and her customary composure settled over her.

The candelabra lit Avondale's luxurious room with a serene glow that infused strength back into her legs.

"Thank God, Fiona you're safe." She moved to Avondale's huge bed and bent to loosen his twisted cravat, which had somehow remained tied. "Stay with me while I bathe this blood from my husband's head, and I will tell you what I know."

Fiona's dress rustled as she perched behind her on one of Avondale's chairs.

Cailin dipped her cloth into the fresh pitcher of water Molly had brought, and then gently sponged her unconscious husband's high forehead. He looked very white and his lashes lay long and thick on his high cheekbones. Had he lost weight? She caressed his lean cheek. Even now, a deep line between his handsome thick brows refused to smooth. Late night stubble pushed through the ruddy skin of his face, and his sculpted lips were slightly open. His big chest rose and fell as if he was sleeping. Even asleep, his great strength looked undiminished.

She glanced at Fiona.

"He could have snapped me in two. Yet, he didna. Though he was taking me against my will, he didna hurt me." She touched his limp hand. "My scratches came from bushes. He took care not to bend my arms. Had I not fought him, I would still be intact."

"But where was he taking you?"

Fiona shrugged. "I don't know. Seems his black spells hurt him more than anyone else. What demon torments him?"

"This time no one was injured. But his…his times of lunacy are becoming more frequent. I'm beginning to live in fear of him." She shook her head, dipped the cloth into the cool water, wrung it, and placed it on Avondale's forehead. "Not fear for myself, but for you, for my baby, for bodyguards, or anyone who dares stand in his way."

"Perhaps we can puzzle out his behavior together. Tell me what you know." Fiona leaned forward in her chair.

Cailin sighed. "You were visiting the dressmaker the day the dowager duchess arrived. We sat down together and had a long chat. I discovered that Avondale's mother attached herself to him during our wedding to keep him out of trouble. The royal mums didn't trust his moods." She turned a wry face to Fiona. "Rather that, than out of over-zealous affection for Avondale and snobbery for me, as I had mistakenly thought."

Finding it easier not to face her sister-in-law, Cailin turned back to moistening her husband's face. "The dowager knew of Avondale's spells. She told me he'd been having them since about the age of nineteen." Cailin sighed. "Prior to that time, Avondale had been a model son, a gentleman, and a highly sought suitor for high born English ladies."

Fiona jumped up. "The old lady knew, and yet she allowed you to marry her son!"

Cailin had thought worse things when her mother-in-law explained Avondale's situation. "I do feel betrayed. I'm afraid they both knew."

Fiona sat tensely on the edge of her chair, her hands tightly clasped.

When Avondale showed no sign of stirring, Cailin hovered over him a few more seconds, and then pulled up her favorite chair and faced Fiona. "I had entirely the wrong impression of the royal mother. She's not at all snobbish. Nor cold. Rather, she felt nervous and on edge, fearing Avondale would create a scene. She's really quite nice."

"Nice! To marry off her—"

"Don't!" Cailin shrugged. "Please don't call Avondale names."

"To marry off her son when he was obviously so ill."

Cailin laid her hand on Fiona's clenched fist. "We both knew the duchess would lose her land and what little money she has left if Avondale failed to marry wealth. The dear lady wanted to give her grandbairns all the inheritance she could."

Cailin caressed the small roundness of her stomach. "The duchess gave my baby an honorable title and extensive lands."

"But not a husband any woman could love!"

Despite herself, Cailin heaved a sigh. "Oh Fiona, I do love him. How could I not? He is kind and loving when we are alone. He's intelligent and even funny at times." She nodded at Fiona's disbelief. "He's a perfect husband except for two major flaws. I still don't know why he snubs me in public, though I think I may have figured out that answer. And he has these times when he's no longer in control of himself. But I do love him."

"But Cailin, you deserve a sane husband!" Fiona wagged a finger so close, her sister-in-law's faint sweet scent overcame the slight smell of blood. "Avondale's a dangerous man!"

"Calm yourself." Cailin pulled in a deep breath.

Fiona plunked back into her chair.

"The royal mother swears this is the very worst she's ever seen her son behave." She frowned at Fiona's unbelieving look. "Something ignites his severe reactions. If I can discover the source, perhaps I can help him." Cailin gazed out the open window into a dark sky. "The duchess advised me to ask Avondale what bothers him." She folded her hands over her stomach. "I shall, just as soon as he becomes…more balanced."

Fiona fell to her knees in front of Cailin's chair and engulfed her sister-in-law in a warm hug. "I'll pray for you and Lord Avondale. Shall I stay here and help you with him?" Fiona whispered.

Warmth crept into Cailin's chilled heart. She clasped the younger lass's hand. "No, dear. I fear there is something about you in particular that stirs up my husband." She turned to peer through tears that suddenly blurred her vision. "Avondale seems to have a particular problem with you." She dabbed at her eyes with her lace handkerchief. "And I haven't the faintest idea why."

"Didn't the dowager duchess have any suggestions?"

"Dear Fiona, always so quick to help. Yes, she did say Avondale started to act rather more strange just before the Culloden Battle last April."

"Then the duchess doesn't think your wedding set Lord Avondale off?"

"No. On the contrary. She said he seemed much better after the wedding. She said he enjoyed the best spirits she'd ever seen."

Fiona's pretty brow furrowed, then she put her finger to her cheek in that adorable way she had when deep in thought. "Really?"

"Actually, I think something about you causes him to fall into his spells. He first began showing stress after you arrived with Megan and Brody."

Fiona opened her mouth and looked about to say something, and then snapped it closed. She leaned forward. Her warm, soft hands curled around Cailin's cold ones.

"I've heard Lord Avondale mention Bloody Billy. Do you know to whom he's referring?"

"Bloody Billy?" Fiona frowned and pursed her lips. "I have no idea."

A moan floated from the bed. Cailin glanced at the athletic form of her husband stirring, his muscles rippling, his fingers moving, and his feet twitching. "You best go."

"I hate to leave you here alone with him. Aren't you afraid?"

"Oh, no. Avondale's never comes close to touching me in any but a gentle and loving way. He's a very sweet man when we are alone. Do go. He's waking."

Cailin heard the rustle of skirts, and then the door closing softly. But she had eyes only for her husband. With the blood cleansed, a huge bump grew purple near his hairline. She perched on the side of his bed and touched his cheek.

Then she lowered her head. No matter how much she loved her husband, her duty now lay with their baby. She cradled her stomach. "I shall do whatever I must to keep you safe," she whispered.

24

Avondale's chocolate eyes slowly opened. "Cailin, what happened?" His words sounded slurred. "I had a bad dream." He put a hand to his head. "Now I have a horrific headache." He stirred and tried to sit.

"Darling, just lie back." She laid her cheek next to his and gently brushed her face along the planes of his masculine one. "You'll be fine. Just tell me what's bothering you."

"Mmmm. I love you, dearest." His smooth baritone almost sounded normal. "You are so good for me. Something about you brings me a sense of peace. Your faith, perhaps?"

Careful not to touch the purple bruise near his scalp, she stroked his hair back from his forehead, luxuriating in the thick texture and the way the slight wave made each strand spring back with a life of its own. She rose from her chair, hitched her day gown slightly, and snuggled next to him on their huge bed. He crooked his muscular arm around her and caressed her shoulder with his long, slender fingers.

She unbuttoned his shirt and ran her fingers over the elegant pattern of hair that dusted his chest. "Who is Bloody Billy?"

He stiffened.

She stroked his chest like she would have a hurt bairn.

"Who told you of Bloody Billy?"

"You did. Won't you enlighten me?"

He writhed on the bed. His free hand bunched the velvet cover until it became a mound between them, but his forehead furrowed as if he was trying to decide.

She crept over the white velvet mound and snuggled as close as she could, one hand stroking his bare chest. His heart beat a strong rhythm under his sternum.

"It's no great secret. Bloody Billy is William Hanover, the Duke of Cumberland, King George's youngest son. He's a cousin. Second cousin."

It took every ounce of willpower not to show surprise. "Oh, yes, of course." She kept her voice soft and moved her hand in gentle circles over the clear definition of the muscles in his chest. His stiffness slowly relaxed.

"Why do you fear him?"

"Dash it all, Cailin!" He pushed her away and tried to sit, but held his head in both hands. A greenish color tinted the area around his mouth. He lay back against the pillows.

She reached over, put her hand on his forehead, gently stroked, and then moved her hand down to cover his eyes. She bent forward to trail kisses down his neck. When she lifted her lips, he'd relaxed.

He sighed. "You're a wonderful wife."

She kept her hand over his closed eyes and made her voice soothing and softened it into a whisper. "Tell me why you fear Bloody Billy?"

She held her breath.

Avondale's body went so still, she feared he had fainted. He pushed her hand off his face. His eyes, darkened to a deep, rich shade of coffee, stared at the ceiling.

She feared he wouldn't answer, but then his chest rose in a deep sigh as if everything hateful inside had come to the surface and he was releasing noxious fumes.

"I don't fear the bloody butcher." His body twisted, and he pushed up to sit back on the numerous pillows lying against the headboard. His Adam's apple rose and fell in his tanned throat. "The man…embarrasses me."

"My darling, how could that fat brother of the King possibly embarrass you?"

Her husband's mobile, sensual mouth barely opened as he spoke quietly, almost as if he was talking to himself. "You may as well know. Before Culloden, the duke ordered me to command his army as his deputy commander."

Not so surprising. Nobility oft times recruited cousins and other relatives to lead their armies. Besides chairing a seat in the House of Lords, gentlemen of nobility were required to lead their retainers and countrymen into battle. There had to be more.

She lifted wooden lips in a smile. "And?"

Avondale laid his forearm across his forehead. His words spouted out. "I wanted no part of his bloody war against the Highlanders." A frown knit his dark brows together. "So, I paid Cumberland half my bank account to purchase a substitute." He grunted. "My money didn't satisfy that thief. The greedy fellow wanted the rest of my fortune or he'd still order me to command his battles." Avondale turned his head away, mouth drawn into a grim line. "I had no stomach for that war. I knew our soldiers, our cannon, and cavalry would decimate the Highlanders. We'd bury their bodies by the thousands in the hills of

Scotland."

She stifled a gasp. He would have been heading the murderous assault that annihilated Brody's family. And he'd wanted no part of that carnage.

Respect twined around her heart like warm bands of honey. Some of the knots loosened in the back of her neck. The baby fluttered inside her womb. Because he refused to take part in slaughter, the horrible, demonic nightmares tortured him? There had to be more.

Avondale's face twisted. "Little did I know that Cumberland would murder the Highlanders who fell wounded in the field. He gave no quarter. Nor did I know that after the battle he would comb the Highlands for survivors and hang each one he found."

His dark eyes blazed straight into hers. "Had I been man enough to command Cumberland's forces, I might have been able to curtail those murders."

"Oh, my dearest, you were brave to stand up for your principles. Never could I think of you as a coward." She kissed his twisted lips until they relaxed and retuned her love. Her heavy heart lightened. Her husband had loftier motives than she could have imagined.

"But Bloody Billy continues to threaten me. He expects more money. More. I have no more money." He gave a grim smile. "Fortunately, until our son is born or your Papa dies, I can touch not a single pound of your inheritance." He squeezed her hand. "Even Bloody Billy cannot wring money from a pauper."

"Papa will live a long time yet. Surely the duke will have forgotten by then." She wondered at her next thought. "Or perhaps he will die." Mayhap one of his captains would murder the brute.

"But the unmanly thief wants money now."

Avondale's voice dropped to a hoarse whisper. "I fear he will storm the castle, kidnap you, and hold you for ransom in the Tower." He pulled her into his arms. "You are too precious for that to happen. I won't let him take you from me." He whispered into her hair, "Especially now, while you carry our son." He held her at arm's length, and stared at her as if she would disappear before his eyes. "That's why I tried to save that beautiful fairy. Cumberland thinks I still owe him. My voices told me he planned to kidnap her. I had to take her to a safe place."

"Fairy?"

"Or perhaps she was a milkmaid. The night of the masquerade…and then again…" He glanced around the chamber as if he'd lost something. "…tonight…or last night." He shook his head. "I'm not sure just when." He rubbed the back of his neck. "I seem to lose track of time. Everything goes black."

"Tell me about the fairy."

"She was the most beautiful nymph…I think she was a nymph. Bloody Billy wanted to snatch her, but…" Her husband's straight, masculine brows wrinkled, and his face contorted into an incredibly sad look of confusion.

Her body chilled, leaving shivers travelling her spine. Dear God, did he not know the difference between reality and fantasy? "But?"

"She disappeared. I don't understand." He sighed. "Sometimes I get confused." He turned his liquid brown eyes away and rubbed the bridge of his straight nose. "Did I dream the fairy?"

She began her circular stroking of his bare chest, but he failed to relax. Muscles at the back of her own neck had grown rigid.

"Do you sometimes find yourself somewhere and you didn't know how you got there?" His furrowed brow and mahogany eyes begged her to say yes. "And you don't even know why you are there," he whispered.

She pulled his head to her breast and stroked his wavy hair. "No, dear." She massaged his stiff shoulders. "That's part of your illness. Sometimes you wander into places where you shouldn't." She lifted his face and bent to kiss his lips. "And you do things you shouldn't. That's why a guard must accompany you wherever you go. To keep you safe."

"Guard?" He pulled away, his spine rigid, his brow deeply furrowed. "Did I do something dreadful to that guard?"

"You knocked him down. You mustn't, you know. He stays with you to keep you safe."

His jaw firmed. "But I won't have a guard. I won't allow it."

Well, Rafe was out of action for a time. She'd have to commandeer the robust Scot who'd taken control tonight. "Think of the man as more of a companion than a guard."

"You shall have to buy him a title, then. I won't be seen with a commoner dogging my heels. People will suspect."

"Yes, my love. You know about such things, and I will procure the money. We shall buy him a title. And a title for Rafe, and another for Hennings." She smiled brilliantly. "You shall have three, true companions…and no watchdogs."

Avondale slid down against the pillow and turned to his side. "I'm very tired."

She nestled her cheek into his arm and began to

massage his back, her heart aching.

Why had God allowed this fine man to be so wounded? What was she to do with him? He hurt others to protect them from imagined threats. He was dangerous.

She bit her lip. Still, she needed to know more. She must push him for answers yet again. "Avondale, why do you avoid me during the day?"

He groaned. "Oh, my very own sweet. I am ashamed to face you in daylight. You are so innocent. You do no evil. And I am such a coward." He half-turned to her, muscles rippled where they stretched down his backbone. "You are so graceful and so perfect. I'm not fit to be your husband. I…I thought you could most certainly see the coward's stripe down my back. I couldn't let you near me in daylight."

Pity wound around her lightened heart. "Oh, Avondale. All this time I thought you were ashamed of me."

"No, my princess." His lips thinned and turned down at the corners. "Once again the craven coward shows his true character."

"Avondale, I do love you so. Together we'll find a way to make the Duke of Cumberland stop bleeding you dry. And I'm quite certain he will not abduct anyone from the castle. I think you a fine, courageous man who stood strong for your principles. You did not want the Highlanders killed, yet you had no power to stop their murder. What you did was right and good."

For the first time her husband's face lost all trace of tension. He sat up, folded her into his arms, and his lips nuzzled her hair as he spoke. "I'm not so certain I did the right thing."

"You did. And you will again. Don't allow the

past that cannot be changed to haunt you." She lifted her chin. "But you must not snub me again. Ever."

He nodded.

Yet from the resumed tightness of his expression she realized he'd not yet gained victory over his demons.

Were there more?

25

The next morning Fiona sat across from Cailin at breakfast. "Will ye come to the broch with me?" Fiona's lake-blue eyes pleaded. The lass was already dressed in a sensible, yellow woolen day gown. "I've been waiting for you ever so long."

Cailin laid her spoon beside her oatmeal. Had she been alone she would have returned to Avondale, who still slept. A rosy mist still floated around her and had since she'd opened her eyes and stared into his sleeping face. His thick brown hair feathered around his face and stood on end at the crown.

She'd pulled in an uneven breath and had difficulty keeping her fingers from tracing his lovely, straight nose and caressing his dark, stubbled cheek. Rumpled and sleeping, his masculine features stole her breath away. How often she'd dreamed of waking with her husband by her side. He lay on his side facing her and sunlight bathed the ridges of his bare torso with gold, outlining the muscles' strong definition. The lump on his forehead had grown larger and darker purple.

He'd looked so peaceful that she'd quickly dressed and come downstairs to eat. Their heart-to-heart talk last night had rewarded him with needed sleep and her with a ravenous appetite.

Perhaps the baby had a growth spurt. She caressed her rounded tummy and decided the bulge had grown.

"Please, Cailin."

She'd hoped to return to her husband before he woke, but she dearly wanted to visit the sweet bairns and how they fared within the old ruin.

And Avondale, no doubt, would continue to sleep. Sleep would help restore his health. Though her heart called out to him, she must let him rest.

While half her mind wrestled through what she'd learned from him, the rest of her yearned to see the bairns.

Though the sun was not yet far above the horizon, she could not deny Fiona's wide blue pleading gaze. So, she opted for her second choice. "Yes. Let's go see to the bairns."

She drank the last of her juice and slipped the final bite of coddled egg onto its finger of buttered toast. The flutter in her tummy acknowledged the baby's thanks.

They rose from the long, formal table, with its snowy cloth and sparkling silver, left the dining room with a nod to the servers waiting behind the chairs, and tossed shawls over their shoulders as they traipsed towards the back castle door.

Cailin pushed open the heavy, outer door and led the way, her boots tapping on the cobblestones. They passed through the portcullis and walked down the faint, still dewy path that led to the broch.

She pulled in a deep breath of the bright, clear morning air, sweet with new mown grass. Butterflies flitted from broken grass stems to the small, pink English roses that lined the way. Already bees buzzed from flower to flower.

"Did ye know some call our Highland bairns, Children of the Mist?"

Cailin picked a rose and held the sweet fragrance to her nose. "Oh, why is that? I thought Children of the Mist referred to the fairies." Perhaps her husband wasn't so off in his thinking as he appeared? Oh, dear God, she prayed not. One day she would explain to Fiona why Avondale had wanted to save her, but not today.

"Aye, and so they do. The wee people. But some folk…" The way Fiona gazed at her alerted her to the possibility that some folk might be Fiona's polite way of saying Lowlanders. "… call our bairns such names."

"Because they are elusive?" A swirl of cool air made her clasp her shawl closer.

"Aye…I mean yes. Elusive." Fiona's sweet smile looked so like Brody's wider grin. "And fair. Ye notice baby Fiona's fine white hair and pale complexion?" Fiona pulled open the curtain door that just a few hours before Lord Avondale had tried to drag her through. "Yes, mostly we are born with that pale hair, and then our tresses darken as we grow."

"Yours are not so very dark yet." She tried to keep pace with Fiona, but the lass continually spoke over her shoulder as she scurried ahead through the meadow.

"Mine will remain blonde until I become a grandmother." Fiona strode faster. "Did ye ken our folk donna…do not like the wee people? Did ye ken that our men wear talismans in their bonnets to ward off the wee people?"

Cailin stopped to catch her breath. The steep climb to the broch seemed more arduous than usual. She fanned her face. "Your brawny Highlanders don't really believe in fairies, do they?"

"Aye…yes. Believe and fear. The old ones are full

of mischiefs."

Cailin pulled in more even breaths. She'd heard King George planned to turn all the superstitious Catholic clansmen into God-fearing Protestants. But she'd seen no trace of superstition in Brody. But then he was not a Catholic, either. "Do you believe in the wee old folk?"

But Fiona had started to run.

"What is your hurry?" Puffing, and lifting her skirts over the dewy meadow, Cailin picked her way through the no longer manicured grass.

The closer she got to the broch, the less well kept was the glen, now overgrown with large purple thistles. Already Fiona had disappeared through the tumbled-down stone walls that circled the broch's keep.

Cailin craned her neck. The crumbling, circular stone tower loomed three-stories straight up. She shivered. Beneath the bright sun, the collapsing boulders reflected deep shadows around her. Had she been so inclined, she might have believed in the wee folks herself.

Fiona peeked back around the stone she'd just disappeared behind. "How old do ye think this place is?"

"I think about fifteen hundred or more years."

"Whatever was it used for?"

Cailin made her way through large stones that had fallen from the curtain around the tower. "No one really knows. Perhaps an ancient type of castle built by the Picts."

They stood close to the small door that even Fiona would have to duck to enter.

"I've never seen one in this part of Scotland

before."

"It's rare. Most were built close to the seacoast. But we own this one and it's in remarkably good condition. Parts of the roof are missing, and you can see gaping holes where chunks of the sides have fallen in."

A sharp wind blew through Cailin's shawl and chilled her arms. She pulled it tighter and hooded the warm tartan around her head. "It seems colder here than out in the glen. Shall we go inside?"

She knocked three times in quick succession, hesitated, and then knocked twice more. Almost immediately, Mikey opened the low, steel-banded wooden door. His work-hardened hand held the door wide.

Fiona ducked and entered.

"Some brochs have entrance passageways. I'm glad ours doesn't. A low tunnel would have made it more difficult to carry the wounded inside." She clasped her shawl tighter and checked the sturdy, wooden door to make certain it was tightly closed behind them.

Mikey held a lighted torch. He ducked his head. "Lady Cailin. Lady Fiona. It's glad I am to see ye." His broad smile somehow highlighted the freckles on his square face. "I'd thought ye'd still be abed."

"Not so, faithful Mikey." Cailin smiled and trudged further inside the room.

"Lady Fiona, the lad, Grady, has been champing at the bit to see ye. Donna' tell the lad I said so."

Cailin stared. Of course that was why Fiona had been in such a rush. How much better life would fare for her sister-in-law if Fiona did not fall in love with a fugitive.

She must think on how to keep Fiona and Grady

apart. Cailin sighed. If Grady were captured, and the soldiers discovered Fiona's attachment to him, the lass would be in grave danger.

Cailin untied the ribbons to her bonnet. She must speedily pair Fiona with several of the eligible young earls who had been so attracted to the girl at the masquerade and steer the lass away from fugitives.

Cailin rubbed her chin and glanced around the interior of the broch. The dank unused odor that usually filled the tower had disappeared. Above her, feet rustled through the straw spread across the old stones to ward off the chill the tower held even in summer.

Mikey's torch lit the lower round room from curved wall to curved wall. The big room looked empty save for torches in their wall niches and an unrailed stone stairway climbing up to all three floors. There were no windows, thus the need for torches day and night.

To the untrained eye the place looked deserted. She shivered at the eerie whistling of the wind through the breaches in the tower.

"I've housed the precious bairns on the second floor and the wounded men on the third."

"Thank you, Mikey. Papa will certainly raise your wages. You've done abundantly more than your share helping."

"Aye, Milady. 'Tis my kinsmen I help, as well." He grinned, showing a gap where he missed a tooth. "But an increase in pay will suit me verra well."

"Who is there, Mikey?" Elspeth, Mikey's tall, muscular wife stood at the top of the stairs. Where Mikey was red and ruddy, she was darker. With her brown hair feathered around her face, she looked like a large brown owl, big eyes shining wide in her face and her dark dress disappearing into shadows.

"The Ladies, Cailin and Fiona, be down here, Ellie. Come to see the bairns, I suspect."

"Good morning, Elspeth. Are the bairns still settling in well?" Cailin followed Fiona more slowly as the lass fairly flew up the winding staircase.

"Aye, Milady. They're roosted in like a nestling of bluebirds."

Cailin turned sideways, her back to the cold stone wall, gathered her long skirts in one hand, and side-stepped up the narrow staircase. The lack of banister always made her leery and peeking down into the shadowy entry hall where torches cast strange shadows didn't make navigating the stairs any easier. When she reached the top, she squeezed her servant's rough hand. "Thank you so much for your labor. You and Mikey are a God-send."

"Nay, Milady. 'Tis ye be a God-send to us. We canna bear to see our Scots, howbeit they are Highlanders, mistreated so. We'll hide these men and these precious bairns with our lives. Ye can trust us."

"I know. But, still I am in your debt."

"Think naught of it. The bairns are all sleeping again. They've had hard days, they have. And they be all but starved to skin and bones. They ate well and we've bathed them. They sleep on husk mattresses on the floor. They are that round-eyed with wonder at the grandeur of this old place."

"I can barely wait until they move into the castle." Cailin peeked into the first floor room, dark except for few rays of sun that glowed in one of the small arrow arches the ancients had cut into the tower for defense.

Elspeth held her torch high.

Cailin tiptoed in and knelt beside each sleeping child.

The baby, toddler really, cuddled a hand-made doll Elspeth had found somewhere. The doll's head rested just beneath the child's chin. Baby Fiona's long pale lashes lay in half-moons on her rounded cheek, and one thumb still half-poked into her rosebud mouth.

Something twisted inside Cailin's breast. She touched the pale hair, fine as a lacy spider web, shining in the candlelight. Her fingers travelled down the silky warm cheek.

How could anyone hurt a little one like this? Her chest stirred. She would fight to keep these little ones safe so they could grow up in peace. Suddenly her mind cleared.

That's what haunted Avondale. Inside his stern façade, the man carried a soft heart. His failure to protect these people was driving him over the edge of sanity. She would again invite him to share her efforts to rescue the Highlanders. Surely, that would help set his mind at ease.

She stroked the baby's silky hair, letting the soft curls twine around her finger. Baby Fiona's tresses shone lighter than the gold overlay on Cailin's wedding dress.

She smiled deep inside the most secret place in her heart. She'd love Avondale's baby even if he was born with his father's malady. She'd love the child as she did the father, and she'd do everything in her power to protect them both.

But her love might not be enough. Avondale might be beyond her help. Still, at last, she knew the name of his demons. Regret. Helplessness. And fear.

He feared his blackouts. He feared Cumberland. He feared his own great strength.

The baby murmured in her sleep.

Gently Cailin pulled her hand away, bent, and kissed the smooth, silky hair. The child's clean baby scent caused a new, curious stirring inside her breast. She stuck her finger into the small curled hand which closed around her finger.

Oh, she couldn't wait for her own precious baby to be born. Not a boy so Papa would have a son to inherit the castle and wield the mighty weapons inside the armory. Not a son so Avondale would have an heir to his title and lands.

But a son, or a tiny lass like this that she could cradle in her arms and love. No matter what happened with Avondale, she'd have a living person who shared the traits and looks of both of them.

She wiggled her finger, clasped with such trust inside the toddler's still bony hand. "This baby is my niece-in-law," she whispered. "She shall have every advantage I can give her." She smiled. "And she shall play with my own child as an equal in every way."

"Aye, Milady."

Cailin slid her finger free, stood, and tiptoed around the room, looking into each lad's sleeping face. How alike they looked. Though painfully thin, they were sturdy built and had the same white hair and long lashes. The cousins could be brothers. The ones close in age could be twins, they looked so alike. They were sturdy lads with open, engaging faces, children that anyone would be proud to call their own.

And they were blood kin to Brody, her dear brother-in-law. She swallowed a lump lodged in her throat. Indeed, as far as she knew, these bairns comprised all that remained of his family.

Surely, Avondale would be comforted when he discovered how he could help these little ones. Raising the children might assuage some of his guilt. Guilt he should not have shouldered. Had he been one of Duke Cumberland's commanders, he could have done nothing to stop the man in his murderous rampage.

"Our nephews." Perhaps a son as first born might be best. A sturdy lad like Avondale. One who would inherit his title and lands. *But please God, not his malady.*

Sharp darts pierced her heart. How many months had she spent wanting her husband to love her?

Before Brody had been wounded, she'd spent too much time with him. They sang together and played their instruments together.

She shook her head, hunched her shoulders and pulled her elbows into her sides. Time she should have spent seeking out her husband. Time she should have spent trying to help him. But she'd been so afraid of his haughtiness. And her dear husband had hid behind that façade perhaps all his life, hiding his differences from his peers.

Dear God, please help me erase those feelings, and help give him the self-respect he deserves. I feel so inadequate.

She'd been so very foolish. Even though she had wed a wounded man, she would help him become everything he could be.

She heaved a sigh, frowned, and gazed into the darkness surrounding the sleeping bairns.

So what was marriage? Really? Was it not being a help mate? Was that not the reason God created Eve? No one ever said marriage was a bed of roses.

"Milady?"

"Hmm?"

"I asked if ye wanted to see the wounded men?"

"Oh, yes. Of course." She stood, smoothed her long skirts, and followed Elspeth's motherly figure out of the big, peaceful room, silent except for the even breathing of the bairns. Then on up the wide-open, second flight of curving stairs. Again she hugged the cool stone wall on the side opposite to the empty vastness of the room far below.

She'd never liked climbing these stairs designed for men dressed in chain mail and wielding swords. Since these stairs jutted so far apart, the better to defend from an encroaching enemy, she had to step high and carefully. The ancients must have battled even more than today's Scots. Perhaps her ancestors had fought, as the Highlanders had at Culloden, to protect wives, bairns, and their way of life.

"Here ye be, Milady."

Cailin had no need of Elspeth's high held torch. The wounded men squatted or lay below low lying torches that lined the round stone wall.

The three men greeted her warmly, keeping their rumbling voices low. They lay in beds of blankets and straw which could be quickly removed if they needed to flee the tower and hide in the woods.

Two men lay with bandaged arms and heads and smiled up at her.

Fiona sat cross-legged in the straw, in deep conversation with a handsome, sturdy youth lying near the curve of the stone wall. His shoulder looked thickly bandaged and another bandage bound his temple.

"That be Grady," Elspeth whispered. "He's the youngest of the brothers. They all favor him. Spoiled he is."

Cailin nodded, certain each brother heard Elspeth whisper. Here the smell was not that of clean, fresh young bodies. Nor the view that of trusting bairns sleeping peacefully. Here men lay with unsheathed weapons close to their hands. Watchful eyes looked upon her with a mixture of gratefulness and uncertainty.

She smiled. "I trust you gentlemen are comfortable and have everything you need."

These men were precious, too. Brody had risked his life for them. Somehow he'd freed these three Highlanders from English soldiers before dragging himself to the castle. How had he done so with that great wound in his leg?

"Aye, Milady." Even with their evident appreciation, the men kept their voices guarded. One tried to rise to his feet.

"No, please, gentlemen, remain seated. I merely called to find if you had any need."

"We are well taken care of, Duchess Avondale."

She started. That name had a far more pleasant ring now that she knew what plagued her husband so. She could now be proud of her title.

"Aye. And ye can be certain, we willna overstay our welcome. We'll be leaving soon as we be fit."

Leave? Where would they go? What did Brody have in mind for these men?

She'd keep the bairns. Somehow she'd coax Papa into keeping them. And she would return to the Highlands to find more beautiful, starving bairns. She frowned. And she was certain Avondale would want to help. Perhaps they could open an orphanage and take in more Highland bairns. Surely this work would help Avondale overcome his guilt.

Of course, he would be occupied with his place in the House of Lords and with running his other estates, but surely he would give time and energy to the care of the bairns of the men who fell at Culloden. If his spells didn't grow worse.

She'd heard how some men lost title, estates, and wealth and had to be committed to the Tower because they exhibited signs of lunacy. She could never let that happen to Avondale. If the king sent soldiers to shackle him in the Tower, she would take speedy measures to…she could not even put the drastic deed into a thought. But she would do what was necessary to preserve her baby's inheritance.

And Avondale would urge her not to lose everything, no matter the cost.

She glanced at Fiona, still deep in conversation. "Um, Fiona, I think we best leave these gentlemen to their rest."

Fiona seemed reluctant to pull her hand from the young man's grasp, but she said, "Ye are right." She bent so her curtain of hair fell over the young man.

"Do hurry." Cailin hustled her from the room.

The men's whispered "Fare thee well," echoed in her ears.

Outside in the warm sunlight, Fiona started singing, her sweet voice low and clear.

Cailin barely noticed. It was past time, and she prayed not too late, to take care of her husband. She would nurse him back to health and give meaning to his life. She would help strengthen his faith in God and be the best wife she knew how. They would have many sons and daughters, as well as protect and care for as many orphaned Highland bairns as she could gather together.

Surely, God would not expect her to take that other awful, drastic step. Though she had learned that simply because she obeyed God with all her heart, didn't mean she would have no difficulties. Those He loved, God tested. She and Avondale had read just two nights past what King David said, "I know my God that you test the heart and are pleased with integrity."

Avondale was her test.

She hurried back to the castle as fast as she dared, careful not to jar the precious life growing inside.

Perhaps Avondale waited for her in their chamber.

26

Avondale wasn't in their rooms.

Cailin hurried to face her other project that couldn't wait.

"People, no matter who they are, or where they are born, are valuable." She thrust out her chin. Here in the brightly lit, cheerful nursery Mums would be in the best of moods, so this seemed the perfect place to approach her.

"That's true, dear."

She hadn't yet caught Mums's attention. Her absent-minded reply while her hands caressed the blue swaddling clothes indicated Mums dreamed of the yet unborn grandbaby.

She settled on the foot cushion near Mums's rocker.

"Please listen to me. I discovered this fact about people's value in a quite personal way." She stroked the top of the nearby hand-carved baby cradle sending the diminutive bed into a rocking motion.

Mums lifted her head, placed the pile of soft clothes into the clothes press, and her cobalt eyes sparked interest. "Will you hold the yarn while I roll it into a ball, dear?" She freed a skein of yarn from the overflowing basket by her shiny boots.

"Yes, of course." Cailin accepted the offered skein and rose to her feet. "When Megan and I attended Miss Hattie's Finishing School for Young Ladies, I learned a humiliating lesson." She placed both hands shoulder width apart through the soft blue yarn. "I never told you what scorn and disdain the snobbish English held for us Lowlanders. A few young ladies at school weren't even titled, yet they looked down their long English noses at Megan and me."

"Really! How dare they?" Mums sat daintily in a white rocking chair and began winding her end of the yarn into a ball.

"Quite." She lifted her own nose imitating the discrimination she'd so often encountered during her three years at Miss Hattie's.

"Untitled lasses snubbed you?" Mums's clear forehead puckered, and she rocked harder.

"Absolutely." She backed a few steps to keep the yarn between her skein and Mums's ball in a neat drape, not quite touching the imported crimson Turkish carpet.

Mums's pretty brows, only lightly sprinkled with gray, drew together. "Actually, that's not so surprising." She smiled, and her forehead effortlessly smoothed. It seemed twenty years of marriage hadn't affected Mums's ability to easily discard worrisome thoughts.

"My point is that people are valuable, regardless of the state in which they are born."

A gleam of wisdom darkened Mums's eyes. She finished rolling the yarn from the skein and dropped the soft ball into her lap. "I see you are heading this chat in a particular direction." She sat back in the rocker, placed her tiny half-spectacles on the lower part of her nose, picked up the blue knitted baby blanket she'd begun, and peeked over her spectacles. "So?"

Cailin's heart fluttered. "We Lowland Scots have

always secretly looked down our noses at the English, though our same blood pumps through their veins. I think it's past time we overcome our barriers of culture and prejudice towards the nobles." She clasped her hands in a half-praying gesture in front of her blue woolen day dress.

Mums's lips thinned. "Though Avondale's quite odd, I've already accepted him into this family. I've treated him like the son-in-law he's become and extended him every courtesy."

Cailin's hand drifted to her heart to press against the pain darting through her chest. "Courtesy, yes. Love, no."

Mums had shown Avondale no love.

And Avondale needed love desperately. From her and from her entire family.

"No? How can you say that?" Mums concentrated on the knitting. "And what of Brody and Ian, then? Your papa and I gave Brody and Megan a lovely suite of rooms off the secondary hallway. We provided Ian and Moira a nice suite of rooms on the third floor. We thought they'd enjoy the privacy." Mums slipped the soft blue yarn into loops over her knitting needle. "And now Ian's gone. And taken my baby sister with him."

"Yes, Mums. Though he's a fugitive Highlander, you did accept Aunty Moira's husband." She couldn't help adding, "After a fashion." She frowned. "And you knew they would have to flee as soon as Ian recovered from his leg wound."

Mums heaved a sigh and finally met her gaze. "I do the best I can. I need time to change my ideas and my behavior."

"That's just what we don't have, Mums. Time."

"Whatever do you mean?"

"I know your heart is much bigger than you let on." Cailin smoothed her gown over the tapestry on the footstool.

"Why, thank you." Mums's voice had an edge Cailin seldom heard from her mild-mannered mother.

She was going about this all wrong. She grasped Mums's hand, taking care not to unravel the loops her mother still counted under her breath. "I need your help."

Mums squeezed her fingers. "I know you're having marital problems. I've never laid eyes on a stiffer husband than Avondale. The man is a cold fish. This castle is a mausoleum since he moved in."

Cailin swallowed and pushed the hurt her mother's words evoked into the deep folds of her heart. She'd deal with her husband's situation later. "Not Avondale, Mums." Now that she'd started this discussion, she became even less sure how to continue. But she really must have permission. Something had to be done soon. "I know you love bairns."

Mums's eyes brightened. She dropped her knitting, and her warm, heavily jeweled hands clasped Cailin's. "Are you expecting twins! Oh, what joy to have two babies in this nursery." Her soft hands squeezed Cailin's fingers again. "I'm so happy for you, darling."

A sick feeling wafted deep inside her stomach. Would she lose her breakfast? She was long past morning sickness. "No, I don't think I carry twins, though the baby kicks like there are two of them."

Mums touched her cheek and gave such a tender look that Cailin's heart warmed. "Surely you carry a son."

"I pray so."

Mums smile faded. "Drat, I dropped a loop!" She jiggled her knitting needles, trying to pick up the stitch.

A giggle worked up through Cailin's tight throat. Probably her nervousness. "I'm sorry, Mums. But I *am* speaking of babies. Actually bairns, rather than infants." She gazed up into Mums's face. "But not my babies."

Mums's cocked head reminded Cailin of their inquisitive sheep dog. "Oh? Bairns? As in more than two?" She dropped her knitting in her lap.

"Mums, I really need your help and permission!"

Mums stopped rocking and sat forward. "I may not always express my love for you, but you are precious to me." Her warm fingers cupped Cailin's face. "I don't recall you've ever before come to me asking for help. You're so capable. Whatever your need, my answer is yes."

Unshed tears clogged Cailin's throat. She rose, wrapped her arms around Mums's slender shoulders and kissed her smooth cheek. "Oh, thank you. I knew I could count on your support. I love you, too."

Would her request shake her mother's love? She'd not realized her own self-reliance had pushed Mums away. In the future she'd make a point to ask Mums for help rather than muddle through her problems alone. And she really needed Mums to love Avondale. Perhaps when she explained his behavior, Mums would open her heart.

Avondale was far from a stiff, cold husband. Except for his injury, he pleased her well. Every thought of him melted her heart like ice beneath an early spring sun, leaving a warm puddle reflecting the life-giving rays.

Yet now she feared more than ever to ask Mums to understand him. One monumental task at a time. She'd hate so to break the fragile web of love Mums had spun to reach out to her.

But she must obtain her cooperation. She swallowed. "I…I wasn't sure you loved me." Her voice sounded thick.

"Of course, I love you." Tears sparkled in Mums's beautiful eyes. "You've always been the sweet, obedient daughter. How could I not love you?" She picked up her knitting and kept her eyes downcast. "But, after your marriage to Avondale fared so poorly, I feared you did not love me." She gazed up. "Papa gave me no voice in your covenant with Avondale."

"Oh, I do, Mums. More than you can ever know." Cailin smiled. "And, we shall discuss my marriage at another time."

Mums leaned forward and embraced her. "Whenever you are ready."

Sweetness stirred inside her chest. She hugged Mums's slender shoulders and yearned to cling to this moment and not let anything spoil it. Yet she must risk just that.

She must act with urgency. Explain to Mums. Lives hung in the balance.

Her heart tripled its beating. She twisted the square-cut engagement diamond on the gold chain around her neck. "So, this is the problem. Mikey brought word just this morning that lobsterbacks will soon patrol our Lowland borderlands. They will be setting up camp and moving from place to place."

"Oh, dear. They're sure to frighten the livestock."

Cailin tipped her mother's chin up so their eyes met. "Brody has more relatives whom I would really,

really like to invite to live with us. There are eight bairns, and they are in danger."

Mums's brows shot to her forehead. Her mouth dropped open.

Cailin bit her lower lip.

"More bairns?"

"Seven more boys and one small girl. You know Brody's two older brothers died in the Battle of Culloden?"

"Yes, of course. Mrs. MacCaulay speaks of little else, poor soul."

"Duncan and Colin had wives and other bairns, besides the two older boys Megan rescued from slavery and Papa sent off to school."

Mums's rocking chair squeaked and teetered faster. She pulled off her spectacles, stuck the needles into the knitting, and stared out the window. "And the women and bairns need a place to stay for a season?" Her words dropped into the silence like beads clinking on a chain. Her hopeful tone as to a short stay wasn't encouraging.

Cailin swallowed. "No. English soldiers took Brody's sisters-in-law away somewhere. They've disappeared. Maybe they were carried to the coast or…." How could she tell her gentle mother that Brody's in-laws had almost certainly been molested and were now being used as slaves, or might even be dead?

Mums gasped. "I've heard stories. Brutal stories. And Brody and Fiona's relatives are missing?"

Cailin leaned forward, letting her eyes beg. "Yes. Duncan and Collin died, and their wives have been taken captive. The soldiers left their bairns to starve."

"Gracious! And you want to bring the whole lot

here?" Mums's yarn ball fell to the floor and rolled across the room, leaving a long strand of light blue yarn trailing across the carpet. "But Cailin, the danger of harboring Highlanders! Think of your baby! Think of the danger to all of us."

"I know. I know. But we have so many rooms inside the castle. And we already protect Mrs. MacCaulay and Fiona."

Mums's expression tightened, and a frown puckered her forehead. "You say there are eight of them?"

"A sweet, small baby girl who just barely toddles. Her name is Baby Fiona."

Mums forehead smoothed, and she nodded. "Yes. By all means bring the baby here. We shall protect her."

Cailin's heart lightened. She smiled. "Thank you, Mums, but…."

"Oh dear. And there are seven boys?" Mums frowned and shook her head.

"Yes, Mums. There are eight children."

Mums closed her eyes. "Eight orphans! Oh, dear God!" She raised her hands in supplication to Heaven.

Cailin nodded. "If we don't take them in"—she gazed at the window—"soldiers will find them and cart them to prison…or sell them to be slaves."

"Good heavens! I simply cannot believe the English are so cruel. I would not have expected them to be so inhumane."

"Remember, the soldiers left the bairns to starve. The Crown wants no more rebellions from the Highlanders, so England is totally destroying them and their way of life."

Mums rubbed her chin and hunched her

shoulders, and then her expression brightened. "You've seen these bairns?"

"Mums, I love you." She pressed her lips against her mother's flushed cheek. "Fiona and I brought them to the broch two days past. Mikey and Elspeth are having a difficult time keeping them in that upstairs room."

Mums's eyes widened. She dropped her head and closed her eyes. "Dear God, help me accept all this!" She lifted her head. "What has Scotland become? I cannot believe all this." Her eyes shimmered. "We must get to work, mustn't we? I'll break the news to your father. Just leave him to me." She rose from the rocker, the blue yarn in her hands. "Lads! God knew how much I wanted a son. Now He's done exceeding abundantly above all I ever asked, or thought." Mums's face looked young and eager.

Surely this was the lass Papa fell head over heels in love with, though their marriage had been arranged. Perhaps if he accepted the bairns, Mums would accept him? Their marriage might yet become loving.

Cailin's heart warmed and expanded. Lightness replaced the fear in her mind. She lifted relaxed shoulders as if a burden had slipped from them. Calm that had so eluded her of late washed over her. "Thank you, Mums." She would explain later that more homeless, hungry bairns wandered the Highlands.

Darkness slithered over her brightened spirit. More bairns seeking roots and berries to fill their empty stomachs and with no roof over their heads. More lads and lasses out in the chill of spring and rain. More broken hearts pining for lost Mums and Papas.

"Shall we call them cousins, kin to your father's sister-in-law?" Mums sauntered to the window, pulled aside the thick drapery, and looked out.

"Yes, Papa's in-laws."

"I had so wanted to help the poor Highlanders. To sit idly by while evil is being committed is a sin. One must do what one can."

"Even though the course is dangerous?"

Mums clutched the window sill. "Yes. We must do what we can."

Cailin strode to hug her mother around the waist. "I love you so much!" She twirled Mums's slender form around the nursery, barely missing the rocking chairs, cradles, and stools.

"You're making me dizzy." Mums smiled up at her and cocked her head. "Listen."

The clip clop of a horse's hooves on cobblestones three stories below sounded faintly through the window.

They both rushed to look down at the courtyard. A single horse walked slowly into the keep.

"Ah, Avondale returned from one of his haunts. I thought it might be an English soldier seeking Highland fugitives already." Mums dropped the curtain and paced the nursery. "I think it's time, dear heart." She paused and the conflicted expression on her face showed she fought some emotional battle.

"Yes?"

"I never could force myself to tell you and Megan, but now seems timely." Mums turned back to the window. The soft morning light streaming through the thick rippled glass made her skin glow. "You and Megan had an older brother."

Cailin dropped the yarn she had bent to retrieve. "What!"

"Your Papa and I had a son." Mums absently

caressed her cheek with her knitting needle. "Our son passed away before he reached a month of age. Papa and I buried him beneath the gnarled rowan tree. We called him our sweet visitor, our baby of the mist."

"I never knew."

"It hurt me too much to tell you and Megan."

"Oh, Mums." The faraway look in Mums's fixed gaze contracted Cailin's heart. Even her mother carried secret pain.

"Every January on the fourteenth day, your Papa and I visit Aiden's resting place. We planted a rambling rose near his headstone and purple heather at his feet. Each year Papa leaves a wooden sword, and I leave a wooden horse by his headstone." Her mother smiled a wry little smile. "That's silly, but it makes me feel better to think he's not alone. That he has something to play with." She sighed. "When Aiden left us, he took a part of my heart."

Cailin brushed at the hot tears sliding down her cheeks. She buried her face in her mother's shoulder. How could this be?

"Now, my dearest, you've given me seven boys to rear." She smiled through tears making trails down her face. "I'll have nine when the other two return from school." She waved her knitting. "Nine fine lads."

Cailin hugged Mums and their bittersweet tears mingled.

She would ask Elspeth and Mikey to make arrangements immediately for the bairns to move into the castle.

Especially since redcoats were beginning to dot the Lowlands.

She'd seen several already today. In case of emergency, she would also ask the two servants to whisk the bairns to six different crofters, so if soldiers did arrive at the castle, they would not wonder why so many bairns would be living with the MacMurrys.

"Oh, it will be so much fun to have bairns underfoot. And Baby Fiona can play older sister to my son." Cailin caressed the small roundness of her stomach. She brushed wetness from her cheeks and shivered.

But what would Mums say about her plans for Avondale?

And would he agree to them?

27

The unborn baby insisted she eat breakfast early, so Cailin rolled out of bed.

Now the first rays of sunlight pushed inquisitive fingers into the dining room window. She wiped her mouth with a napkin, pushed back her empty bowl, rose from her chair, left the dining room, and rushed through the hall and up the grand staircase. Her heels clattered on the granite floor of the passageway, then stopped abruptly as she knocked lightly on their bedchamber door.

No answer. She knocked again.

When Avondale didn't call for her to enter, she turned the decorative handle and slid the door open. No one looked up smiling from the overstuffed settee by the crackling fire. No one had partaken of the tray of inviting breakfast things waiting on the low table in front of the two couches. The sitting room was empty.

Perhaps he still slept.

She opened the door to the dressing room. Empty. She worried her lip as she walked through the room with the large clothes presses on both sides, and her hand touched the door handle to their bedroom.

Oh, God, please let him still be in bed.

She tiptoed inside. A shadow stole over her heart. The sunshine-filled room felt abandoned. But the privacy curtains were still down enclosing the bed. Oh, if only he still slept. She reached out and pulled the red velvet drape open.

Empty, rumpled bedclothes. She collapsed on the edge of the bed, cradled her womb, and rocked.

****

Hand on the banister, Cailin stood at the top of the staircase. All day she'd kept busy with tasks that must be done, and now she could barely stand with her shoulders back and her head held high. After their talk last night, she'd so expected to see Avondale today.

She only had dinner to endure. She would sneak her hand into her husband's under the damask tablecloth and give him a silent message that she desired him to join her in their suite immediately after they dined.

And if he refused her invitation—what? Pain would rip into her heart again. She thinned her lips. But she would risk more suffering. After she forced herself to take the first step down, the remaining descent seemed easier.

The others, already gathered around the table, looked up with smiles and greetings.

The dining butler behind her chair seated her.

When Avondale strode to his place at the end of the long table, despite how tired he looked, she couldn't keep the wide smile from her face.

"Hello, my love." After he settled himself, his knee brushed hers. Hidden by the long tablecloth, his warm hand closed around hers.

She placed her other hand over his, gently squeezed, and gave him another bright smile.

Yet something was wrong.

His jaw was set. His face too ruddy. His frown too

deep, the bruise on his forehead hidden by thick, mahogany hair. He nodded at her and smiled. "I trust you spent the day well."

Though he acknowledged her publicly, he seemed troubled.

"Yes, well. But I had hoped to see you."

"I'm sorry. I was called away on an urgent matter." The moment his gaze left her, his smile faded, and a cleft deepened between his dark brows. The slight stubble on his cheeks shifted as the muscle in his jaw clenched.

She'd seen that tense expression before.

Oh, dear God, please, not another of his spells.

He barely tasted his soup and soon waved the server to remove his bowl. His back looked rigid as an iron post, and he shook his head as the waiter offered the lamb savory.

Her husband stared down the long table at Papa. He cleared his throat. His tense manner curtailed conversation among the family and various guests.

Heads turned in his direction.

Papa lowered his fork.

"This news comes straight from the lion's mouth." Avondale's voice sounded raspy, as if the news hurt his throat. "A friend, a royalist in a government regiment, sent word via secret dispatch that the Duke of Cumberland ordered his dragoons and his Kingston Horse to widen the search for rebel Highlanders. He's searching the Lowlands. Beginning tomorrow."

Cailin's heart sped. She glanced at Brody, sitting across the table.

According to Megan, he'd gotten the news late last night and had whisked the men hidden inside the broch away to some secret places—Brody thought best that none of them knew where. Fortunately the men's wounds were healed enough they were now mobile.

The English guests barely nodded and went back to their eating, flirting, and conversations.

Avondale heaved a deep sigh and raised his voice. "Cumberland ordered the soldiers to search every square inch of the Lowlands, castles and cottages, burghs and farms, because three of their soldiers have recently been murdered." He glanced at Brody and his mouth thinned. "The duke thinks some Lowlanders are abetting the rebels. He is searching every single cottage and castle for fugitive rebels."

Cailin's hands grew icy.

Brody chewed more slowly, his eyes downcast.

Megan's face drained of color.

Fiona blushed wine red, dropped her fork, and arranged and rearranged the silver fork across her plate of uneaten food.

The English gentry gazed at Avondale. "Surely not our castles and estates," several of his peers spoke together.

"You will need to fly your colors. But yes, they will search your estates. I suggest you return to your lands to guard your holdings in person." Her husband's shoulders slumped as if the weight of the world burdened him. "Cumberland believes the Highlanders are mounting a new irregular type of warfare, using ambush and murder." Avondale's strong hand trembled as he sipped water from his glass. Some spilled on the white ruffle of his shirt. "Cumberland means to track any fugitive Highlander who escaped after the battle and found refuge in other parts of Scotland. Since he's already scoured and plundered the Highlands, he'll begin tomorrow with the Lowlands."

"Wasn't destroying the Highlands enough for them?" Megan's green eyes flashed. "Aren't his soldiers tired of searching? Don't they ever want to return home to their families?"

No one else spoke.

Red stained Fiona's neck and face all the way to the roots of her hair.

Brody rose from the table and bowed. "Ye will please excuse me." His boots clattered in the silence as he strode down the long table past the other diners, and then from the dining room.

Every servant craned his neck to watch, and then jerked back into attention.

Was her mouth filled with cotton? Cailin wet her lips. The napkin she put to her mouth trembled.

Papa picked up his fork, gave a meaningful glance at the servants, and stabbed his meat. Obviously, he meant for the family to take little notice of Brody's leaving, so as not to bring more attention to him.

Several long minutes later Megan folded her napkin and glanced at each of them. "I love you all so very much." She rose from the table and rushed from the dining room.

Cailin pushed her lamb with her fork, but couldn't force another bite down her tight throat. Megan would follow Brody into hiding. Would she ever see her sister again? Oh, she hated this war!

Abruptly Papa dropped his napkin, rose from his place, bowed to Avondale, and, boots striking the granite floor like a blacksmith's hammer on the anvil, he left the dining room.

Finally, the awkward dinner ended, and family and guests departed to wherever they fancied.

Cailin and Avondale met in their chambers.

"Come sit with me." He held out his hand and patted the side of the large, overstuffed chair.

She nodded and curled at his side. The elation she'd expected was dampened by the set of his jaw and the dark shade of his eyes.

Would the news he'd delivered send him over the edge?

Would she worry the rest of her life about what would send him into one of his spells? His future looked so bleak. But, no matter what he did, to her or even to their bairns, she would never, never allow Rafe to carry out his plan of her dear husband's accidental death. "I so appreciate what you did for our family tonight. Do you think your banner will keep Cumberland's soldiers from searching our castle?"

"No. He'll search. Pray God he finds nothing." His chocolate eyes deepened to onyx. "You must remain in our chambers. In our bed. With a cloth over your eyes. You will feign sickness."

"That will not be difficult. I am sick at heart."

"Obey me in this, Cailin. Do not leave our bed tomorrow. No matter what happens." His lips parted in a sad smile. "You and our baby are too important to risk." He took her hand. "Promise me."

She nodded.

He went to a chest in the corner, pulled a key from his vest, unlocked a drawer and withdrew a length of royal blue silk. Slowly he unfurled the banner, royal blue embroidered with three gold stags, and using the stairs to the bed, draped the royal banner of the house of Avondale over the red velvet canopy at the foot of the huge bed. From the door, the silk emblem would be the first object anyone entering would see.

Soldiers could not miss the message.

He returned to the chest and removed a small box from the drawer, closed the door, and walked slowly to her side. He took her hand and slid a gold ring with the royal blue seal of the house of Avondale onto her index finger. It was a small replica of the gem he wore on his own finger.

He bent and kissed her forehead. "With this ring I give you my heart. No one dare touch you as long as you wear this ring. This seal is second to the Duke of Cumberland and third to King George himself. This ring holds power and authority."

Darkness touched her heart. Did his preparations mean he feared a bout of blackness? Did he expect he would be unable to defend her? "Will you not be here beside me?"

He turned his face away. "I don't know what tomorrow will bring. But if you obey me, you shall be safe."

What did he fear? What did he know that she didn't? Why was he not open with her? Would he run, rather than face his nightmare, Bloody Billy?

Avondale's tight lips and frown forbade her asking. She wouldn't push him over the edge by forcing him to speak.

He settled in his accustomed double chair next to the crackle and snap of the fireplace. She twirled the ring on her finger watching the gem flash and sparkle in the reflection of the flames. The fit was loose, so she must be careful not to let the seal slip from her finger. Well she knew the significance of this ring. With this emblem, he empowered her to act in his stead. He'd given her his heart, and he fully trusted her. Madman or not, he'd deposited far more power into her hands than she'd ever before experienced. Her hand shook.

What did he expect would happen tomorrow?

His face was set with determination.

"But you will be by my side tomorrow, will you not?"

"You shall be safe."

Though he still evaded answering her question, the darkness on his face kept her from asking yet again. Since the morning would certainly bring evil into the castle, tonight she would speak to him of his protection. Whatever put the tension in his stance, the rigidness in his broad shoulders, the tight set to his lips had to be dangerous. Especially for a man subject to periods of blackness. He needed what she'd yearned to speak to him about since the day they wed.

She slipped into the chair beside him. Cuddled into the one big seat in front of the roaring fire, she cupped his strong face in her hands. "Let us read together from the Holy Scriptures. Our earlier reading has taken us to the book of Romans."

He nodded, his eyes on the fire, his face tense.

She found the place she wanted in the fifth chapter.

"For the wages of sin is death, but the gift of God is eternal life in Christ Jesus our Lord." She looked up from reading and raised a brow, trying to keep her expression calm while her heart beat so fast she feared he might detect the sound or see the palpitation.

"Yes, I am well acquainted with sin." His voice deepened, "I walk with a load strapped to my back every day."

"Why not, here tonight, receive God's gift?"

"How can losing the guilt be as easy as taking a gift?"

"Easy for us, but not easy for God's Son." She leafed back in her worn Bible to the book of First Peter.

"Who his own self bare our sins in his own body on the tree, that we, being dead to sins, should live unto righteousness: by whose stripes ye were healed."

"I know of Christ's suffering terrible agony and dying on the cross. More agony than any man should ever bear." He rubbed the stubble on his cheeks, making a small rasping sound in the silence.

A log broke in the fireplace and fell with a comforting thud.

She skipped back in her Bible to Romans again. *"That if thou shalt confess with thy mouth the Lord Jesus, and shalt believe in thine heart that God hath raised him from the dead, thou shalt be saved."*

They talked long into the night.

He promised he would think on the words she had read.

She would remember his sweet lovemaking for a very long time. It was as if he thought there might not be another opportunity to show his love.

Yet, the next morning when she opened her eyes, his pillow was empty.

Throwing a robe over her nightdress, she ran into the dressing room…and stumbled over the two bodies sprawled on the floor. She gasped and the room spun.

Hennings and Rafe.

28

Avondale snatched off his hat and wiped sweat from his forehead. After last night, he'd risen early and ridden all day. Thus far, the hordes of soldiers had not bothered any of Castle Drummond's people.

When the soldiers began their search of the castle, he'd stood outside the front door, hand on his sword, praying Brody and the wounded men had disappeared without a trace of their having been inside the broch.

But he'd had to ride off before the two bodyguards regained their senses. He'd left a note pinned on the insides of Hennings' and Rafe's jackets. They must not follow him. At the risk of their own lives, they must protect Cailin and the babe. When the laudanum he'd administered them wore off, they would guard her with their lives.

He'd seen from his perch on the distant hilltop that the redcoats had thoroughly searched the castle and grounds. Some still lingered, but he couldn't. Urgency drove him.

Scores of redcoats were underfoot everywhere, popping out from the forest, riding up over the hills, threading through Kirkmichael's streets. Hundreds stalked the Lowland countryside on foot. Others thundered past on horseback.

He'd raised his coat of arms to fly over each cluster of cottages dotting the great estate, and King George's soldiers had respected his banner. They searched homes, but had taken no prisoner on MacMurry lands.

He beat dust from his shoulders. His tongue clung to the roof of his mouth, and, all but falling from his saddle in weariness, he'd ridden further afield to the cottages in Kirkmichael, the adjoining burgh.

He heard rumors that soldiers rounded up one or two Scottish peasants at each cottage they rode up to, ravished the women, and pillaged the farms and stores. With no opposing army to protect the peasants, and the redcoats goaded by the duke's proclamation, the people were at the mercy of the soldiers.

And he had long since crossed the boundary of MacMurry land.

He stiffened his back and put his hand on his sword. Yet another band of soldiers herded a group of men and boys, hands bound behind their back, up the carriage road in his direction.

Blood dripped down homespun shirts and from the foreheads of several of the men. Some limped. The soldiers were singing, shouting and laughing.

One dragged a young woman by her arm, her gown torn and hanging from one shoulder, the other exposed to the sun and the leering eyes of the soldiers.

Avondale urged his horse forward, and then turned his steed and blocked the narrow road.

"Let us pass, sir." The face under the tall military hat was almost as scarlet as the man's uniform.

"Where are you taking these people?" His dry throat sounded a tad weak, so he raised his volume. "Answer me, soldier."

"Cumberland said round up any Scot sympathizers to the fugitives hiding out in the Lowlands. These men fit the bill." The soldier stomped his polished boot on the road. "We're taking them to be sold as slaves and sent to the colonies."

"The duke promised you could keep any monies you received, so you rounded up these innocent people." He'd practiced that sneer in his voice and manner all his life. Never had he used it for better service.

The soldier ducked his head. "Yes, sir, he did. He did do that."

"Do you know who I am?" He let his horse prance close to the embarrassed soldier's side.

"Yes, Your Grace."

"So, where did you find these prisoners?"

"In yon village." The man shuffled his feet and jerked a thumb back over his shoulder.

"Blairsville, was it?"

"Don't know the name, Your Grace," he mumbled, glancing at his men as if to see if any knew the name of the burgh where they'd captured the peasants.

"Of course, you don't. If you did, you would know these people are under my protection." He glanced at the six men and two boys who stood heads down, shoulders heaving as if they'd been running.

The girl looked up, tears streaking her face. She tried to raise her ripped gown to cover her naked shoulder, but the man gripping her arm jerked her so violently she fell at his feet.

"No, Your Grace. We didn't know. We thought—"

"You didn't think." Avondale raised his voice and urged his horse close to the soldier.

The man had to step back. He collided with another of his men.

"I want these people freed." Avondale put an edge on his voice.

The soldier's mouth dropped open. "But—"

"Now!"

A sullen expression dropped over the faces of the soldiers, but they turned to slash the ropes binding the men and boys. They muttered and growled low in their throats, but they freed the prisoners.

One of the freed peasants hurried to the girl, helped her to her feet, and thrust an arm around her waist. He balled his fist, veins in his red face all but bursting.

"Look to your right and to your left, soldier, as far as you can see." Avondale quieted his side-stepping stallion.

All the soldiers gazed around the glen, eyes wide.

"This is my dukedom. None of the people who live here was involved in any way with The Jacobite Rising. Not a single one. Each man, woman and child is loyal to King George. Not a one of them is to be harmed. These are loyal, hard-working crofters and merchants. Not a Jacobite among them." He rattled his sword. "Now leave my glen and my bailiwick."

The soldier managed a bow. "As you say, Your Grace." Looking more eager to be off than to stay and apologize, the squad of soldiers headed down the road in the direction of Castle Drummond.

"Wrong way, soldiers. From here to the Highlands belongs to me."

The soldiers cursed, but turned and, in a faint-hearted march, headed away from the castle towards the midlands.

Avondale sat his horse and watched them leave, dust and grit from their march settled over his shoulders and in the hair of the people he'd freed.

They bowed in the dust at his horse's feet. "Thank

you, Your Grace."

The man with his arm around the woman looked up. "Might we know Your Grace's name?"

He smiled and pulled a banner from the diminishing stock in his saddle bag. "Raise this in the center of your village. I am the Duke of Avondale. This banner will protect you from illegal seizure."

As he rode away, they still knelt in the dust, their heads bowed, his banner held high in one man's work-worn hands.

Avondale sighed, lifted his water skin, shook open the lid, and lifted it to his mouth. Nothing. Perhaps he'd find a stream somewhere.

He rode up yet another hillock. Smoke rose just behind the thicket of trees. Shouting and the clash of weapons wafted to his ears. He had no power outside his estates, but he could not let these atrocities continue and do nothing. Not again. Never again.

Ducking his head from low branches and sharp twigs, he urged his mount through the trees, and burst through to the clearing.

A heather-thatched roof smoldered, raising black smoke. The acid scent burned his nostrils.

Three redcoats on horseback, sabers flashing in the setting sun, surrounded a young peasant. One soldier had a noose about the man's neck, and the other two penned him in with their steeds.

Avondale spurred his horse to block the soldier tightening the noose. "Stop. Release this man."

The soldier's mouth dropped.

Avondale wiped dust from his jacket to reveal his coat of arms. "I am the Duke of Avondale, and I demand you free this man."

The soldier snapped his mouth shut, narrowed his

eyes, and stared.

Back stiff, hand on his sword, Avondale returned the glare. "This man had no part in The Rising. He, his people, and his property are under my protection. If you doubt my word take your case to King George."

Slowly the soldier lowered the rope. The peasant's hands jerked upward, and he tugged at the loop around his neck. His face slowly lost its purple color, and he drew in great gasps of air.

"You're the Duke of Avondale?" Disbelief pitched the redcoat's voice high.

Avondale held out his hand. The powerful ring on his right index finger sparkled in the dusky light. "You disbelieve me? That would be a grave mistake. You will find yourself stripped of rank should you and your men fail to leave this burgh immediately." He glanced around the small clearing.

Two soldiers, trews around their ankles, knelt over a female, her skirt hiked above her head. A pile of tartans and plaids burned in front of the humble doorway.

Another soldier led a cow away from the byre.

The sound of a whip slashing into bare flesh floated from behind the cottage.

"At once, Captain," he ordered.

The soldier bowed, slid his sword into his saddle scabbard, put his fingers to his lips, and shrilled a whistle.

All around the clearing soldiers froze.

The woman's soft crying and the fire crackling through the thatched roof filled the silence.

The soldier leading the cow dropped the rope, and the animal turned and plodded back to the byre.

The two men hitched up their scarlet pants and

sauntered over to face their captain.

Three men hurried around the corner from the rear of the cottage, a blood-stained horsewhip in the tallest soldier's hand.

After they all assembled, Avondale forced every ounce of authority he could muster into his voice. "Do not return to this property or to this burgh." He waved to the other houses clustered nearby, each surrounded by a small clearing. "These people are crofters. Simple farmers. Lowlanders, faithful to the king. Take the word of the Duke of Avondale. These people did not fight at Culloden. You have no right to trespass."

"But Milord, they are sympathizers." The captain waved a weak, uncertain hand, as if to prove he had a right to pillage unarmed villagers.

"And you have proof of this, Captain?" Avondale fought exhaustion creeping over his limbs, numbing his hands and feet; over his voice, making it rasp; over his resolve, making him stiffen until he thought his back would break. He stared the man down.

"No, Your Grace. We shall leave at once." The red-faced captain bowed.

Avondale nodded.

Slowly the men on foot marched after the mounted officers. As they disappeared into the woods, he slumped in the saddle. He had to rest, but he would not return to the castle until he could protect as many peasants as he was able. He would spend the night here in this burgh and start early tomorrow.

Bloody Billy would not have the freedom to murder, rape, pillage, or take captives of any more innocent people as long as he could bluff his way. He had no power to protect these people so far from his own lands and estates, but he could no longer sit idly by while that evil man emptied the countryside of Scots.

He already owed Cumberland. If the duke discovered these actions, the king's brother would seek his blood.

But Bloody Billy no longer ruled his soul. He'd given himself to a much Higher Power.

29

Cailin had ticked the minutes off, measured the hours in counting the English guests as they finally left the castle, one by one, to return to their lands to protect their holdings and their crofters from the redcoats.

She'd ticked the days off by the routine of the household and her duties. She and Mums selected the week's menus, assigned the various household chores and supply purchases, and together they took food and clothes to their own crofters who had need.

The only bright spots in the two weeks since her last night with Avondale arrived as she spent time with the bairns. After they moved into the castle, they'd not wanted separate rooms.

So she, Mums, and Fiona assigned Duncan's four lads to one room.

Though Baby Fiona spent cheerful hours in the nursery, she demanded to sleep in the same room as her three older brothers, so Collin's four bairns received an adjoining room. Mums placed a small bed beneath the biggest, brightest window for Baby Fiona.

The bairns big eyes took in every nook of their rooms and grew larger when they discovered each would have their own bed.

Already they had woven their way into Cailin's heart. She felt a special fondness for Baby Fiona, who liked to climb up into her lap when she took a minute or two to rest in one of the white rockers Mums had the servants bring to the bairns' rooms from the nursery.

Cailin scarcely recognized the energetic, warm, smiling woman who supervised the servants, telling them where to place the clean sheets, comfortable chairs, desks, toys, and throw pillows. Mums had never seemed happier.

She and Mums no longer had any emotional barriers distancing them. She'd never before felt so completely comfortable around Mums. And Mums obviously felt the same way. The looks, hand clasping, and smiles they shared drew them into a new closeness.

Cailin painted the plaster in the two rooms by grinding color pigments in oil until it became a stiff paste. She used bright yellow for the walls and royal blue for the trim. Some of the servants brushed the paste on the wall. The exuberant bairns helped as well. Baby Fiona came for a cuddle with yellow paint dotting her face.

Cailin laughed for the first time that week. She distributed cushions and tacked up oil paintings to accent and add warmth and welcome to the rooms. For Baby Fiona's new bed she used all sweetly girlish, bright and pastel pinks.

When they viewed the finished rooms, the boys clapped and grinned.

Baby Fiona, cleaned of her paint and resembling a fairy in her long peach gown, her almost iridescent blonde hair floating to her waist, danced around the room like a will-o-wisp.

Liam, the oldest by six months, appeared to be looked upon by the other bairns as leader and spokesman. So after they calmed, Cailin turned to the sturdy blond whose face seemed covered with light freckles. "Is there something more I can bring to make this room home for you?"

Liam shuffled a foot on the polished granite. He tucked his hands behind his back and raised his chin to look her in the eyes with his brilliant blue gaze. "Aye, ma'am." He swallowed. He straightened his shoulders and took a deep breath. "We'd verra much like to have some books."

Cailin grinned. Delight spiraled from the roots of her hair to her toes. "I'm so pleased to hear that!" She reached a tentative hand to weave her fingers through his springy, red hair. She wanted to hug him, but, though he was only about seven, he stood almost to her shoulder and she was not at all certain how he would react to being hugged. "We shall take a carriage to the book store in Kirkmichael and you shall each select some books that appeal to you."

Oh, how she missed Megan. Her sister would so have loved the upcoming outing. But, as days passed and the castle received no word of Megan and Brody's capture, her worried heart lightened for them. Though she prayed for them often during the days since they'd escaped, her prayers became more and more optimistic. But her sister would have loved spending time with these bairns. Cailin could only pray to one day receive a letter.

"And," Cailin turned to the task at hand, "Mums and I shall see that a suitable tutor is brought to begin you on your studies."

The lads clapped.

Baby Fiona wrinkled her nose. "What is too-too?"

Cailin knelt beside the lass and explained. Then she turned to the boys. "But Liam, Dougal, Gavin, and

Tevish, you four brothers and Ewan, Angus, Kameron, and Baby Fiona must all begin calling me Aunty Cailin. And we shall begin today teaching you to speak in the English manner. Though you live here in the castle under Lord Avondale's protection, there might come a time when you are away and redcoats might question you. You cannot let your Scottish brogue betray you." She looked long at each one of the eight serious faces turned up to her. "Will you do that for me?"

"Aye, Aunty Cailin." Liam grinned. Already his sturdy body had begun to fill out, so different from the skinny, dirty, lad with the large, frightened eyes whom she'd brought to the broch.

She snatched a moment during the bairns' rest time to take her quill in hand and pen a note to Pastor Fergus.

Dear Pastor,

I plan to start an orphanage for the bairns of deceased Culloden warriors. Do you know of any proper and sizable facility I can purchase to renovate for the yet-to-be-rescued orphans? I know of one qualified couple who will live full-time with the little ones. Do you know of any others? Thank you for any advice you can offer.

Yours sincerely,

Cailin Mountebank, Duchess of Avondale

Her heart sang. The future orphanage shone as a bright guiding light in her tense, worrisome days. She had a new mission. The Highlands as they had been before Culloden no longer existed. But she could save the bairns.

Though she remained excited about her planned orphanage and her newfound joy in Mums's company, still time crept by. One slow minute ticked away after another slow minute. She played with the bairns, prayed, fretted, paced, and watched the sun slowly descend in the sky.

Her heart stuttered. After yet another day with no word from Avondale, she must make another foray and rescue more of the motherless, homeless, bairns wandering still in the Highlands. She must return to where the hillside homes were burned to ashes. Where little more than prickly thistles and fields of broom had been left for the people to live on.

She would not leave the needy bairns to die. As long as Mikey would drive for her and Elspeth would cook for the homeless ones, she would search out all she could find. She glanced at Fiona, who sat on the floor surrounded by her nephews and niece.

Fiona's eyes met hers and she nodded, agreeing to Cailin's silent question.

Having settled that, she sank into one of the comfortable, upholstered chairs scattered in the big sitting room between the bairns's rooms and leaned back to enjoy the youthful laughter and roughhousing. So, she spent much of the long, slow days and lazy evenings with the bairns inside the castle, learning about each one.

Yet her mind spiraled from one dark worry to another. The days slipped past, and she received no sign or word from Avondale. Where was he? Had he experienced another dark episode and been unable to break free? She gazed out the window at his banner flying proudly in the breeze, unfurling his protection over the castle.

Had he been injured? Thrown from his spirited stallion? Did he lie in need in some forsaken place?

Had Bloody Billy caught up with him and thrown him into the Tower?

She shivered.

Surely, he would have gotten word to her somehow.

Or was he dead?

30

"Rafe, you and Hennings, please go out again and search the countryside. We must find Avondale." Cailin could barely keep from breaking down in front of the two newly knighted bodyguards. "Please find him. Take a good riding horse from the stable." She bit her lip. "You might start in Kirkmichael. See if anyone has news of him."

"Yes, Milady. We shall do our best." Hennings bowed.

"Thank you, Hennings. Please be on your way." She turned to the tall, muscular Scotsman standing with his head bowed, his massive fists doubled behind his back. "Rafe, please stay. I need a word with you in private."

"Aye, Milady."

Both stood at the drawing room door until the valet, his massive muscles partially hidden by his tailored swallow-tailed black suit, turned and left.

She faced Rafe. "Regardless of the kind of mess you find Avondale involved in, you are not, under any circumstances, to arrange a hunting accident. I want my husband back alive." She stood on tiptoes and stared the rugged Scot straight into his gray eyes. "You understand?" She shook a finger in his face. "He is not to be harmed."

"But, Milady, he—"

"Under no circumstances!"

****

Someone knocked at her chamber door. Fully dressed, though the night was half passed, she opened the door.

Dust covered and gaunt, Rafe bowed.

Heart beating fast, she asked, "You've news?"

"Nay, Milady. I've ridden two days in every direction, and I know not where His Grace is. I've had no news of him." His hands were fisted.

Her hand flew to her throat and she dropped her gaze.

Rafe went down one knee. "Please forgive me for letting the duke out of my sight. Regardless of how God decides the future, I will serve milady with all my heart until the day I die."

"Thank you, Rafe. I appreciate your loyalty." She sighed. "I trust you will be more vigilant in the future."

"I pray my suggestion might not be forgotten, should you have need of it."

"I shall never have need of that. We shall never speak of it again."

"If the duke's behavior puts anyone else in danger—"

"Not another word of that!"

"Yes, Milady." He bowed his head. "I shall lay down my life for you. And, I vow I shall never be taken unawares by the duke again."

"Thank you, Rafe. You are a good man. Now, please get some rest, then go out and search for the duke on the morrow."

Rafe rose from his knees, his face grim. "I shall do as you bid."

She closed the door and listened as his footsteps echoed down the hall.

****

"Milady." Molly, Megan's personal maid, stuck her head through the dressing room door. "There be a huddle of people wants to see ye at the back door."

Cailin stirred, raised herself from the pillow on the settee, and wiped her wet cheeks with the back of her hand.

She had taken the dispirited Irish girl as her own personal maid after Megan fled, and she still needed to handle the woman with kid gloves. Any little thing could set the plain-faced Irish girl off into an assault of crying. And Cailin had had her own fill of crying today.

"People?"

"Yes, Milady. Men, women, and even bairns."

"For what purpose?"

The pale, russet brows raised and her blue eyes rounded. "They have gifts."

"What on earth?" Cailin stood and smoothed her brown summer weight day gown. She took a step towards the dressing room door. "Who are the gifts for?"

"You, Milady. They be asking for the duchess."

"Are there any soldiers about?"

"No, Milady. I haven't seen nary a hide nor hair of them soldiers about for a couple of days now."

"Well, come with me, then. We shall see what our visitors want."

Cailin hurried down the grand staircase and through the castle to the back entrance.

Why would visitors appear at the rear door?

A group of her servants had gathered just inside the hall in front of the door. They were smiling and chatting like a gaggle of song birds.

Cailin's heart lifted.

So the visitors must be pleasant, not harbingers of bad news.

As she reached the open door the servants parted to let her pass through. Why had they not invited the visitors inside? Who could they be?

Afternoon shadows lay softly over a much larger gathering than Cailin had expected. Why, there must be twenty-five or thirty people standing on the stone porch. Whatever could they want?

At her appearance they swept low in bows. The group consisted of mostly men, sprinkled with a few women, and several bairns. They were plainly dressed in clean, peasant apparel, the men in trews and linen shirts with belled sleeves, and the women in simple arisads.

And several carried bouquets of flowers with the bulbs still embedded with rich dirt. A few carried sacks, which, from the earthy odor she figured contained seeds. Others held armfuls of dressed pelts. The women held beautifully worked wicker baskets filled with sweet-smelling baked goods.

She held out an inviting hand. "Do come inside."

"Oh nay, Yer Grace." The woman speaking was comely, and her cheeks blazed. "We dropped by to give ye our thanks." She gazed at the crowd around her for support. "We donna have much, but we're beholden to ye. As long as ye live, ye have our devotion and our hearts."

The men bowed onto one knee. "You have our

faithful fealty."

Cailin raised her brows. She opened her mouth, but no words came out.

"We shall never forget what ye've done for us." The woman gave a deep curtsy and held out the basket crammed with mouth-watering baked goods.

"But…but I don't understand."

"'Tis the Duke of Avondale we owe, Milady. He saved my son."

Another woman stepped forward, a wide grin on her slightly wrinkled face. "And my husband."

"He saved me and my cottage, and my livestock." A stout man stood from his kneeling position, shifted a huge bag of grain from his wide shoulders, and set it carefully at her feet.

A dozen other cries rose up together so mingled that Cailin could not make out a single sentence.

A merchant, by the cut of his clothes, stepped forward. "He saved my family, my shop, and myself. I can never repay the debt I owe him."

"I…I thank you all." She could barely catch a breath. Avondale had done all this?

"Is he here, Milady? We'd like to thank him in person." The merchant gazed at her with twinkling eyes and a broad smile.

"Uh…no. He has not yet returned. Do come inside. We'll share a beverage, and you can tell me how my husband helped you." Her thoughts whirled. Her head spun. She held a hand against the doorpost to steady herself.

All these days had Avondale been out riding the countryside saving these people? Had he stood up to the redcoats all by himself? Had he opposed the Duke of Cumberland's explicit orders? Was he in danger?

31

Avondale guided his tired steed towards London. He had one more duty before he returned home to Cailin.

He shrugged, flipped the reins to the right of the horse's neck to turn back to the castle. He'd done as much as could humanly be expected of him. He couldn't handle the confrontation in London.

A bright sunset to his right already touched the tip of the far off grassy glen. He would soon be swallowed by night. Magic gloaming, Cailin called the time of day. How he missed her loving presence.

In three days' time he could be back inside her castle. He could hold her in his arms and breathe in her sweet fragrance and kiss her luscious lips. And—

The horse had trotted but one hundred yards. He tugged gently on the reins, pulling the stallion to a stop. "Whoa."

No, he could not gaze into those lovely eyes until he'd finished his mission. Once he walked back into her warm, sweet presence, he'd never have the strength to leave her again. She was his anchor, his talisman, his mentor, his…oh-so-obviously better half.

God had given him Eve before the temptation, perfect without blemish, walking with God.

It was so extremely difficult to face her perfection in broad daylight, his own flaws so obvious. His own failures so blatant. His own future so insecure.

His stallion pawed the dirt road, anxious for home and food and rest.

Still he sat rigid in the saddle, reins tight. His shoulders ached, his head ached, his stomach rumbled. Saddle weariness snaked along every limb of his body. Everything urged him home to Cailin. But something inside his soul insisted no.

His work was not yet done. He knew it, but would give almost anything to avoid what he had to do. Bile rose up into his throat. Yet, he would not return to her half a man.

He turned his horse's head back in the direction of London.

****

Avondale's horse's shoes clopped sharply off the London cobblestones just as the sun crested the horizon. First he must rest and have a fresh change of clothes. So, he turned his horse towards Avondale House.

His royal mother was away taking refreshment at Bath, so she could not impede his mission.

Piccadilly was quiet this time of morning. No carriages, no vendors, no people on foot. His steed's hoofs clicked on the wide cobblestone street. The rising sun painted the white statuary of Cupid, Venus, and the Graces pink as he passed by.

His stomach flip-flopped as his horse trotted past Devonshire House and headed to Hyde Park corner.

He'd suffered his first spells while reaching the age of accountability at Avondale House. He'd plummeted from being the most sought-after bachelor in London to the least, after only one of his more devastating blackouts. He shook his head. He would not revisit that time. He needed all his courage to tackle today's objective.

A single carriage rumbled along the cobblestones, drowning out the chirp of birds. Soon he directed his horse to the left. Avondale House. His steed's nose all but touched the gilded entrance gates, their cornerstones topped with seated sphinxes.

The gates were closed and locked. Of course they would be. He shrugged his tired shoulders to ease some of the tension and steered his horse down the broad street. The gates enclosed three acres of garden and the monstrous mansion. Around his neck Avondale wore the key to the small, hidden gate at the northeast corner.

The house, like so many in London, was modeled after their country estates to show wealth and power rather than being comfortable homes. He'd never liked the square, plain Palladian style flanked by service wings that hid the sumptuous interior. But that was today's fashionable design.

He opened the side gate and trotted through. The grounds were a bit overgrown, showing his absence, but the place had never welcomed him like Castle Drummond.

Still his royal mother loved the London house with its proximity to court and the whole London social scene.

He'd always preferred any one of the country estates.

The horse's hooves dislodged bits of dirt as he trotted slowly up the winding road which ended at the back door. He preferred the back entrance rather than the exterior front stairs that led to the two-story entrance hall.

A stable boy ran out and gazed up at him. "Welcome home, Your Grace."

"Thank you." He dismounted and handed the reins to the lad.

Avondale entered the house and took the inconspicuous stairs tucked behind the library two at a time. He strode to the central hall that led to a suite of connecting receptions rooms circling the top-lit stair hall. He'd never liked the design that allowed a large gathering of guests to circulate through the reception rooms, library, and ballroom.

His riding boots clicked loudly as he took the lesser hall to the baroque apartments and finally, to his own suite of rooms.

It was strange how coming here brought evil memories rushing to the surface. He dare not stay longer than a quick bath and change of clothing, or he would lose his nerve. The voices always spoke while he stayed here. He would refuse to let them put odd thoughts into his mind.

His butler approached and bowed.

"Good to see you, man. Please have the formal carriage brought around. And send up my old valet. I'll need a bath drawn."

While servants scurried around making a racket doing what he bid, he chose what he should wear.

The old man arrived, his white hair neatly tied behind his neck, his uniform impeccable, as if he'd been expecting Avondale. Did the man dress that way every day?

"I shall not wear a wig, but bring the powder."

"Very good, Your Grace." His valet nodded to his assistant who rushed from the dressing room.

"I want the new embroidered silk frock coat that is cut away from the waist with no buttons. The royal blue one. My best jabot. My tightest white breeches. And jackboots rather than buckled shoes."

The old man smiled and nodded. "Have you been well, Your Grace?"

"I have, Robbins. Married life agrees with me." He smiled. "But I have not long to tarry. So please hurry."

"Very good, Your Grace."

While Avondale waited, he shaved and brushed his teeth.

When he finished his toilette, he scowled into the cheval mirror. He hated the popinjay of court clothes. Country life was far more to his taste, but today he had no choice. The ensemble was tight, restraining, but the result nothing short of glorious. Today, he needed this.

At the crunch of wheels on the gravel drive, he pulled the gold pocket watch Father had bequeathed him from his silk waist coat. Not too early. He needed to catch the man before he started his daily activities. He needed undivided attention.

Soon he was ensconced on the brown leather coach interior, perspiration already pooling beneath the tight jabot. He twirled the signet ring on his index finger.

Surely Cailin was secure as long as she wore his ring. He must not let thoughts of her vulnerability impinge on his mission. He must keep his mind clear. Resolutely he gazed out the window at the passing scenery, large mansions set back from the broad street, each one inside a quite sizeable garden.

He knew all the dukes, duchesses, lesser princes, and princesses who lived on this street. Most, like himself, who spent the majority of their time at their country estates, only visiting London during the season. The green, lush view smelled of wealth.

Cumberland Lodge was close by in Windsor Great Park.

Since Duke Cumberland had been made Ranger of the Park, he would be in residence.

Avondale settled his shoulders more comfortably inside the tight-fitting frock coat. Today he would face his nightmare. Throw off the man's hold over him. Take charge of his life. Or lose his freedom. Terror and excitement spiked his blood. Sweat beaded his forehead. Today's outcome would change his life.

If he were thrown into the Tower for his past actions and these last three weeks' activities, Cailin was still free and would remain so. His title was safe. His child would inherit. This was the day he would face his demons and, Lord willing, overcome.

Cumberland Lodge's gates stood open. Swaying side to side, Avondale's carriage drove through and up the long, curving drive to the imposing mansion. The country house was located a bare three and a half miles south of Windsor Castle.

King Charles II had declared the house the official residence of the Ranger of the Great Park—a Crown appointment always held by someone close to the Sovereign. The Duke of Cumberland now enjoyed that exalted position, and the lodge had been renamed in his honor.

Not for the first time Avondale wondered at the ornate building's plain name. This was no hunting lodge. The lovely architecture housed the cruelest man he'd ever encountered, the second surviving son of King George, a fat, greedy, killing brute who led a profligate, whorish life. The man was responsible for the murder of hundreds of Highland men, women, and children. He was single-handedly ending life as it was known in the Highlands. He'd destroyed the clan system, murdered or enslaved the young men, and agreed to the rape and pillage of their wives and homes.

And I did nothing to stop him. My sin is as black as Cumberland's.

But, thanks to his dearest Cailin, he'd stopped punishing himself and finally found forgiveness. Now he must take the next step.

The carriage groaned as he stepped down to the gravel. "I shall not be long, I think," he said to the footman holding wide the door.

The man in royal blue livery bowed. "As you wish, Your Grace."

Avondale strode to the double entry doors, letting his boots crunch heavily on the gravel. He blanked out the beauty of the mansion and surrounding garden. He must focus on his mission.

A butler bowed before Avondale could strike the large gold knocker on the inlaid door. "Your Grace." The servant moved aside and held out his hand.

Avondale swiped off his hat, stripped off his gloves, and slapped the lot into the butler's hands. "Cumberland receiving?"

"For Your Grace, of course. Please wait in the main drawing room."

Avondale's boots clicked authoritatively over the granite floor as he stalked through the portico into the entrance hall. He passed the famous crystal staircase with its glass handrail and glass newel posts, and went on into the vast gilded drawing room designed to impress and cower the highest noble.

Not this time. He refused to grovel to this man, though portraits of kings, queens, and princes lined the walls. Only Cumberland's ailing older brother and his father, King George, held more power in the land than Bloody Billy. Billy the Butcher.

Yet, Avondale would not be intimidated. Not this time.

Moving to the long bank of windows that overlooked the vast grounds, he stood, hands clasped behind his back and gazed out. English landscaped acres undulated before him, peaceful and real. This was no nightmare.

His task was mortal.

Minutes ticked by.

Finally a tall, obese man, still in dressing gown and robe, limped into the drawing room.

Avondale forced himself to bow. "My Lord."

"Ah. I thought you were still in Scotland."

"I was, but found it necessary to see you. On business." He firmed his jaw.

Bags encircled Cumberland's bloodshot eyes. He tied his robe around his fat frame, and motioned to the servant standing by the door. "Bring some refreshment."

"I shall not take up much of your time."

"Nonsense. It's been way too long. Take a chair." Fat fingers motioned to several chairs clustered beside a small table near the enormous fireplace.

Avondale walked to the nearest and dropped down to perch on the edge of the Queen Anne wing-back, both boots planted firmly on the marble floor.

Cumberland limped over to the matching chair. "Blasted wound. Makes sure I'll never forget the action at Dettingen. Never healed properly." He kicked over a priceless stool, dropped awkwardly into the chair and propped his foot on the stool. "So, what brings you here so early?" He glanced at the empty doorway. "My latest mistress, Marianne, is still abed, and your early arrival has made her grouchy."

"I'm afraid I don't care about the mood of your latest damsel." He leaned forward. "And don't expect me to fawn over you in order to erase that scowl from your face."

Cumberland's face grew mottled red, and then unexpectedly he leaned back in his chair and laughed. "You're feeling lucky today, are you not?"

Avondale shook his head. "You expect more money from me in order to exempt me from your army. Instead, I have come to volunteer my service."

The butler brought in a serving table loaded with food as well as assorted drinks.

"Ah. Breakfast. Fill my plate, James. And I'll have the port." He frowned at Avondale. "What is your pleasure, man?"

No one else in England dared address him in such a way. He tamped his temper. "I have eaten."

"Port, then?"

"No thank you."

"So, rather than pay, you wish to join my army?" Cumberland took a huge bite of stuffed quail.

"That is correct."

"Hmm." Cumberland chewed and took several more bites, and then a long drink. "I have a second-in-command that I am quite pleased with." He wiped his mouth. "I have no need of your service."

"Then we are agreed." Avondale held his shoulders straight. "I am not in your debt. When you have need of my service, I shall ride with the Army. I shall not pay you another pound."

Cumberland smiled. "We are agreed on that point." He took another long drink. "But there is the small matter of you overriding your Duchy and claiming to protect Lowland Scots far outside your boundaries."

So Cumberland had heard of his interference. Well, best to take care of that business while he was here. Sweat ran down his armpits. He clenched his fingers to keep from gripping the arms of his chair. "Yes. Those people were not involved in The Jacobite Rising. Nor were they harboring fugitive Highlanders. They are completely loyal to the King."

"Perhaps a visit to the Tower would change your mind on that."

"Perhaps a gift of twenty of the finest racing horses ever bred would change your mind about the Tower visit." Sweat ran down between his shoulder blades, but he kept his eyes steadfast on the bulging eyes of the man who could lock him away for the rest of his life. He would not allow the man to enslave his soul again. The horses on his estate in Berkshire were his last assets.

Cumberland's fat mouth opened in a wide grin. "Ah, yes. I accept your gift with many thanks. They should go a long way towards making your time in the Tower a good bit shorter."

Avondale stood to his full height and towered over the sitting Cumberland. "I understand your failure to clear the woods at Fontenoy lead to the defeat of your forces by the French. Should word of this get around, you might find yourself relieved of your command and any future command."

Cumberland's face drained of color.

"Your reputation in London has suffered as well. I hear the name Bloody Billy bandied about in all the best clubs. You're not popular. And your elder brother is ailing. If you aspire to become king when your father passes, you'll discover that adding my name to the list of people you've wronged will not be politically helpful.

"Parliament and the people may well decide to choose your nephew to reign as king rather than you." Avondale unclenched his hands and slapped his thigh. "It's unwise to lock up a fellow duke."

Cumberland choked. His face grew scarlet. He pounded his fist on the low table.

32

"I took that gift you told me about."

Cailin noticed every move Avondale made. Every shift. Every quiet laugh. A living, breathing force arced through the air between them. She felt soft and fluttery inside and couldn't drink in enough of his hard masculine strength sitting just inches away. It was so delightful to have him back. And judging from the movement inside her womb, the baby felt the same.

His dark chocolate eyes made her heart pound. "Are you sure?"

"I've never been more certain of anything in my life."

They sat there, gazes locked.

He laced his fingers with hers.

She was riveted by the sight of his large, strong, tan hand holding her small pale one. Her heart thudded a wild reaction to his words. "And your heavy burden of sin?"

"Forgiven and forgotten by God."

A sense of rightness flooded her. A sense of completion. A sense of all being right in her world.

Perhaps he would have other times he couldn't remember. Perhaps he'd have times when he disappeared. Perhaps he'd make wrong decisions in the future. But he was a forgiven man. A child of God. A new creation in Christ. A husband she knew loved her.

Perhaps his demons were gone. Perhaps he'd never have another spell. But if he did, he belonged to a higher power Who could help him through his trouble. A power Who could guide him in the way to go. A power Who could strengthen him.

This was the man she loved with all her heart and soul. He wasn't perfect, but he knew the Man who was perfect. Just looking at him made goose bumps shiver on her arms. She stared at his beautiful lips. "Tell me again."

"I am a child of the everlasting King. I'm forgiven. I'm a new person in Christ, and I love you with all my heart, now and forever into eternity."

She tilted her head and raised her lips. "Kiss me again."

And she had learned that just because she loved God with all her heart didn't keep bad things from happening to her. Bad things did happen to committed Christians, but God was faithful, and He would work out all things according to His will.

She'd not been able to make this marriage happy, hadn't been able to make her husband happy, hadn't been able to make him love her. She had even thought about having her husband murdered, but her faithful God worked all things out well.

And now along with his duty caring for the estates, taking his place in the House of Lords, and caring for the orphanage he'd promised to help create, he would become a father himself.

Already her bulge showed through her afternoon receiving gowns. She relaxed against the cushions in her chair. And if this child was not the expected son, well, she and Avondale had many years ahead of them.

And with all Mums's adopted lads running about the estate, surely one of her own future children would be male. She smiled a secret smile. She would so love to have a baby girl.

They sat together in the rose arbor where they had promised their vows.

Sunlight touched the mahogany in his thick hair with shafts of gold. He held both her hands and gazed into her eyes.

All around them invited guests, English and Scottish nobles, chatted, drank, and ate together, and glanced at them sitting together in broad daylight and so very obviously in love.

Haggis

Ingredients
1 sheep stomach
1 sheep liver
1 sheep heart
1 sheep tongue
1/2 pound suet, minced
3 medium onions, minced
1/2 pound dry oats, toasted
1 teaspoon kosher salt
1/2 teaspoon ground black pepper
1 teaspoon dried ground herbs

Directions:

Rinse the stomach and soak overnight in cold salted water.

Rinse the liver, heart, and tongue. In a large pot of boiling, salted water, cook over medium heat for 2 hours. Remove and mince.

In a large bowl, combine the minced liver, heart, tongue, suet, onions, and toasted oats. Season with salt, pepper, and dried herbs. Moisten with some of the cooking water so the mixture binds. Remove the stomach from the cold salted water and fill 2/3 with the mixture. Tie the stomach closed. Pierce the stomach several times to prevent the haggis from bursting.

Place the filled stomach in a large pot of boiling water. Cook over high heat for 3 hours.

Thank you for purchasing this White Rose Publishing title. For other inspirational stories, please visit our on-line bookstore at www.pelicanbookgroup.com.

For questions or more information, contact us at customer@pelicanbookgroup.com.

White Rose Publishing
Where Faith is the Cornerstone of Love™
an imprint of Pelican Ventures Book Group
www.PelicanBookGroup.com

May God's glory shine through
this inspirational work of fiction.

AMDG